# ROCKEFELLER
## & THE DEMISE OF
# IBU PERTIWI

Published in Australia by Sid Harta Publishers Pty Ltd,

ABN: 46 119 415 842

23 Stirling Crescent, Glen Waverley, Victoria 3150, Australia

email: author@sidharta.com.au

Phone:     +61 3 9650 9920

Fax:       +61 3 9545 1742

First Published: September 2017

This edition published 2017

Copyright: Kerry B. Collison

Design, Typesetting, Graphics: WorkingType Studio

Cover Design: Luke Harris, Working Type Studio

Illustrations: Pawel Nowacki

National Library of Australia Cataloguing-in-Publication entry

Creator: Collison, Kerry B., author.

Title: Rockefeller and the demise of Ibu Pertiwi : West Papua / Kerry B. Collison.

ISBN: 9781921030987 (paperback)

Subjects: Rockefeller, Michael C. (Michael Clark), 1938-1961--Fiction.

Political fiction.

Papua New Guinea--Fiction.

Indonesia--Fiction.

Australia--Fiction.

# ROCKEFELLER
## & THE DEMISE OF
# IBU PERTIWI

### KERRY B. COLLISON

# ALSO BY KERRY COLLISON

## Non Fiction

*The Happy Warrior — an anthology of Australian Military Poetry*
Co-edited by: Kerry B. Collison & Warrant Officer Paul Barrett

*In Search of Recognition — the Leo Stach Story*
(Biographical)

## Fact-based Fiction

*Crescent Moon Rising*

*The Fifth Season*

*Indonesian Gold*

*The Asian Trilogy*
consisting of:

*Jakarta*

*Merdeka Square (Freedom Square)*
(book of the month, Singapore)

*The Timor Man*
(book of the month, Singapore, Hong Kong, Australia)

**KERRY B. COLLISON** followed a distinguished period of service in Indonesia as a member of the Australian military and government intelligence services during the turbulent period known as 'The Years of Living Dangerously'. This was followed by a successful business career spanning thirty years throughout Asia.

Recognized for his chilling predictions in relation to Asia's evolving political and economic climate through his books, he brings unique qualifications to his historically-based vignettes and intriguing accounts of power-politics and the shadowy world of governments' clandestine activities.

Further information is available on the website: www.sidharta.com.au

Photo: Courtesy of Dominion Newspapers, N.Z.

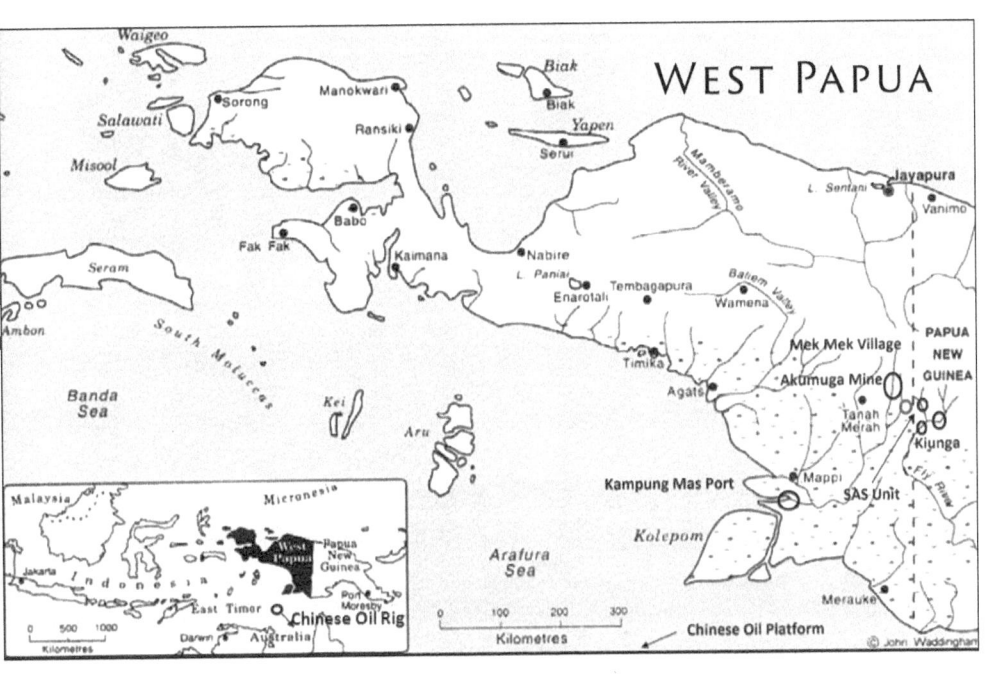

*For my grandchildren*

*Zara Angelina, Oscar Boyd & Maxwell Ray Collison*

# PROLOGUE

1961–1962

Michael Rockefeller clung precariously with one hand to the overturned catamaran, wiped salt-stung eyes, and then craned his neck towards Western New Guinea's blurred shore. The 23-year old adventurer sensed that the current was dragging him further away from land. In that moment he became fearfully conscious that these waters were populated with both sharks and crocodiles. *Could he swim the five miles to shore as the two native guides had attempted or should he remain with the useless hull being tossed around in the roiling sea?*

With his free hand, Rockefeller tested the ropes tied to the two empty gasoline cans he had managed to salvage before being thrown into the Arafura Sea. He turned his attention to Rene Wassink, the Dutch anthropologist, who had accompanied him on the expedition on behalf of the Rockefeller Museum. The intention had been to collect artefacts from the Stone-Age peoples of the Asmat tribe who occupied the southern coast of the world's second largest island.

'I'm going to try to make it to shore,' Michael shouted to Wassink.

Unable to swim, the Dutchman appealed to the younger man. 'You will never make it. The current is far too strong! Stay here with me. Someone is certain to come along and take us to safety.'

Michael was not to be dissuaded. 'I'll come back for you,' he promised.

Stripped down to underwear and with his glasses clenched between his teeth, Michael released his grip and struck out through the challenging waters, paddling towards the mangrove-covered shoreline.

Wassink watched in dismay and offered a silent prayer as Rockefeller quickly disappeared amidst the turbulent seas. It had been at the Dutchman's urging that Rockefeller had acquiesced and agreed to purchase the motorised catamaran, despite being advised that the vessel was unsuitable for the open ocean.

The anthropologist was aware that he would be held responsible for permitting the scion of one of the most prominent families of industrialists and philanthropists to perish, on his watch.

*　　*　　*　　*

# Irian Barat
# (West Papua)
# The Reluctant Colony

Umar Suharjo raised the Soviet SVD high-powered sniper rifle and nestled the weapon against his cheek. The assassin peered through the PSO-1 scope at the scene unravelling below, where an advance patrol of *KOPASSUS* Special Forces paratroopers had occupied the isolated highland village. His eyes traversed the scene and then narrowed when his attention focused on a group of high-spirited soldiers gathered around something on the ground. Closer scrutiny revealed the object of their undivided attention to be a woman. A sneer curled Suharjo's upper lip when it became apparent that the victim was white.

He concluded that she was most likely a foreign missionary and was aware of their scattered numbers and often isolated presence, throughout Indonesia's eastern frontier.

Suharjo remained unobserved; a camouflaged backdrop high in the forest canopy, three hundred metres from where the paratroopers jostled for turns to rape their victim. He waited patiently in a dispassionate mood as he saw a child kick and flail at the attackers, only to be punched and then thrown viciously aside.

The sniper bided his time until the soldiers had finished their brutal engagement. When the last of the men rolled off the woman, rose and commenced buttoning his trousers Suharjo's forefinger caressed the SVD's sensitive trigger. As the barrel air-penciled a path across his targets, he paused, inhaled slowly and sent the first soldier to his death. Then, in rapid succession, he dispatched the remaining three men; their bodies crumpling under his deadly fire and their surprised expressions testament to the assassin's lethal skill.

Moments passed until the surreal silence was suddenly pierced by shrill screams as the villagers abandoned their dwellings and fled, leaving the unconscious woman and her six-year-old son terrified at her side. Suharjo monitored the landscape for several minutes, to ensure that the entire patrol had indeed been exterminated, before climbing down from his canopy perch and descending down to his killing field.

He hesitated at the village's perimeter, tilting his head when he detected the approach of others. Withdrawing into the jungle growth from where he could survey the developing situation, Suharjo waited impatiently, adjusting the rifle now at his hip, to automatic fire.

Angry voices signalled the arrival of a group of armed Papuans. Concluding that he was observing a band of freedom fighters and likely members of the *Organisasi Papua Merdeka,* the Free Papua Movement, Suharjo estimated their numbers were small and, as they were generally undisciplined and poorly-trained, there were not too many for him to confront. He crouched forward, observing the one whom he assumed to be their leader bending down to calm the wailing child. The woman moaned and struggled to a sitting position, reaching out to the light-skinned child. Suharjo frowned.

The assassin considered the opportunity. His mission was to create confusion as the interim province was dragged towards the United Nations-supervised plebiscite to determine whether Papuans would remain within the Indonesian republic or seek independence. Suharjo's master, General Nathan Seda, acting unilaterally, had decided to influence the outcome to benefit another agenda in East Timor. Suharjo had been ordered to the former Dutch territory to disrupt the proceedings; the choice of targets left for him to determine as he criss-crossed the mountainous outposts, indiscriminately killing. His elimination of the Special Forces patrol would guarantee the severest of reprisals against the indigenous population which, in turn, would further obfuscate the security situation for the UN-sponsored plebiscite.

As it turned out, not all of Suharjo's missions were successful. Some months earlier, he had been thwarted while attempting to execute a Jakarta-based Australian Embassy official, Stephen Coleman who, at the time, was conducting an information gathering tour of the province in anticipation of the referendum. Suharjo's bullet had been deflected, hitting the Australian in the shoulder. Stephen Coleman had survived the assassination attempt.

Refocusing on the scene in front of him the assassin saw that the child was now cradled in his mother's arms. Suharjo raised the SVD to his shoulder, adjusted the scope and fired rapidly until none of the Papuan soldiers were left standing. Satisfied, he then lowered his sights marginally, steadied his aim and settled the cross-hairs on the foreign woman. Suharjo could clearly see tearful eyes as she cradled her child. His bullet sent her reeling backwards, spilling the boy onto the ground. The killer considered the child and, in an out of character gesture, lowered his weapon and slunk back into the jungle leaving the boy alone, but unharmed.

Suharjo would not survive to witness the ramifications of his decision to permit the boy Julius to live. The outcome was destined to profoundly impact the course of Indonesia's future relationships across the region.

*   *   *   *

# JAKARTA

## EMBASSY OF THE UNITED STATES OF AMERICA

The Deputy Head of Mission's annoyance was evident at the meeting, that Henry Kissinger had convinced President Nixon to visit Indonesia at the most sensitive of times. Delegating this responsibility he had summoned the departmental heads to discuss the myriad preparations which needed to be addressed.

'Before we move on to discuss the President's program we'll hear updates on West Irian,' the career diplomat directed, passing the chair to the senior political adviser.

'You will recall that our May monthly intelligence brief reported the surrender of the rebel leaders who have been fighting the Indonesians over the past two years.' His eyes flicked around the polished table before he continued. 'The Arfak tribe uprising drew a heavy response from Jakarta, with the military mobilizing an additional two infantry battalions from Sulawesi to quell the resistance. Jakarta's propaganda machine insists that the Papuans are attempting to undermine the approaching vote to determine the question of Western New Guinea's sovereignty, and that the increased Indonesian military presence is necessary to maintain the integrity of the plebiscite.'

The senior adviser was aware of Jakarta's heightened concern regarding the deteriorating situation after popular rebellions had erupted across West Papua's Western Central Highlands in April forcing the Indonesian military onto the defence. One hundred well-armed Papuan policemen mutinied and joined the Free Papua Movement. The adviser also recalled that General Sarwo Edhie, the territory's Indonesian military commander, had ordered B-26 bombers into the theatre, and Indonesian paratroopers from West Java were flown in to hunt down the resistance fighters. The American official was also cognizant of the Indonesian counter attacks that had driven more than fifteen thousand Papuans into the hinterland and that demonstrations had flared across the territory resulting in Indonesian troops being attacked on the Bird's Head Peninsula, and in Merauke.

'What, if anything, will be the result of the Dutch entreaty to the UN?' The CIA station chief wanted to know. He had been ostracised for not having indigenous agents on the ground, with the Agency dependent on US citizens within the missionaries to provide current information. Should the UN be receptive to the Dutch proposal, he envisaged the easy planting of CIA operatives among a multi-national presence.

'UN Secretary General U Thant has dismissed the Dutch request to send in an expeditionary force, despite the Dutch arguing that such a move would neutralise the intimidation tactics employed by Indonesia's armed forces. His refusal to consider the call reflects another clear illustration of the UN leadership's collaboration with Indonesia to legitimise President Sukarno's intended takeover of West Irian.' The senior adviser paused then added cynically, 'Not that Washington disagrees with U Thant's position.' Smug smiles accompanied nodding heads in silent concurrence. It would not be in the United States' interests for the Papuans' political rights as guaranteed under the terms of the 1962 New York Agreement to become a reality.

The meeting continued for another hour before discussions of White House matters commenced. When the Deputy Head of Mission was satisfied that at least some of the issues arising from President Nixon's impending visit had been resolved, the diplomat left the meeting and, moving with his customary casual gait to the upper level, met with Ambassador Galbraith. That afternoon, within minutes of the embassy communications officer encrypting the ambassador's sensitive report to Washington, the cable was in the hands of the recently-appointed Secretary for State, William P Rogers.

The transmission read:-

*"Subject: The stakes in the upcoming "Act of Free Choice."*

*The Act of Free Choice (AFC) in West Irian is unfolding like a Greek tragedy, the conclusion preordained. The main protagonist, the Government of Indonesia, cannot and will not permit any resolution other than the continued inclusion of West Irian in Indonesia. Dissident activity is likely to increase but the Indonesian armed forces will be able to contain and, if necessary, suppress it.*

*The Free Papua Movement (OPM) is not the all-pervasive revolutionary organization some believe it to be. ... anti-government dissidents have virtually no liaison with each other, receive no outside assistance or direction, and are generally incapable of mounting an insurrection in the face of the relatively large Indonesian military establishment in West Irian. Grievances and anti-GOI (Gruppo Operativo Incursori) sentiment are quite real, however, and there is little question that a great majority of the non-Stone Age Irianese favour a termination of Indonesian rule. Opposition to the GOI stems from economic deprivation over the years, military repression and capriciousness, and maladministration. Limited efforts of the GOI to rectify these problems to date are generally "too little and too late," and it is uncertain whether the Indonesians will actually try to ameliorate the sources of local discontent in coming years.*

*The Free Papua Movement (OPM) is widely believed to be the core of opposition to the Indonesian Government in West Irian. But it is difficult to track down the OPM as an organization, although not because its security is tight or people are unwilling to talk. On the contrary, everyone talks about the OPM; it has few, if any, secrets, and many Irianese proudly proclaim they are "members" of the OPM. A foreigner travelling in West Irian has no difficulty in contacting anti-government activists. They stop you on the street and groups of them gather around when you visit a native village; in short, no one is reluctant to discuss the OPM and their reasons for disliking Indonesians. One American missionary explains this by saying that "the Papuans simply are unable to keep a secret." Of course, information known to foreigners is also available to the Indonesian authorities, the Army, and even to the most casual observer. ... Regarding the magnitude of the opposition to Indonesian rule, probably a decided majority of the Irianese people, and possibly 85 to 90 percent, are in sympathy with the Free Papua cause or at least intensely dislike Indonesians.*

*As the Indonesian government firmly rejects a one-person, one-vote plebiscite in West Irian, insisting instead on a series of local 'consultations' with just over one thousand hand selected tribal leaders (out of an estimated population of eight hundred thousand), conducted throughout this month with between six thousand to ten thousand Indonesian troops spread throughout the territory. Past abuses have stimulated intense anti-Indonesian and pro-independence sentiment at all levels of Irian society, suggesting that "possibly 85 to 90 percent" of the population "are in sympathy with the Free Papua cause." Moreover recent Indonesian military operations, which have resulted in the deaths of hundreds and possibly thousands of civilians, has stimulated fears and rumours of intended genocide among the Irianese..." (United States State Department Archives)*

\*    \*    \*    \*

# BRITISH EMBASSY

On the third floor of the British Embassy in Jakarta political affairs First Secretary, Lawrence Nelson Whitehead sat pondering how he would occupy his spare time, after his wife returned home to England. With the end of her second trimester rapidly approaching, and British Airways' policy banning pregnant passengers beyond their sixth month, it was time for Emily to depart.

Contemplating her upcoming absence, the MI6 station chief felt some consolation that at least he would not be subjected to his wife's outlandish cravings. How Emily could devour those heavily-spiced Sumatran dishes was beyond him. He was pleased that at least she would be home with their extended family and on a more accept-able diet than chilli-pepper lung, brain and other disgusting offal dishes she had their houseboy smuggle into their residence from 'kaki lima', mobile food vendors that roamed Jakarta's streets. The resulting reflux she endured worried the diplomat and constantly reminded him of the absence of decent medical facilities or advice. Although there was Doctor Mitchell, a British surgeon and Subud sect convert who had embraced Islam upon taking up residence in the capital, officially he was unlicensed to practice. This left Her Majesty's Embassy staff reliant upon a former medical missionary the Australians had relocated from Port Moresby. The doctor had been engaged to provide basic care for embassy officials and their families. Whitehead mused the doctor's services were available only when one was fortunate enough to find the man sober.

The intercom on Whitehead's desk squawked as a subordinate attempted to communicate. He grabbed the antiquated box with one hand while slapping it with the other.

'Lawrence?' the speaker crackled. 'Can you hear me Lawrence?' The MI6 chief could hear the male voice cursing; the broken, one-sided conversation ending as the frustrated agent surrendered to the idiosyncrasies of the archaic system. Broken some six years earlier during his predecessor's time, when embassy staff were preoccupied destroying files before abandoning the building, the system had never been updated. Having completed his training with the Secret Service in 1963, the British and Indonesians were engaged in a secret war known as *Konfrontasi,* Whitehead's recollections of the time remained fresh in his mind. The country's founding president, Sukarno, had declared unofficial war against the British Commonwealth nations of Singapore and Malaysia. British Gurkhas and Australian Special Forces were deployed along common borders with Indonesia. The Republic had been armed extensively by the Soviets with long-range bombers and other sophisticated weaponry. As these TU16 bombers had the capacity to strike Australian capital cities as far south as Melbourne the Royal Air Force positioned two Vulcan bombers in Singapore to counteract the threat. The British ambassador had been instructed to present his government's message to the recalcitrant Sukarno and, when the president learned that Vulcan bombers were armed with atomic weapons and would fly regular missions over Indonesian airfields, he capitulated. The petulant leader then orchestrated elements of the powerful *Partai Komunis Indonesia* to demonstrate against the British, with the *PKI's* leadership losing control over the unruly mob which proceeded to burn down the embassy and forty eight diplomatic residences. Whitehead recalled that it was during this low point in their relationship that Sukarno had ordered the nationalisation of British properties valued at more than $400 million. The gutted embassy had eventually been restored, but it was not until General Suharto had wrenched power from Sukarno that there were any significant steps taken, towards a rapprochement between the two powers.

'Bloody intercom is on the blink again,' the station chief's senior field agent complained as he swept into the First Secretary's office, bumping against a side cupboard in the cramped surrounds and knocking a recently depleted bottle of Johnny Walker on its side. 'Don't know how we are expected to operate efficiently under these conditions.'

Whitehead softly tapped his front teeth with a pencil. 'What's up?' he asked, amused when the bottle rolled across his office. Jakarta's buildings floated atop a soft layer of earth cushioned by a water table that rose to within a metre of the surface. When the Intercontinental Hotel had been built on the other side of the *Selamat Datang* welcome roundabout, the pressure exerted by the eight hundred-room structure caused the British Embassy to rise, and fall lopsided, more than thirty centimetres at the end closest to the hotel.

'Had a call from Sander,' the agent commenced, 'Seems there's quite a mob gathering outside their embassy.' "Sander" was Alexander Hoffman, the First Secretary's Dutch counterpart. Whitehead listened, the possibility of demonstrations at the Netherlands Embassy not unexpected.

'Send Wilson,' was all the MI6 chief had to say. The agent nodded and turned without further discussion, returning to the crowded quarters he shared with Wilson, the third member of the MI6 contingent based at the embassy.

Whitehead's agents operated from a small discrete cell within the embassy, known as "the station". Equipped with its own highly-secure communications systems and frequently swept for listening devices, the station was only accessible by the agents.

As head of station, traditionally Whitehead would function under the guise of a Foreign and Commercial Office Counsellor and his activities would be declared to *Badan Koordinasi Intelijen (BIN)*, the Indonesian equivalent of the CIA, as much of his activities only involved general liaison. The other officers such as Wilson remained undeclared because they would spend a significant part of their time spying against the host country.

While reflecting on the competency of his two agents, Whitehead slipped into a ruminative mood, reassessing the successes (and failures) of MI6 operations in Indonesia. The British Secret Service maintained some fifty stations around the world and he was aware that Third World stations usually consisted of only one officer and a secretary. The size of a station reflected the importance of the host country in relation to Britain's interests. Jakarta, due to Indonesia's evolving pro-Western stance, had been upgraded to a three-man-station with a personal secretary, as President Suharto's 'New Order' fascist regime was, potentially, a major customer for Britain's weapons industry. London, he knew, was preparing the groundwork in anticipation of a revitalised Asian arms race. Indonesia was prioritised as its armed forces were desperate to replace their antiquated Soviet arsenal with Western product. Also, should the possibility of Indonesia losing West Irian to an independence vote in any way compromise Britain's military sales' prospects, then Her Majesty's Government would support and encourage Jakarta to absorb the territory by whatever unobtrusive means possible.

Whitehead's eyes canvassed the wall of his domain, drawn to a wall plaque that he had inscribed as a constant reminder of any nation's vulnerability, when overly dependent on its intelligence-gathering apparatus and personnel.

*"In the eyes of posterity it will inevitably seem that, in safeguarding our freedom, we destroyed it. The vast clandestine apparatus we built up to prove our enemies' resources and intentions only served in the end to confuse our own purposes; that practice of deceiving others for the good of the state led infallibly to our deceiving ourselves; and that vast army of clandestine personnel built up to execute these purposes were soon caught up in the web of their own sick fantasies, with disastrous consequences for them and us."*

**Malcolm Muggeridge**
**May 1966**

The MI6 station chief's secretary knocked once then entered. 'Your wife called ... again,' she informed, not without a hint of annoyance, '... to remind you not to be late.'

Lawrence Whitehead checked his wrist. 'Might not be such a bad idea to leave a little earlier for the airport, what with the demonstrations gaining momentum. Have my car brought around then call my wife to inform her I'm on my way to take her to the airport.'

\*    \*    \*    \*

# ROYAL NETHERLANDS EMBASSY

Army recruits dressed in civilian attire scrambled from army transports parked in an adjacent street. They jogged towards the Dutch Embassy, their crew-cut hairstyles and military boots obvious to onlookers parked not so discreetly in diplomatic-plated vehicles, snapping photographs, monitoring the demonstration. Amongst these were British, American and Australian observers whose countries shared common interests in the world's largest Moslem nation's recent shift towards democracy. The Soviets had long lost interest following President Sukarno's downfall, his demise spiraling the world's third largest Communist party into oblivion. Having provided (and lost) hundreds of millions in both military and commercial aid Moscow now maintained a more pragmatic approach to Jakarta, diverting much of their energy to North Vietnam.

The soldiers infiltrated the scene waving placards demanding the Dutch Government withdraw its request for United Nations troops to be stationed in West Papua. Within minutes the gathering degenerated into a hysterical mass of screaming demonstrators, when military provocateurs commenced throwing missiles over the entrance's two-metre walled barrier, into steel-shuttered windows.

Chants of *'Belanda pulang!'* and *'Belanda jangan campur tangan!'* could be heard reverberating along the street, the calls for the

Dutch to go home and cease interfering in domestic issues gathering momentum as another truckload of agitators joined the fray. Dutch Embassy staff had commenced implementing Level Two readiness orders which effectively shutdown all Consular services to the general public.

*   *   *   *

Although it was unlikely the demonstrators would breach embassy security, First Secretary Alexander Hoffman, or "Sander" as he was more commonly called was, nonetheless, reminded of the recent attack against the nearby Singapore Embassy in the elite central suburb of Menteng. At the time, even he had been surprised with the viciousness of the assault, recalling that the retributive attacks were in retaliation to Singapore's hanging of two Indonesian commandos. The men had penetrated the island's defences and detonated a bomb at the Hong Kong & Shanghai Bank, killing two — and partially destroying the Australian High Commission. He had seen Jakarta's normally gridlocked streets transform eerily into traffic-less avenues when the soldier's bodies were transported from Kemayoran to the hero's cemetrey, Kalibata.

Sander had anticipated the demonstrations having received warnings from informants. He had assessed the volatile climate and the potential for spillover from the current Malaysian riots which, since erupting the month before, had already claimed two hundred lives. As a senior intelligence officer, it was his responsibility to monitor not only Indonesia's domestic situation, but also that of neighbouring countries. He had read the briefs concerning the Malaysian

State of Emergency, surprised when the Malaysian Parliament had been suspended. He and others amongst the diplomatic corps had expressed concern that the racially-driven unrest might spread across the Malacca Straits and result in a repeat of the 1965-66 purge, which near-decimated Indonesia's ethnic Chinese population. Sander was also disquieted by the opportunity such instability offered the military-driven Indonesian Government to implement covert, state-sponsored terror campaigns as it had so effectively initiated over the past three years since General Suharto's *coup d'etat* in March 1966.

\* \* \* \*

Sander's eyes remained transfixed on the dossier's contents — the First Secretary momentarily mesmerised by the lifeless, black and white imagery of the murdered Dutch missionary Jeanne Heynneman. He remained in silent contemplation, the tips of his right hand unconsciously brushing imaginary dust from the stark photograph, his mind wandering back a year to when he had last spoken to the woman.

\* \* \* \*

'Then you won't reconsider?' Having learned of Jeanne's missionary appointment which would take her to West Irian, Sander had invited her to the embassy to seek her cooperation in providing regular, on the ground information which might be of value to the Dutch Government. Sander was a serving Dutch Army officer actively engaged in security matters under the auspices of LAMID, the Netherlands Army Intelligence Service. As was the situation with other Western nations, they were bereft of intelligence assets across the huge West Irian expanse, the Dutch marginally ahead in the game benefitting from missionaries who had remained in the territory, subsequent to the effective annexation in 1963.

Jeanne Heynneman's in-country presence had become known to embassy officials some three years earlier when she had pleaded for The Hague's intervention on behalf of her Papuan husband, Johannes. He had been arrested following the September 1965 failed Communist takeover, falsely accused of participating in Left Wing subversive activities and, along with some twenty-thousand other political detainees, incarcerated without trial at the infamous Nusa Kambangan prison.

'I'm sorry, Mister Hoffman,' she had refused adamantly. 'I would not be comfortable doing so. My work as a missionary for the Council of Churches cannot be compromised.'

Sanders, disguising his disappointment persisted. 'I cannot give you any guarantees, Jeanne, but your support in this matter might encourage our government to reconsider your husband's situation.'

A year had passed and yet Jeanne Heynneman's response still reverberated in his ears.

'Then you haven't heard?' was her accusatory response. 'My husband Johannes was transported to Buru Island Prison.' Sander recalled the pit forming in his stomach as she rose, preparing to leave. 'Where he survived only a few weeks.' Hesitating at the doorway she turned, fire in her eyes. 'You will forgive my being bitter. All I have left now Mister Hoffman is God's work and my son, Julius. Please do not approach me on this matter, again.'

Sander returned to the present reminded that Jeanne had a child. He rifled through the dossier photographs but found nothing except a file annotation referring to one Julius Heynneman whose birth had been recorded with the consular section. The First Secretary was not surprised that the boy's mother had registered Julius with her maiden name, concluding that the father, Johannes, as was the custom in Indonesia, most likely never used his family surname.

A telephone rang interrupting his introspective mood.

'Ambassador has summoned everyone to his office,' the Consul alerted. 'The demonstration appears to be getting out of hand.' Sander filled his lungs slowly, initialed the report and closed the file, clearing his desk of all sensitive material which he then had locked away in the central registry's vault, the fugacious thought of Julius Heynneman's whereabouts lost to more pressing priorities.

\* \* \* \*

# AUSTRALIAN EMBASSY

*"Our aim is not to be impartial (with respect to Indonesia) for the sake of impartiality but to have the appearance of impartiality so that the message we want to deliver will be delivered successfully."*
**Paul Hasluck, Australian Minister for External Affairs, during the period known as The Years of Living Dangerously.**

'*Selamat datang, tuan.*' The seemingly ageless Indonesian security guard known as Pak Ali welcomed the frequent visitor. Holding the pale blue Holden sedan's rear door open with one hand and saluting with the other he enquired, courteously, '*Kapan datang tuan?*'

Special envoy Jonathan Meyers' limited *Bahasa Indonesia* vocabulary let him down. Although he understood the question asking when he had arrived, the Canberra intelligence bureaucrat reached into a trouser pocket and passed an unopened packet of Camel cigarettes to the beaming seventy-year old.

'*Terima kasih, tuan.*' Pak Ali's head bobbed with gratitude as he thanked the dwarfing figure, leading Meyers up the embassy steps to the lobby.

Meyers approached the reception desk manned by a Commonwealth Police officer.

'The Counsellor is expecting you, Sir.' The guard's rehearsed one-sided working smile jacked a lower cheek as he rotated the visitor's book around for signature.

'Ah, you're here,' Meyers was greeted by the Counsellor, who ranked directly below the ambassador in seniority. 'Perfect timing.'

They shook hands, the Counsellor nodding perfunctorily in the guard's direction before escorting the envoy through yet another security door to the unmanned elevator. The Counsellor pressed the button for the second floor, the pair rising in silence as the four-passenger lift which resembled an oversized dumbwaiter, carried them slowly upstairs.

Jonathan Meyers was taken to the Counsellor's office and asked to wait there until the others assembled. Alone, he eased his corpulent frame into an executive chair and angled his head to enable a clear view of protocol avenue, Jalan Thamrin where children frolicked, splashing vehicles playfully, as they ploughed along the partially flooded thoroughfare. Meyers had seen the capital's roads inundated before, never ceasing to be amazed how the street urchins survived exposure to raw sewage that eructed from inadequate and overflowing canals.

Two hundred metres further up the street and adjacent to an open *kali* stood the Soviet-styled monument depicting a youthful couple, hands held in welcoming gesture, their statue centered in the roundabout's neglected fountain. To the left he could see the British Embassy, dwarfed by the skeleton-like outline of the abandoned Wisma Nusantara skyscraper. He mulled sadly; the structure reflected the demise of the Indonesian economy in every way. The project had been poorly conceived, badly designed and now, with the funding misappropriated by corrupt officials, destined to remain an incongruous marker of how business was done in this country.

His thoughts returned to matters at hand. The weekly "prayers meeting" with the Ambassador and department heads had been postponed to permit the special envoy the opportunity to brief senior embassy officials regarding Canberra's policy shift in respect to the forthcoming West Papuan vote. Meyers was all too familiar with the historical references that predicated Australia's current dilemma. Subsequent to the cessation of hostilities following the ousting of President Sukarno, with relations between Jakarta and Canberra on the mend, Australian bureaucrats and the business community now advocated nurturing relationships with Suharto's New Order elements; even if this resulted in West Papuans losing sovereignty to Indonesia.

Just months before, the newly appointed Australian External Affairs Minister, Gordon Freeth signalled Australia would accept the results of an act of self-determination in West Irian even though only one thousand representatives of the indigenous population would be selected to vote. Aware that the decision to support Indonesia's proposed methodology in implementing the so-called Act of Free Choice would polarise many across the political and intelligence spectrum, Meyers, the Department of External Affairs SE Asian theatre special envoy, was there to discuss the ramifications of the revised policy.

Canberra was now confronted with how to accommodate Indonesia's self-interest in moving to assume sovereignty over West Papua, whilst balancing the benefits of consolidating relationships with Suharto's pro-Western "New Order". Meyers accepted that this positioned Australia between two irreconcilable outcomes. Meyers knew that the Indonesian leadership, apart from any nationalist designs it held over the disputed territory, with General Suharto assuming power, the armed forces' economic tentacles had already reached far into the area. Preempting the plebiscite's outcome by issuing mining licenses two years before to the powerful American mining conglomerate, Summit Gold, the envoy understood why ABRI, the armed forces, were so profoundly opposed to West Papua's separation.

The Counsellor returned to find Meyers deep in thought, gazing out through the double-glazed windows. 'The ambassador and department heads are ready,' he announced, one hand extended to usher the visitor down the passageway to the meeting. The envoy followed, nodding and smiling at familiar faces when he joined the gathering of the embassy's most senior advisers.

Meyers had attended meetings in this inner sanctum before noting that nothing in the décor had changed since his most recent visit. An ornately carved desk separated the ambassador from the others, the attachés and others occupying a leather suite of armchairs positioned in a crescent row facing the Head of Mission.

'I believe that introductions are not necessary?' The Counsellor commenced as all present had attended such meetings together over time. 'With your permission, Ambassador, we'll ask Special Envoy Meyers to commence.'

The ambassador nodded affirmatively and Jonathan Meyers assumed the floor.

'Gentlemen,' he commenced, abandoning the customary acknowledgement to the ambassador. 'On behalf of the Minister I wish to offer some insight as to how Canberra will proceed in support of Indonesia's imminent assumption of sovereignty over West Papua.'

Without referring to notes, Meyer reminded those present of events which, over the previous months clearly reflected Indonesia's determination to have its way.

'When this country's Foreign Affairs Minister Adam Malik declared that the "one man, one vote system" proposed by the United Nations was impractical and therefore not acceptable, one could say that this was the opening round in Indonesia's more militant stance in securing the outcome over West Papua that we had previously wished to avoid. As you are aware, last month our ambassador challenged Adam Malik on if it were true that he had accused Australia of establishing training camps in Papua New Guinea close to the shared border with West Papua. Although Malik rescinded his earlier statement he did, nevertheless, suggest that such a development to be of concern to his government. 'Part of my brief today is to confirm that we are, in fact, continuing to covertly expand our military presence directly along the shared border area, in response to the increased number of Indonesian military incursions into our mandated territory of New Guinea.'

None of the three defence attachés so much as raised an eyebrow, aware of the Australian Special Forces jungle-warfare training camps in the New Guinea highlands. SAS presence had commenced along the border earlier that decade when Indonesia had unofficially declared war against neighbouring states, dragging Australian troops into direct confrontation with Indonesia's finest. SAS soldiers also undertook intensive training in the tropical environment to provide assimilation opportunities prior to taking up operations in Borneo and Vietnam. The attachés never discussed the black ops conducted by the SAS which often required cross-border search and destroy missions, resulting in deep penetration into Indonesian territory. Armed with the knowledge that border delineation both with Malaysia and New Guinea had never been clearly defined, in the unlikely event that SAS elements were captured, they were instructed to claim that they were not aware that they were on Indonesian soil.

'Documented reports demonstrate that the Indonesians remained determined to ignore our objections to their military incursions into New Guinea. In April, fifteen uniformed Indonesian soldiers followed a group of West Papuan refugees to Wutung, firing at the Patrol Post constabulary who later reported several of the refugees being killed in the skirmish.'

'And these attacks will continue unless we take them to task,' the Army Attaché interrupted.

'No doubt,' Meyer affirmed. 'The very reason we are beefing up our SAS presence along the border.' Those present were all too familiar with the extremely arduous treks SAS troops endured across the New Guinea highlands, their presence not only a flag-raising demonstration but ostensibly a deterrent, as Australia was still responsible for New Guinea's security. 'As we see it, the mobilisation of additional forces will be revisited once the outcome of the Act of Free Choice has been accepted internationally which, hopefully, will result in a cessation of any further incursions.'

The three military attachés glanced at each other, unconvinced. Jonathan Meyers' words were destined to return and haunt the next generation of Australian soldiers.

\*   \*   \*   \*

One hundred miles north of the Indonesian capital, Jakarta, the modified long-range Boeing 707 Air Force One's crew signaled to President Nixon's aides that they would be making their final approach within the next minutes. An attendant moved swiftly through the aircraft and stopped at an appropriate distance before addressing the leader of the Free World.

'Excuse me, Mister President,' she smiled broadly, 'the captain has advised that we shall be landing shortly.' Nixon nodded without eye contact and returned to his notes prepared by Henry Kissinger, who had, only minutes before, completed his final briefing on the Republic of Indonesia.

President Nixon's eyebrows squeezed together in a frown as he recalled Kissinger's specific comments. He mentally revisited these, his adviser's words coming back to mind; *"General Suharto is a moderate military man, committed to progress and reform. When in discussion with Suharto you should not raise the issue of the West Irian plebiscite except to respond if Suharto mentions the territory. You need to demonstrate that the US is sympathetic to Indonesia's concerns."*

Jet-lagged yet only partly into his Asia tour which would take him across SE Asia into Vietnam before returning to Washington, the furrows of Nixon's wrinkled face deepened, lost in geo-political confusion. 'What the hell has Iran got to do with this fellow Suharto?' he had asked the US National Security Adviser.

The President did not detect Kissinger's inaudible sigh. 'Irian, Dick, not Iran. The Indonesians call West New Guinea, West Irian.'

Despite being advised of Indonesia's real intentions and the obvious flaws evident in the Act of Free Choice, Nixon agreed with Kissinger's position that it was imperative for the US not to create obstacles for the Indonesians. Since the Washington-Jakarta rapprochement following Suharto's successful *coup d'état*, Kissinger knew the US was on the path for the Suharto-regime becoming increasingly pro-United States.

The recently elected president looked out the cabin window as the Boeing banked — his first imagery of the world's largest Moslem country spread out below prompting the question in his mind. *'How could this bankrupt nation be capable of paying for the military hardware they would undoubtedly require, to maintain their sovereignty over the fractious archipelagic nation?'*

\*   \*   \*   \*

27

# WEST IRIAN (WEST PAPUA)

## THE PLEBISCITE — THE ACT OF NO CHOICE

### 1969

Widespread rebellions erupted across the Western Central Highlands with the potential to jeopardize the integrity of the imminent voting process. Indonesia responded by increasing its military presence. In April, one hundred Papuan police mutinied and joined the Free Papuan Movement, OPM.

General Sarwo Edhie, the territory's Indonesian military commander, came under fire when his plane flew over the area. Livid at the audacity of the attack the General responded in the same bloody manner as he had in the aftermath of the failed Communist takeover in 1965. Ordering his forces to punish the OPM to the extreme, B-26 bombers strafed hamlets, and paratroopers from West Java were flown in to sweep the territory clean of all resistance. However, superior numbers and weaponry failed to break the Papuan spirit and the Indonesian counter attack faltered with nationalist demonstrations flaring on all fronts.

\*    \*    \*    \*

In an isolated enclave dominated by snow covered peaks, dusk passed. Darkness now masked the permanent mantel of clouded forest and verdant, fluorescent-green landscape, blanketing valleys below. Plumes snaked lazily from open timber-fuelled fires, flames illuminating the communal centre where ageing, betel-stained-teeth women gathered to watch barefooted children play. Surrounded by oak-brown thatched huts, young men sat within earshot of their elders, shoulders wrapped against the brisk highland air as they listened intently to Tomas Karma who had come to confer with the tribal council.

The Reverend Natan Tabuni's discerning eyes locked on Tomas Karma's movements from the moment he had entered the village. Natan had learned from others associated with the Council of Churches' missionary activities that Tomas had often been sighted mingling with Jakarta's dreaded Special Forces and members of *BRIMOB*, the brutal Mobile Police Brigade. During an earlier visit when he had challenged Tomas, the thirty-year-old, self-appointed *ondoafi*, or traditional head, had simply shrugged off the question, leaving Natan sceptical as to the man's sincerity in supporting the OPM. The Reverend's travels occasioned visits to Tomas' home area of Sentani where whispers of the large numbers of Papuans killed were directly accorded to Tomas' association with the Indonesian military. Natan considered the man an enigma; deeply concerned that Dutch-educated Tomas harboured a secret political agenda which could threaten the overall independence movement.

Natan continued to eye the visitor who sat crouched, squatting on haunches, arms crossed, seemingly absorbed by youngsters wrestling in the flickering campfire light. Natan's attention was momentarily distracted by Bennie, as the light-skinned child wrestled his opponent, Jules, to the ground in laughter.

Natan never tired of watching the adopted seven-year-old boys at play, content that they had integrated successfully into village life. As the boys frolicked Jules gained the advantage over his adversary Bennie. Unable to break his hold Bennie yielded to Jules who rose to his feet and playfully beat his chest.

Natan smiled, the moment reviving a memory he wished he could put to rest.

Several months had passed since news of the Dutch missionary's slaughter had reached Natan's village. The elder had hurried to the scene and, upon viewing the carnage, had his men bury the Dutch woman where she had died. Julius had been taken to Natan's community in the highlands to be cared for until, as Natan had mistakenly assumed, the authorities would repatriate the child. As the months passed the infant became part of the village mosaic; his assimilation into Natan's community unobserved to the outside world.

The village elder considered the two children. It was not uncommon for mixed ethnicity to be evident in Papuan families. During the Dutch presence there were numerous liaisons with native women. And, as the Dutch society across the *Indies* perceived a mixed marriage a greater evil than concubinage, and men married to native women and their offspring were barred from returning to Europe, the fruit of these relationships were invariably left behind.

Natan's thoughts turned to Bennie who had been delivered into his hands by Brother Tobias, following the disappearance of the American explorer Michael Rockefeller.

Charged with keeping Bennie's origins secret, Natan had undertaken to never reveal the truth of Bennie's parentage; the boy's past would remain buried, a pact sworn with the missionary, Tobias.

\*     \*     \*     \*

Tomas Karma moved closer to the camp fire, shadows flickering across his figure when a villager stoked embers to life.

'Before I leave,' he addressed the older men, 'I remind you again what is expected of this village.' Assured of their attention he continued. 'Soon there will be others who will come. These will be representatives of the great world power, the United Nations who will oversee the plebiscite. You must do as they say.'

With the majority of the elders' eyes dropping subserviently, Tomas remained confident knowing that yet another village community would comply with the voting procedures he had adumbrated earlier in the day. With his connivance, West Irian would remain a fiefdom to the Javanese.

Long after Tomas Karma had departed on his continuing quest to convince West Papuans that the model proposed to conduct the plebiscite would provide fair representation, the Reverend Natan Tabuni remained deeply troubled. He ruminated through the night as he considered the ramifications of the proposed, flawed-voting procedures which would undoubtedly deliver the three hundred Papuan tribes into Indonesian arms. Natan accepted that the Papuans would be tempted to take the line of least resistance, having been subjected to partial Indonesian occupation since the betrayal of 1963, when Jakarta mobilised large concentrations of rapacious military personnel to the territory. He had witnessed Indonesia's denigration of the Papuan people; the degradation by racial discrimination. It was clear to Natan that the Javanese looked down upon the indigenes as being inferior because of their darker skin and lack of civilized attributes. He had seen how the presence of Indonesian troops had placed an unendurable burden on the local economy with military commanders plundering produce creating life threatening shortages of fruit and vegetables, crucial to the local population for their survival.

Natan had learned that the occupying armed forces had mobilised close to ten thousand troops in West Irian, the bulk belonging to the *Cenderawasih, Hasanudin, Brawidjaja, Siliwangi* and *Merdeka* Divisions with a support group of Mobile Brigade police. Faced with such formidable forces he accepted that it would simply be a matter of time before the occupying forces mopped up the fractured elements of resistance, as his people had few modern weapons, ammunition or supplies.

He prayed that a groundswell of world opinion would prevent the ongoing brutal repression. However, as Jakarta had never heeded the international community when crushing other secessionist movements in the past, Natan was far from optimistic. When his thoughts returned to what might lay ahead for Papuans, he rested his chin on calloused hands and prayed.

Saddened by what appeared to be inevitable, Natan continued his silent deliberations, sitting alone in the village square whilst others slept, until crowing roosters broke the silence of dawn.

* * * *

# AKUMUGA MINING SITE

## MAKOE MOUNTAIN RANGE

Sitting amongst the high slopes of the Makoe Mountains within the Akumuga Mine complex, Brother Tobias gazed moodily across the improvised school grounds, wondering how the children could maintain their playful activities, in the oxygen-starved outpost.

The missionary unconsciously fiddled with a loose overcoat button until it dangled then fell to the floor. Cursing painful joints as he bent down to recover the chipped, wooden disc the movement exacerbated the headache resulting from a mixture of high mountain air, and the remnants of a bottle of home-brewed *arak*.

Tobias rose and leaned back in his wobbly, plastic chair now stretched under his oversized frame, his thoughts distracted by a child standing forlornly watching others at play. The image resurrected past events and his mind momentarily tracked back to the fair-skinned child born seven years before. Recollections of the young American dragged from crocodile-infested, muddy reaches along the Asmat shores, reminded Tobias of events that he hoped would remain buried and forgotten.

Michael Rockefeller had been mauled and not expected to survive. Limited medical resources were available to tend to his wounds however, under the attentive eyes of the village women the man gradually recovered.

Several weeks convalescing had passed when, suddenly, approaching Christmas Eve, Michael Rockefeller disappeared without any trace. It was as if he had never existed. Or at least, not in *that* village.

Neither Tobias nor the villagers were aware of the American's importance until foreign teams appeared and scoured the mangrove-ringed coastline searching for the missing heir, Michael Rockefeller. Tobias had never understood why Rockefeller had not revealed his identity, arriving at the conclusion that this was withheld, because the wealthy and educated explorer knew that his family name would have no significance, in this distant and unfamiliar corner of the planet.

When one of the village women, who had been in close attendance with the handsome explorer later died giving birth to a light-skinned child with obvious Caucasian features, the elders took the mother's death as a sign and threatened to sacrifice the newborn.

Tobias remembered moving quickly to remove the child from the village. Previous contact with a highland community that had converted to Christianity drove him to take the infant there, for safety. When he arrived at Natan Tabuni's doorstep, the baby was close to death. With a surrogate mother identified the child survived its ordeal. Prior to Tobias' return to the Asmat community, he and Natan had christened the boy, naming him Bennie.

Upon his return, Tobias remained in the Asmat area for a further five years before being assigned to overseeing the spiritual needs of the burgeoning, mining population at the newly-created Akumuga mining village.

\*   \*   \*   \*

Mobilisation for the Akumuga Mine had commenced within months of the US-based consortium signing with the Indonesian Government. A one-hundred kilometre road had been carved out of the challenging terrain followed by the construction of a pipeline from the newly-created port facility and airstrip on the southern coast. A township had emerged embracing the port development, aptly named Kampung Mas, which translated literally as "Gold Village".

The entire landscape became peppered with Indonesian Special Forces *KOPASSUS* soldiers.

Tobias' mind glazed back to the scene outside as another helicopter arrived disembarking expatriate engineers. He knew these foreign workers would remain on site for their two-week stint, accommodated in converted containers, before being shuttled back to Kampung Mas, where charter flights connected to home destinations.

Military barracks providing support facilities for the one hundred Indonesian soldiers were strategically placed towards the main gate entrance. Along the outer perimeter shanty-dwellings had already appeared. These were occupied predominantly by prostitutes transported to the site from poverty-stricken environments throughout the Nusa Tenggara Islands, although a small number of local indigenous women from the three Akumuga tribes also worked in the brothel.

The missionary occupied one of the converted container dwellings. The elongated structure partitioned to provide for basic living quarters at one end, whilst the remaining half was presented as a small, makeshift chapel.

Tobias managed himself upright and over to the first aid cabinet.

He squinted inside the small cupboard, his brow collapsing into furrows upon discovering the bottle of *arak* was not in its customary hiding place. Stumbling around the cramped quarters he found the bottle lying in the sink, alarmingly empty, and he cursed aloud, raising an index finger to the heavens then sulked.

\*    \*    \*    \*

# AUSTRALIA

## CANBERRA

Director John W. Andersen returned from his one-on-one with the larrikin Prime Minister John Gorton, somewhat relieved that the former RAAF pilot shared his views with respect to the United States and, closer to home, Indonesia.

Andersen opened his briefcase, extracted a file bound with bright red tape signifying the contents' level of secrecy, and re-read the report he had earlier tabled for the PM. The communication was headed "Secret, AUSTEO (Australian Eyes Only) — Australian Special Forces' West Irian Cross Border Intrusions".

Although joint members of the 1947 UK-USA Security Treaty which established an alliance of Anglo-sphere countries for the purpose of sharing intelligence, it was unusual for the Australian intelligence agencies to withhold information from their ally, the United States. The Australian Security Intelligence Organization (ASIO) and the Australian Secret Intelligence Service (ASIS), the equivalent to both the CIA and MI6 were very closely integrated at most levels of the intelligence exchange apparatus. In fact, Andersen encouraged ASIO and ASIS agents to develop even closer relationships with their foreign counterparts, as it was undeniable that both agencies identified ideologically with the CIA's right-wing elements. Nevertheless, Andersen and his predecessors had gone to extreme measures to protect the integrity of the existence of ASIS which, as of that time, was known only to a limited few, the exclusion including New Zealand until only four years before. ASIS members, upon sighting any communication or file that bore the heading "OYSTER" knew immediately that the contents were the product of the real Secret Service.

Since its inception, ASIS had been involved in a number of projects designed to destabilise Indonesia's pro-Communist president, Sukarno which, inarguably, resulted in the mass murder of hundreds of thousands of Indonesians during the turmoil that followed. Now, undeniably supporting the recently-installed Suharto regime, ASIS continued with its clandestine operations across the archipelago, directed from the First Secretary Political Affairs office in the Australian Embassy on Jalan Thamrin, Jakarta.

\*   \*   \*   \*

Andersen's meeting with John Gorton had lasted just under an hour. The Prime Minister's derogatory anti-comments during their discussion were not entirely in concert with the Director's own position.

'I don't trust the bastards,' the PM had reiterated, as Andersen recalled the somewhat undiplomatic statement being made by Gorton to the American Secretary of State, Dean Rusk on an earlier occasion. 'And I am sick and tired of being reminded that we should be obligated to their so-called nuclear umbrella!'

The PM continued his diatribe. 'It's time we did something constructive about developing our own nuclear weaponry.' Andersen remained silent, permitting the PM to vent. 'We shouldn't fall into the trap of believing that the Americans would keep their side of our treaty, the event of any nuclear threat.' Andersen was aware of the heated exchange between Rusk and Gorton which had resulted in a searing recommendation by Rusk to Washington comparing the Australian PM to France's Charles de Gaulle. The Americans were deeply annoyed with Gorton's insistence that Australia should serious consider constructing its own nuclear arsenal at a time the USA was lobbying for a nuclear non-proliferation treaty, and pressing Canberra to sign.

John Gorton scratched at a phantom itch on the side of his cheek. 'There's no doubt about their intentions to remain the only player in our backyard,' he continued. 'This business of Washington urges us to crank up our efforts in establishing military cooperation with Jakarta. It's just so bloody obvious. On one hand they don't wish to be perceived as having any influence over the outcome of the Irian vote, yet they have all but guaranteed the Indonesians that not only the UN, but Australia as well, will support a pro-Jakarta outcome.'

'We all know why Washington wants it that way,' Andersen reminded him.

The PM continued to scratch as he considered the US Navy brief he had been privy to, even before assuming the leadership from the interim Prime Minister, Jack McEwen. 'Well, providing the Americans with free passage through Indonesian waters for their nuclear submarines has certainly come at a price.'

Andersen sensed where the conversation was heading. Unbeknown to the general public there were two deep ocean passages that joined the South China Sea and Pacific Ocean to the Indian Ocean, both imperative for the undetected transit by nuclear submarines. The Lombok Strait was one such channel and the other, the lesser known trenches of Ombai and Wetar which touched the island of Timor, were more frequently traversed by US warships.

The ASIS Director was *au fait* with US submarines and the missiles they carried. He knew that currently, these boats were armed with the Polaris A3 which could strike any target within two thousand, five hundred nautical miles which placed most of SE Asia and China within range. Operating from the nearest submarine base located on Guam, nuclear-missile carrying submarines could choose between the Ombai-Wetar or Lombok passages to access targets in the Middle East, and Diego Garcia in the Indian Ocean, saving some eight to ten days steaming time.

The Director was also aware, however, that the submerged passage of submarines through the Indonesian archipelago contravened the 1958 Geneva Convention on the Territorial Sea and Contiguous Zone, which provided that vessels passing through territorial waters were only entitled to the right of 'innocent passage' which obliged the crew to navigate on the surface and show their country's flag.

The PM dry-washed his partially disfigured face with hardened hands. The scars were a reminder of a time when he piloted a Hawker Hurricane and had crash-landed during the war against Japan. Gorton's face had slammed against the gun sight and windscreen mutilating his nose and breaking both cheekbones. He thumbed open the 'OYSTER' report Andersen had wished to discuss.

'Are the Americans aware of our incursions?'

Andersen shook his head. 'They don't have any assets in New Guinea. Besides, even if it did become known that our Special Forces crossed into West Irian we would merely shrug it off as the delineation of the border is far from clear to either side.' Andersen moved to reassure. 'And we have a legitimate reason for our troops to be stationed in the New Guinea highlands. Apart from our UN responsibility to provide New Guinea with defence and security, it's a perfect environment to train our men in jungle warfare, and preparation for their Vietnam deployment.'

'And what about those engagements between our troops and the Indonesians?' the PM wanted to know. Typically, Gorton was seeking confirmation of what he had been told by the Chief of Army.

'Nothing that's been relayed through our people in Jakarta,' Andersen reassured. The SAS troopers operated under the strictest guidelines. Should Indonesian forces be caught crossing into New Guinea then they were dealt with expeditiously, their bodies buried deep in the jungle. In the event of any Australian casualties inside Indonesian territory, wounded or dead, bodies were never left behind to avoid the potential for political fallout.

\* \* \* \*

Having returned to his office, Director Andersen sat alone quietly chewing over the dramatic shift in Australia's policy towards Indonesia since General Suharto had seized power, acknowledging that

Canberra's about face over West Irian to support Jakarta was in Australia's long-term interests.

Andersen accepted the premise that whoever controlled New Guinea and West New Guinea had the capacity to greatly influence the security of shipping to Australian ports, this consideration soon to become paramount with New Guinea's independence to be granted in five years. He had read his agents' reports from Jakarta expressing the Indonesian military's concerns that New Guinea would become a hotbed of rebel, if not communist activity, once independence had been achieved.

Andersen appreciated Indonesia's tendency to suspect the West's motives from a historical perspective. Jakarta secretly resented the United States and had done so dating back to when the Eisenhower Administration, obsessed with the eradication of the Indonesian Communist Party, had decided to attack and invade with the support of rebels in Sumatra and Sulawesi. The United States had provided funds, weapons, training and backed by the Seventh Fleet with air support out of the Philippines, had moved to overthrow the Sukarno regime. Incredibly, the plan failed. Then, in the following eight years, six US-sponsored assassination attempts made on President Sukarno left no doubt as to the Americans' determination to expand their sphere of influence, displacing the British and French across SE Asia.

\*   \*   \*   \*

# INDONESIA

### HANKAM — INDONESIAN DEFENCE DEPARTMENT — JAKARTA

The Brigadier General signed the document then watched officiously as the order was sealed by a junior officer. 'Ensure a copy is hand-delivered to *Jalan Cendana*,' the Brigadier General ordered. 'Inform the Palace Guards you are on the way.'

Alone with his thoughts the general remained at his desk contemplating the momentous increase in troop numbers across the restive territory known as Irian Barat. In preparation of the imminent Act of Free Choice vote his troops had engaged in widespread killing to annihilate Papuan resistance. At first, he had believed that last month's aerial bombing of the Wissel Lake District had been successful, with more than fourteen thousand villagers fleeing into the jungle, only to learn that the event had hardened the Papuan resolve swelling the ranks of the resistance movement. He accepted that the three-thousand-strong Papuan Battalion formed by the Dutch in earlier times offered a serious threat to the outcome of the imminent vote to determine the territory's future. These guerrilla units were collectively known as the *Organisasi Papua Merdeka* (Free Papua Movement; OPM) and the general was determined to have them annihilated, to a man, as the President had ordered the military to take whatever measures necessary to ensure an outcome that would favour Jakarta.

The OPM had too many successes in opposing the brutal Indonesian occupation army. Two years earlier, the OPM had overrun the former Dutch capital, Manokwari and held it for several days until retaken by the general's paratroopers.

In light of the *KOPASSUS* Special Forces' presence in the operational theatre and their achievements, he was reminded of the recent report claiming thousands of Papuans had been killed by *KOPASSUS* troops during an uprising in the Kebar Valley, and Paniai District.

The Brigadier General mentally counted the numbers he could still draw down upon from commands in other provinces. In order to achieve the required result troop strengths in Irian Barat his Indonesian security forces had been increased to forty-thousand, of which five thousand were members of the Mobile Brigade (*BRIMOB*), the paramilitary brigade. The general considered this elite unit necessary in dealing with the ongoing, deeply-annoying mass demonstrations currently occurring in major West Irian centres.

Deciding a face-to-face with the relevant commanding officers would be more appropriate, he summoned an aide and ordered a vehicle to stand by to take him across the city to Cijantung, home of the revered Special Forces.

*　*　*　*

# INDONESIAN SPECIAL FORCES (*KOPASSUS*)

## GROUP 3 SANDI YUDHA

## CIJANTUNG, EAST JAKARTA

Elements of Batallions 31, 32 and 33 were present when their commanding officer, an infantry colonel, briefed the select assembly of soldiers from the *KOPASSUS* (a portmanteau of *Komando Pasukan Khusus*) Special Forces Group 3, *Sandhi Yudha*. This highly-secretive command specialised in clandestine operations, the gathering of combat intelligence and counter insurgency. The unit had been operational for two years, headquartered amongst other commands at Cijantung in the outer-eastern corridors of the capital, Jakarta.

The Colonel scanned the serious-faced men before him as if searching for any that might disappoint, a problem the unit had occasionally experienced when some of its number displayed excessive behaviour. He accepted that it was not always possible to weed out those with maverick tendencies.

Soldiers selected for membership of Group 3 had not only completed the demanding basic ten weeks *KOPASSUS* entry training, but had also completed specialist training undercover operations and advanced martial arts. Many of these soldiers had been selected to attend military intelligence education centres abroad in the United Kingdom, Germany, Israel and the USA.

Due to the secrecy of the unit, its members were ordered never to reveal their activities to any, including family.

Group 3 elements were essential to providing on-the-ground

theatre combat intelligence prior to any military incursions. Often operating in civilian attire with the appropriate documentation, these *Sandhi Yudha* operatives acted as fifth columnists and undertook subversive actions. On occasion, the State Intelligence Agency (*BIN*) utilised *Sandhi Yudha* personnel due to their expertise, when shadow operations were required.

The Colonel accepted that penetrating the Papuan communities with secretive agents would be extremely difficult due to the absence of any indigenous Papuans within his organisation. To overcome this hurdle, he had decided to utilise several of his specialist undercover agents to assume the role of black marketeers in the targeted areas, and ingratiate themselves with the local traders. These operatives would be separated from family and friends, frequently for extended periods.

When the unit had been dismissed and the briefing completed, the Colonel examined his notes, satisfied that his highly-skilled soldiers would complete the clandestine operations ordered by Central Command, and other more delicate missions he personally had authorised.

An uncommon smile curled the officer's upper lip as he nodded sagely to himself; satisfied that amongst his bag of dirty tricks, the introduction of pigs infected with the very contagious swine flu across the Papuan environment would exacerbate food shortages across the undeveloped territory. Several hundred infected animals had been moved from Bali by freighter, the virus to be introduced into the animals prior to the ship's arrival in the far eastern destination known as Irian Barat.

*     *     *     *

# USA

## Phoenix Arizona

Chubby fingers held a Cuban in one hand and a near-empty tumbler of Southern Comfort bourbon in the other. The Summit Gold Mining president peered out across the city of Phoenix two miles north, where the Phoenix Corporate Tower stood supreme. Soon, he mused, the title of being the tallest skyscraper in Arizona would be passed to another, the Wells Fargo Plaza, as it was completed in just over a year.

He turned to the former diplomat and, consciously tapping ash from the cigar to the floor, raised his glass. 'To our good friends in Jakarta,' he toasted.

The former United States Secretary of Defense nodded. '…and to a clear and prosperous path ahead.'

The Summit Gold president nodded knowingly. His associate had been instrumental in orchestrating Washington's substantial increase in military aid to Indonesia, which was delivered with the customary "facilitations fees" to that nation's generals, via Langley financial conduits. President Nixon had returned from visiting Jakarta where behind closed doors, he assured President Suharto that the United States fully supported an outcome when the plebiscite was held, whereby Indonesia would legitimately absorb West Irian.

When President Sukarno had been overthrown in a coup, there had been a rush to invest in the emerging economy, and Summit Gold had been amongst the many USA interests that had immediately invested in Indonesia. The new regime under General Suharto had thrown open thousands of square kilometres of offshore oil fields to US multi-nationals such as Atlantic Richfield, Mobil Oil, and Union Carbide. Stock markets responded favourably and, amongst those that benefited, was the US listed Natomas Co whose shares were listed in 1968 at sixteen dollars, and within one year had increased in value by eightfold.

The Summit Gold board members wielded considerable influence in Washington and had Pentagon assurances, that arms shipments destined for the illegal campaign in Cambodia would be redirected to the Indonesian military, to consolidate their presence in West Irian. Publicly, the US Government had supported almost $400 million in grants and loans to Jakarta, accepting that much of this would be siphoned off by the so-called New Order's quasi-military regime.

When the initial Contract of Work to commence operations was signed, the Summit Gold founding shareholders accepted that an allocation of fully-paid shares would be allocated to selected members of Jakarta's powerful elite. Summit Gold had negotiated a seventy-five percent share in the new Indonesian mining entity, P.T. Akumuga Mining. The Indonesian Government was gifted ten percent, and the remaining fifteen percent was held by a nominee entity, on behalf of undeclared local interests. Akumuga Mining's investment agreement with the government provided for Summit Gold to carry out exploration, mining and production activities, across an area of some twenty-five thousand acres, on a site adjacent to the border with Papua New Guinea.

The company's operations had been in progress for eighteen

months, and capital expenditure had already exceeded $100M with expectations that a further $50M would be required in the coming year.

The former United States Secretary of Defense topped-up their tumblers. He was conscious that his associate had reservations about the outcome of the imminent plebiscite. 'The situation will be much clearer once the United Nations observers leave the area in August and the military can consolidate its presence at the mine.'

The company president suppressed a sigh, recalling what his associate's Pentagon contacts had suggested would be the impact on the indigenous tribes, once Jakarta officially assumed control over the former Dutch outpost. 'I just wish we could have accommodated the Papuans without all this bloodshed.'

'Forget about those stone-age bastards,' the Secretary countered. 'Once their environment has been fully developed and they're dragged into the twentieth century, they'll come to appreciate the downstream benefits from the mine's development.'

The Summit Gold president turned back to the window and stared out into space, his conscience reminding him that this was unlikely to be true.

*       *       *       *

# WEST IRIAN

Indonesia's General Murtopo had warned the Papuans that if they voted against Indonesia *"their accursed tongues will be cut out and their evil mouths wrenched open"*.

As the commencement of polling approached, elements of Jakarta's ruthless and highly-trained Police Mobile Brigade *BRIMOB* and the army's *KOPASSUS* Special Forces swept across the territory, to ensure the desired outcome. Jakarta's strategy cut off resistance groups from supporting the village populations, thereby destroying their food supply. Thousands of Papuans were killed as the occupying army inaugurated a system of relocating smaller village communities into designated and more manageable, but agriculturally-poor areas. Deprived of their traditional food supplies many perished. As the military round-up of Free Papua activists continued, intimidated villagers quickly fell into line.

However, strong pockets of resistance remained in the more isolated, mountainous regions. In April, rebellions erupted in the Western Central Highlands, when one hundred armed Papuan policemen joined the rebels. The Indonesian military's response was brutal. When a gathering of demonstrators near Jayapura proclaimed a "National Republic of West Papua" the group was dispersed by machine-gun fire leaving many dead, and others to be imprisoned. Unconstrained, a platoon of Indonesian soldiers forced their way into the United Nation's post and arrested Marshal Williams, the UNRWI's black American Chief administrative officer, mistaking him for a Papuan.

Jakarta despatched nine ground-force task units to Irian Barat.

Uprisings continued throughout the territory; air fields were sabotaged to prevent Indonesian troop landings, which precipitated the poorly-conceived aerial drop of four battalions of Red Beret paratroopers from Hercules aircraft. Most of the soldiers drowned in Lake Paniai when the pilot missed the target, and those who survived were killed by Papuan Resistance forces.

*   *   *   *

On July 14, 1969, the Act of Free Choice finally began as the sound of democracy faded.

An assembly of only one thousand Papuan members, selected to represent the entire Papuan population, had spent several weeks before the day under guard by the authorities, and isolated from the rest of the community. Most assembly members were either threatened or bribed by Jakarta's presiding general, choosing specific individuals who had rehearsed pro-Indonesian speeches to speak at the assembly. These representatives were to create a collective consensus to remain with Indonesia and, in turn, each stood and made similar statements proclaiming they recognized the Indonesian Constitution.

When the Act's implementation was complete, Jakarta announced all the Papuans had elected to remain with Indonesia. Tomas Karma was one of the thousand delegates to the 'Act of Free Choice'. He would become a member of Suharto's political wing, *Golkar* and serve as a member of the West Papuan provincial parliament.

The sham referendum was ratified by the UN General Assembly paving the way for the betrayal of the people of West New Guinea which then became absolute, and West Irian became Indonesia's twenty-sixth province.

The Indonesian military moved quickly to establish a permanent presence to control the indigenous population, now agitated by the influx of Javanese immigrants brought in under the government's transmigration program, to dilute the native presence.

The Free Papua Movement (OPM) rejected the referendum result, advocating unification with neighbouring Papua New Guinea (PNG), and commenced an ongoing low-level insurgency operating from sanctuaries along the common border, under the watchful eyes of Australian Special Forces.

Fifty years of repression, reprisals and genocidal behaviour would pass before the flawed plebiscite would be revisited by the United Nations, dragging Indonesia and Australia once again, to the brink of war.

*       *       *       *

# THE PRESENT

## LONDON

The crowded Westminster auditorium, filled with politicians, members of the international business community, diplomats, and the media had attracted the attention of intelligence circles.

Indonesian State Intelligence agents from BIN *(Badan Intelijen Negara)* continued their surveillance on the *de facto* leader of West Papua's Government in Exile, Bennie Tabuni.

At the rear of the hall, Anne Whitehead stood alongside Jules Heynneman. When polite applause followed Tabuni's introduction as the closing speaker, she tilted her head closer to Jules. 'You need to press him to take the warnings more seriously,' she said, *sotto voce*.

Jules turned and whispered in response. 'Already taken care of … Don't worry.'

Anne slipped a hand to his elbow and pinched lightly. 'That applies to you also.'

Jules glanced sideways and winked. 'I have it covered.'

They then both stood silently listening to Bennie continue his address to the assembly.

' … and the primary purpose tonight is to encourage all who support democracy to sign the global petition calling upon the United Nations to revisit the flawed so-called Act of Free Choice, by intervening in Indonesia's brutal repression, and providing for West Papuan's legitimate claim for independence.

'It was not so long ago Parliamentarians from around the world signed up to the International Parliamentarians for West Papua (IPWP)'s "Westminster Declaration", calling on the UN to over-see a new independence referendum. Since that landmark, historic moment, seven countries have collectively voiced their support for our struggle. We thank the people of Nauru, the Marshall Islands, Tuvalu, Vanuatu, the Solomon Islands, Tonga and Palau for their contribution towards the formation of the Pacific Coalition for West Papua ...'

Jules watched Bennie approvingly, pleased with his "adopted" brother's performance. Although he had attended countless, similar appeals before, Jules still marvelled at Bennie's capacity to motivate his supporters. Jules had never felt envious of the attention this attracted recognising from the very beginning of their journey together that each enjoyed their own specific skills, and ambitions.

His thoughts wandered, carried to a distant place by the famil-iar voice at the podium, an image of their childhood village and the family that had raised them as their own, coming to mind.

\*   \*   \*   \*

Bennie and Jules' relationship grew from what set them apart from the other village children. Both enjoyed a mixed, European parent-age and physically, they stood tall amongst their village peers. When Natan Tabuni believed the timing was appropriate Jules had been informed of his origins. Bennie, however, was told that he had been adopted immediately following his birth, and that his parents were unknown.

Although the same age as Jules, Bennie assumed the role of elder brother from the outset, the two inseparable companions making their mark scholastically in Jayapura. Under kinship care, Natan Tabuni had arranged through the Council of Churches for both lads to be educated in the city as isolated village schools were inadequately provisioned, with textbooks and quality teachers.

Both had attended the old campus of the Cenderawasih University in Jayapura, again with the support of church foundations that provided scholarships. Bennie had covertly become politically active whilst serving in the provincial government. Jules' interest in commerce however drove the young men along different paths initially, until they realised that there was a common thread in the direction both were heading.

Applause reverberating throughout the assembly brought Jules back to the present, and again he focussed on Bennie's address.

'Even against almost impossible odds with fifteen thousand Indonesian troops stationed across our homeland, the people of West Papua are determined to reclaim the voice that was denied in 1969. If you are serious about defending human rights this is the moment to stand with West Papua. We seek to make up for the mistake in allowing Indonesia to take control almost fifty years ago. We ask that you join us now to support our quest for the United Nations to pass a resolution sponsoring an internationally-supervised vote, to return West Papua to the rightful owners and grant their claim for independence.'

Bennie turned and pointed to the Free Papua Organisation flag, *The Morning Star* with its white five-pointed star at its centre, spread against the backdrop. 'The Indonesians imprison West Papuans who fly this flag of defiance. But, proudly, we still do!'

Many amongst the audience had risen to their feet and applauded loudly. Enjoying the response Bennie nodded in appreciation then closed his address. Stepping down from the dais he was engulfed by eager supporters, many already pledging their financial support for his cause.

Anne tugged at Jules' sleeve. 'I have to leave for a meeting. I'll call you at the hotel later to fix a time to catch up in the morning. There's much we need to discuss before Bennie returns to Amsterdam.'

\*    \*    \*    \*

Anne Whitehead gathered her coat, stepped into the cold English night, and hailed a taxi instructing the driver to take her to a Hampstead address. Rain fell heavily and blurred street lighting and buildings in a mesmerising fashion. Anne consciously ignored their passage, concentrating on how she would frame her recommendations to her superior, now awaiting her arrival.

The taxi slowed and came to rest and with each movement of the windshield wipers she caught a glimpse of flashing red lights ahead. When the driver slowly shook his head in exasperation, Anne resigned herself to the delay and called her destination. Settling back into her seat she permitted her mind to take her back in time, reflecting on the origins of her relationship with Bennie and Jules.

Often captivated by her father's many anecdotes relating to the time he had served with Her Majesty's Embassy in Jakarta, Anne had developed an early interest in Asia, with a special interest in SE Asia's archipelagic regions. Armed with graduate degrees in South Asian Studies and Anthropology from the University of Edinburgh,

Anne had entered the workforce, engaged by the multi-international behemoth, Anglo American Aerospace Defence Technologies Inc. When an opportunity arose to fill a position with a subsidiary unit in Singapore, Anne had applied and was accepted for the post. During her three-year posting with the company which specialised in the engineering of mining operations, and studying part-time, Anne earned an MBA at the Nanyang Business School in Singapore. It was there she had met and entered into a relationship with the brash, young Julius Heynneman whose trading network across the Indonesian archipelago had earned him the agency rights, for Anglo American Aerospace Defence Technologies Inc. products and services. Their affair was casual, one more of convenience than commitment, and had, over time, developed into a mature relationship that surpassed their sexual liaisons.

Acting on Jules's invitation to visit the sites across Indonesia where engineering systems designed and installed by the Defence Technologies Group were operating, Anne spent two weeks crisscrossing the vast archipelago, completing the tour by visiting the Akumuga Mine. She recalled how during the West Papua journey Jules had become withdrawn and introspective, and even with her cajoling he had remained reserved and distant. It was not until they had returned to Singapore that Jules revealed the story of his early life, and relationship to the man he accepted as a brother, Bennie Tabuni.

Anne learned of the hardships and opportunities the boys of mixed blood had experienced, appreciating how their fair features had set them apart from the other children. Jules recounted how they had been raised initially in a remote highland village then sent to school in Jayapura, and educated under the patronage of the Council of Churches, the path providing access to university studies. During this period, Jules had explained, both were cognizant that if they were to succeed outside their environment, they would need to become fluent in English. This, they achieved, albeit with noticeable accents, a product of their non-native-speaking English teachers.

As her company's commercial activities blossomed across the Indonesian mining sector due to Jules' association, so too had her fondness for both men.

At the outset, Bennie had remained an enigmatic, shadowy figure to Anne. It was not until the following year when Jules arranged a discreet gathering across the Causeway, in Johore Baru, that she had any real one-on-one direct communication with Bennie. It was then that she became aware of the significance of Bennie's role in Indonesian politics, specifically those relating to West Papua.

Anne recalled her surprise with Bennie's knowledge of the parent company that indirectly employed her, the Anglo American Aerospace Defence Technologies Inc's (AAADT). It became evident that his interest lay with the arms and weapons division.

The British-American multi-national had long been a major global arms supplier and via its predominant client, Saudi Arabia, the group had successfully penetrated the Indonesian military market. Due to AAADT's sensitive operations, both the British and United States' governments enjoyed oversight positions within the company's structure. The weapons division operated as a semi-autonomous business unit within AAADT, under the watchful eyes of MI6 who were obliged, but did not always adhere to, sharing operational information with their counterpart, the CIA.

Anne had signed the mandatory Official Secrets Act during the embryonic stages of her career. She discovered how the British conglomerate successfully avoided compliance with mandated sanctions against potential client states or organizations. To circumvent such rulings AAADT often dealt through so-called arms-length operatives such as mercenaries.

Anne understood that the British Government was not alone in its concerns how destabilised Indonesia had become since East Timor won its independence from Indonesia. With an international groundswell supporting a United Nations review on the question growing beyond expectations, AAADT commenced supplying arms to the rebels. The British had commenced the covert weapons delivery via Belgium conduits with an expectation that, eventually, West Papuan independence would become a reality. The AAADT senior executives believed that such an outcome could also improve its current military sales to Indonesia. Looking ahead, AAADT's projections were that any future, independent West Papua with such natural resource wealth would naturally wish to build a defence force to defend its borders. As AAADT's weapons manufacturing arm produced an array of armoury along with combat vehicles, missile launchers, artillery systems and munitions, the long-term potential for military sales was substantial.

Anne felt the taxi move forward. She checked the Tag quartz watch on her wrist, frowned, and chewed on the inside of her lower lip, annoyed that she would have to cancel her scheduled hiking event, yet again.

Calling ahead to alert her party that she was on the move again, Anne dismissed the temptation to resurrect further memories of those past, special moments with Jules. Instead, she mentally prepared for her arrival to discuss how her masters, Anglo American Aerospace Defence Technologies together with the British Government, could exploit the relationship she had developed, over some twenty years.

*   *   *   *

Jules remained behind at the event until he was comfortable that Bennie had been surreptitiously escorted by his own security team, to the private address in West Brompton. Satisfied that the Indonesian security agents had been unable to follow, he departed to the discreet accommodations to prepare with Bennie, for their crucial meeting with Anne Whitehead's masters and their clandestine British Government associates.

Jules was ushered into the two-storey dwelling set in the leafy and tranquil environment where Bennie waited impatiently. He gestured for Jules to approach, handing a stapled document for him to review.

'The updated version,' he offered.

Jules moved to a contemporary, living-room chair and commenced reading. Less than a minute passed when he raised an eyebrow and waved the document in Bennie's direction. 'We're moving the timing back again?'

'Yes,' Bennie confirmed. 'Another six months. There's a problem with double-handling the final shipments from Port Villa.'

'Will Coleman have the capacity to handle such transhipments?'

'I've already discussed this with him. He's suggested moving the final delivery to the border staging point as before, then breaking down the volumes for more secure passage into the holding depot.'

Jules locked eyes with Bennie. 'We were getting close,' he stated. 'And I, for one, am losing patience with having to move the deadline back yet again.'

'We can't risk jeopardising everything for the sake of a few more months.' Bennie admonished. 'And if that means waiting another three, even six months once the final delivery has been completed then that's the direction we will take.'

The men were under no illusion as to the enormous risk they were undertaking. They recognised the futility in even considering confronting the might of the Indonesian military and, in consequence, their strategy to draw other nations into a border conflict had always been the foundation of their long-term strategy. Indonesia's four hundred thousand-strong military combined with the might of its hardware would not be challenged directly. Instead, orchestrated guerrilla-tactics had been the methodology, Bennie's small teams able to strike then disappear, a clear advantage over the invading forces.

Jules' demeanour reflected his dissatisfaction with another delay. Bennie stepped across from the desk and placed a hand on his shoulder. 'Let's see what the outcome is tomorrow then revisit the timing. If the Brits baulk then that would impact on our next move.'

Jules nodded. 'We should have given Anne some warning.'

'She doesn't always need to know the complete picture.' Bennie pondered momentarily carefully selecting his words. 'We must be careful, Jules. There's too much at stake not to be reminded where her first loyalty lies.'

Jules sat thoughtfully before responding. 'She's been a good friend. To all of us.' Bennie's daughter Alice immediately came to mind.

* * * *

Although Bennie's concerns for his daughter and only child, Alice, had been alleviated by taking the necessary steps to disguise their relationship very early in life, her safety remained paramount in his mind. As Natan Tabuni and his wife had fostered Bennie, he had assumed their surname prior to leaving for Jayapura to commence schooling. Upon graduation he married Natan's niece, and was gifted a daughter from that union.

About that time, although a peripheral participant, Bennie had already been identified, along with Natan's son Markus, for this political activism, their names listed in the Indonesian State's BIN secret dossiers as agitators, and placed under constant surveillance. During a flag-raising rally which Bennie had been unable to attend, both Natan and Bennie's wife were amongst the many killed, when *BRIMOB* elements opened fire on the crowd.

Marcus had been arrested, charged and incarcerated at the infamous Wamena Prison under the provision that outlawed *"makar"*, or rebellion. Markus challenged the charge, one often used against persons arrested for their alleged participation in, or support for, separatism. His lawyer explained that the crime of *makar* was listed in Indonesia's criminal code in a section entitled "Crimes Against the Security of the State" (*Kejahatan Terhadap Keamanan Negara*) which should not have been applied, particularly as the articles authorise prison terms up to twenty years for the such offences.

The appeal failed.

Sentenced to fifteen years and after serving five of these, Marcus' assisted escape by boat to Darwin placed him out of Indonesian reach. However, his status in Australia continued to be precarious having not been granted asylum out of political concerns, that such acceptance would jeopardise Canberra-Jakarta relationships.

An accumulation of these events had become the catalyst for Bennie's commitment to actively support the independence movement, then joining a group involved in armed insurgency, bringing his life and those associated, into extreme danger.

Jules' wife was incapable of bearing children and, as Alice was but an infant, Jules and Bennie decided to conceal her true parentage. She was given Jules' family name, Heynneman and Bennie then deliberately distanced himself as her father, passing the role to Jules and his wife, to raise Alice as their own daughter.

Bennie accepted this was but one of the many sacrifices required to ensure her safety. Though saddened that Alice had been deprived of a natural, father-daughter relationship he was relieved that she had not expressed any sense of abandonment as he had sometimes experienced, when the revelation of heritage had finally been explained. The decision to unveil their secret when Alice reached maturity had carried deep reservations. Bennie had prayed that in doing so she would understand the dangerous impediment her father's name could bring. Bennie's fears assuaged when Alice had tearfully accepted the rationale and undertaken to maintain the status quo.

The frequency of their contact remained constrained. However, Bennie had never failed to ensure his daughter's future would not be disadvantaged by the distant relationship. Through Jules he had orchestrated for Alice's education overseas, grateful for the role that Anne Whitehead had played in achieving this outcome.

Anne had been instrumental in having Alice employed when she graduated from the University of Sydney under the reinstituted Colombo Plan. Graduates who had enjoyed full funding under this programme were obliged to return to their country of origin, and work for a minimum of three years. Encouraged to seek a position with the Akumuga Mine, Alice was now engaged as an on-site systems engineer on the West Papuan site.

Bennie stood and stretched. 'Anything else we need to discuss as I could really do with a few hours' sleep?'

Jules rose, slowly rotated his head, until a distinctive "crack" emanated from his neck. 'Only what the final figure will be to satisfy those usurious customs officials in Belgium.'

Bennie opened his briefcase and locked the documents inside. 'Guess we'll find out soon enough.'

*   *   *   *

# JAKARTA

Agus Winarko silently cursed his affliction when again struck by shortness of breath, as the city's heavily-polluted air continued to hang limply, across the windless realm. He inhaled twice, then slipped the puffer back inside a trouser pocket, his eyes narrowing as he swept subordinates sitting meekly across the oversized Java-teak desk.

Agus was an ugly man; ugly in appearance and more so in his demeanour. However, extreme wealth provided a pathway that enabled the feared entrepreneur's faults to be overlooked by many, over whom he exercised absolute control. The product of a corrupt regime, Agus feared nothing except his place in Indonesian society where, due to his military connections, he dominated much of the country's economy.

In the corrupt world of Indonesian commerce, Agus stood tall amongst his contemporaries. Ranked as one of the wealthiest players in SE Asia his peers would secretly cringe at having to deal with the man whilst publicly lauding his achievements. Amongst his ambitious endeavours were acquisitions across the mining industry that had brought many a foreign investor to their knees. Underpinned by a clique of generals and close financial bonds with the dominant political parties he enjoyed the privileges of power that accompanied extreme wealth. Amongst his fortune Agus held a commanding shareholding in P.T. Akumuga Mining, acquired over time as the foreign shareholding had been watered down and acquired, under pressure by the nation's nepotistic rulers. Currently, the Americans via Summit Gold still held the controlling interest of fifty-one percent. The Indonesian Government had "sold" its accumulated interests to Agus Winarko at the time the remaining fifteen percent held by nominees, also mysteriously changed hands. Effectively, including what he held on behalf of others, Agus controlled forty-nine percent of the wealthy mining enterprise. He wanted it all.

Further exploration drilling had proven additional reserves adjacent to the existing concession areas. Before Summit Gold could arrange for P.T. Akumuga to acquire the new area Agus had stepped in and submitted an application in his wholly-owned entity, the purpose of this morning's meeting with the Minister for Mines and his senior directors.

'*Bapak* Agus.' The Director General addressed the mining magnate respectfully, attempting to pacify. 'The eastern boundary line is contentious. The area marked on the application encroaches upon the border with New Guinea. The area directly on the line cannot, by law, be allocated for general use.'

The statement attracted a maelstrom of invective, Agus rising on his toes and castigating the public servant to the extreme. White-faced, the Minister for Mines raised open-palm hands in acquiescence and offered a compromise. '*Bapak* Agus, what if we issue an order marking the questionable area as "subject to final consideration by the Department of Mines" to avoid any future disputes?'

Agus returned to his chair and crossed his arms defiantly. 'I want you to understand that however you treat the problem, no other party can ever attain access. Is that clear?' All in attendance agreed, subserviently. Agus nodded to his personal assistant standing to the rear of the office who immediately stepped forward, signalling the meeting was concluded. Once the government officials had been ushered from his presence, Agus removed a file from his personal safe, and made several entries relating to the meeting. Then, satisfied that the outcome would achieve his desired result, the billionaire smiled smugly, leaned back in his seat, closed his eyes and formed a mental image as he visualised what half a million tonnes of copper and one million ounces of gold, would do for his wealth; the figure representing the overall production of the Akumuga Mine, the previous year. Alone with his fantasy a thought annoyingly penetrated. Agus abruptly returned to his miserable self when reminded of the Chinese presence that could interfere with his long-term goal.

At the time China negotiated the creation of the Kampung Mas City Special Autonomous Zone, he had been vociferously against the Indonesian Government granting such a concession. He argued, citing examples of what the Chinese had implemented in many African destinations. However, as the greasing process had been in play for several years and successfully facilitated preliminary approvals, Agus had been incapable of blocking the mammoth investment of $35 billion.

The port city of Kampung Mas, gateway to the eastern highlands of West Papua and the Akumuga Mines, now effectively belonged to Mainland China. Within one year the population of Kampung Mas had grown by eight thousand, almost all of these, Chinese nationals, many of questionable credentials.

With the potential to determine ore export handling fees and other associated costs, Agus knew he needed to address the issue of handling the Chinese presence, when he finally achieved control over the Akumuga Mine.

*　*　*　*

# KOPASSUS (INDONESIAN SPECIAL FORCES) GARRISON HQ
## CIJANTUNG — JAKARTA

With the restoration of joint military training exercises with Indonesia's Special Forces, senior members of the United States Embassy in Jakarta had, for the first time, been invited to attend a *KOPASSUS* graduation ceremony. In attendance and representing the USA were the Deputy Chief of Mission and the Military Attachè for Defense Cooperation, both men cognizant of the many jaundiced views relating to the history of the group.

In 1975, it was a *KOPASSUS* officer that ordered the execution of five journalists, known as the *Balibo Five*, during the Indonesian invasion of East Timor. And, during the May 1998 riots of Indonesia, renegade *KOPASSUS* members were involved in carrying out acts of murder and mass gang-rapes of Sino-Indonesian women and girls across Jakarta. The attaché knew that members of this Special Forces group were legally exempt from the jurisdiction of civil law, a fact that was highlighted in the confidential brief.

As impressive lines of red-beret soldiers marched past in review, the defence attaché leaned closer to the embassy Deputy Chief. 'We have our eyes on that officer,' he said, indicating a Special Forces Lieutenant

Colonel standing alongside the armed forces commander. 'His star is on the ascent.'

'Who is he?' the Deputy asked.

'Didi Sumantri. He's married to the President's youngest daughter. That's his father, General Sumantri, *the* Commander of the Armed Forces.' The attaché continued once a number of loudly shouted commands abated. 'Counting Didi, the family can now boast four generations that have served in the Indonesian military.' Again he paused waiting for the public address system announcement to pass. 'His grandfather served with Suharto in the Western New Guinea campaign in 1962, and the Indonesia-Malaysia Confrontation following that. His father was involved as a young officer during the East Timor invasion in 1975'

'Will he be invited to the States?'

'We're working on that. Didi is currently slotted to lead one of *KOPASSUS*' five brigade level groups. That's Group 1 Para-Commando. We intend on having a word in his father's ear to have Didi attend our Army Special Forces Training Course at Fort Bragg.'

'Good,' the Deputy nodded then winced with another announcement blasted over their heads.

Not fifty metres from where the Americans were seated, Didi stood proudly erect alongside his father. Straight-faced and pumped with pride, none could detect from his outward appearance that inside the young officer's head was the mind of an ambitious, self-centered creature who, since childhood, suffered from a deep sense of self-entitlement.

Enjoying the hidden envy he expected of his peers, Didi Sumantri openly flaunted the power he enjoyed as a Presidential son-in-law, and beneficiary of his father's powerful office. Often, even his superior officers would accede to requests that would normally be denied to others. And socially, women with whom he secretly flirted often felt obliged to accept his advances.

With the parade coming to a close Didi was introduced to the American officials, the orchestrated opportunity lost on none that were present.

*   *   *   *

# INDONESIAN MINISTRY OF DEFENCE

General Sumantri teased an aching molar with the tip of his tongue, shocked, when the unconscious manipulation was rewarded with excruciating pain. Cursing the Minister of Defence's summons that required rescheduling his visit to the surgery, he fumbled angrily with a bottle of pain-killers, twisting a child-proof cap without result.

'Wahid,' he bellowed. 'Get in here!'

When his aide entered and immediately identified the problem, he opened the bottle and looked questioningly at his commanding officer.

'That's all!' General Sumantri summarily waved the junior officer away as he awkwardly extracted several tablets from the container and swallowed. Once the pain had subsided he again turned his attention to preparing for the Minister's briefing.

The growing insurgency was impacting on Indonesian troops in a manner he and his peer officers had never envisaged. Deeply concerned with deteriorating troop morale, not only amongst the regular army soldiers but also within the *KOPASSUS* and *BRIMOB* rank and file, General Sumantri decided to seek presidential approval to increase troop numbers to fifty-thousand. Although greatly out-numbered, over the course of the previous twelve months rebels had punished the occupying forces with multiple attacks on outposts, ostensibly fleeing into neighbouring Papua New Guinea.

Attacks had primarily targeted the lesser-manned outposts leav-ing headless corpses for the Indonesians to find. The effect had been successful, striking fear amongst the occupying forces deployed to the dense, intimidating, highland jungle.

Repeated demands by Jakarta had not resulted in PNG patrols addressing the porous border issue. Covertly the general had given permission for his patrols to follow the insurgents into PNG to track and kill the rebels. Disappointingly, these intrusions had resulted in a line of United Nations Peacekeeper posts being established dur-ing recent months to monitor the situation. The presence of UN forces had only exacerbated the problem, as the rebels could now easily disappear into safe territory with the knowledge they would no longer be followed.

General Sumantri had been stunned when it was reported that another Indonesian post had been destroyed, resulting in the bor-der crossing being temporally closed, after a shoot-out between his troops and rebels. Adding to his anger was the foreign media revela-tion that the rebels had been dressed in blue berets to mirror United Nations personnel at the time. The general was deeply concerned that the Indonesian shadow war in West Papua had his forces on the defensive. It had become increasingly difficult to suppress informa-tion, his obsession with keeping the mounting losses from online social media near impossible, with the increased presence of mobile devices.

His aide appeared to remind the general of the appointment with the Minister for Defence. He knew he would be expected to offer a feasible strategy to address the rapidly deteriorating situation in West Papua. He motioned to the aide then returned to the remaining intelligence update, hoping for some content that may reinforce his case when reporting to the Minister of Defence.

Becoming Commander of the Armed Forces Sumantri had required endorsement by the Indonesian House of Representatives, and without the financial influence provided by Agus Winarko, he recognized that the appointment would never have been approved.

General Sumantri's expectation that the customary military line of succession would ensure that he eventually be appointed as Defence Minister, one of the country's three most powerful and coveted positions. Aware that the Ministry is explicitly mentioned in the Constitution, Sumantri, as a dedicated military officer, agreed with the provision that prohibited the President from either dissolving or replacing the office. With such power, the general knew that the possibility of even ascending to the presidency would not be an impossible reach. If the President and Vice-President were to die, resign, or be unable to perform their appointed functions, the Minister of Defence, together with the Ministers of Foreign and Home Affairs, would jointly hold the position of president and vice-president until the succeeding president and his VP were elected by Parliament. However, the General accepted that such aspirations would never be realized unless he resolved the current crisis in the restive West Papuan provinces, before it spiralled into anarchy.

Although initially troubled with his senior advisers' suggestions that there was evidence of foreign intervention in support of the Papuan freedom fighters, General Sumantri had reviewed reports of the growing number of sightings of Westerner presence in the restive territory.

The Javanese crossed his arms and frowned, and although mentally dismissing the latest report with scepticism, he couldn't shake the feeling that there must be some substance to the *KOPASSUS* Special Forces Group 3 *Sandhi Yudha* operative's statement that there were several sightings of an elderly *bule* living high in the provincial highlands. He had heard rumours of similar sightings over time but, not unlike his predecessors, he gave no credence to the stories.

As was common with his generation, the general more often referred to Caucasians as *bule* to describe white foreigners, oblivious to the feeling amongst Europeans living in his country, that the term was derogatory, racist, and offensive.

There had been earlier reference to native albino contact causing the general to draw the conclusion that the agent's sighting was of an albino, and not a *bule*. Aware of the many witchcraft-related killings in the distant province, he mused that if the long-white-haired albino was not a figment of the agent's imagination, then why had the villagers accepted this manifestation in their midst?

Dismissing the report, concluding that there was no correlation between this imagined sighting and the upsurge in rebel attacks against military posts, General Sumantri turned his thoughts to his youngest son, Didi. The handsome young officer's photo stood proud on the general's desk, a constant reminder of yet another generation of soldiers who would continue the family's history of military service.

\*    \*    \*    \*

# JAKARTA — PASAR MINGGU

### INDONESIAN STATE INTELLIGENCE AGENCY
### (BADAN INTELIJEN NEGARA -BIN)

Abdullah Siregar was, in reality, Indonesia's senior spook. Returning from consulting the President and receiving approval to pursue a number of sensitive issues during their weekly briefing session, Siregar the head of Indonesia's State Intelligence Agency, *Badan Intelijen Negara* (BIN), commenced initiating those actions.

Tasked with the implementation of operations in the field of domestic intelligence he was responsible both for coordinating operations between other intelligence agencies, and for mounting operations on his own.

Under Abdullah Siregar's capable leadership the agency's clandestine activities had achieved a level of competence his predecessors would have envied. Siregar had managed to sweep many of the agency's indiscretions into the past, although there were exceptions which continued to haunt, due to their international implications. He had been aware, but not complicit, in the Munir Said Thalib assassination. Thalib, a prominent Indonesian human-rights and anti-corruption activist, was poisoned on a Garuda flight from Jakarta to Amsterdam, dying two hours before arrival in Schiphol

International Airport. An autopsy would reflect that his body contained extreme levels of arsenic. Siregar felt fortunate that he was not included in the subsequent investigation when top-level agency officials were implicated in Munir's murder. Learning from that experience, Siregar was determined to ensure the highly-sensitive order approved by the President would not be revisited in any detrimental manner.

The top secret directive which lay on the intelligence chief's desk was the approval to have Bennie Tabuni terminated, and if necessary, with extreme prejudice.

*   *   *   *

# CAMBODIA — PHNOM PENH

Bambang Sutejo knew that if discovered, he could never return to his village in Java where, for over six decades his family had been employed by the thriving Javanese textile mill that manufactured most of Indonesia's military uniforms.

Having expanded its operations into Cambodia, the textile manufacturer had been producing uniforms, the predominant product, for the past three years, supplying the military across the ASEAN landscape. Often, to accommodate facilitation payments to senior officers in the Defence purchasing departments, part-orders to produce Indonesian uniforms would be placed on the Cambodian plant, where siphoning off payments could be more easily orchestrated and hidden from superiors.

As the shift change commenced, Bambang Sutejo continued to

monitor the movement of the batch of *loreng*, camouflage uniforms that had been duplicated within the production system. Having switched the production numbers down the line, the shift supervisor had only then to ensure that despatch would deliver the items, to the designated address in Koh Kong Port. The Indonesian knew he would be paid as well as before, to supply the uniforms to the warehouse just inside the Cambodian border, from Thailand's Hat Lek. What he did not know was that the Koh Kong facility, being a major border crossing for overland shipments, belonged to a Jules Heynneman freight forwarding company.

Bambang remained at the plant personally overseeing that the designated shipment had left then texted confirmation to a nominated number in Bangkok. Saddened, but in some part relieved that this would be the final order, Bambang had long decided not to dwell upon his betrayal, justifying his actions in view of the substantial compensation received.

\*   \*   \*   \*

# MEK MEK VILLAGE

## PAPUA HIGHLANDS

The Mek Mek village chief rose at the conclusion of the religious ceremony ensuring that the male tribal members would undertake their assigned tasks. A distant, high-pitched clicking sound caught his attention and when this was immediately followed by another closer by, the chief recognized the call of a black sicklebill, his eyes searching for the bird of paradise high amongst the forest's canopy. Suddenly his lower jaw cracked into a toothless smile when a familiar shape of a young boy formed, naturally blended amongst the forest foliage, maintaining his post as lookout. Emulating bird calls to alert whilst disguising one's presence was taught from early childhood.

Waving an acknowledgement, the chief turned his attention towards the two men sitting amidst ironwood stilts that supported an elevated tree-house dwelling. He nodded sagely, and although unable to understand their exchanges he knew that there was warmth between the foreigners, curious that the older of the men the villagers called *Lapun Buna* would always become withdrawn, whenever the other departed.

Having inherited the existence of the bearded, grey-haired white man, the chief accepted, as did the entire tribe, the honorific position the elderly figure enjoyed. Children bowed their heads in respect when passing the grandfather figure. Village women were always present fussing around his person, the old man's integration into village culture evident from the facial animal bone piercings, he had undertaken back in time.

Having mastered the dialect, *Lapun Buna* now acted as interpreter for the other foreigner who the Mek Mek reverently referred to as *Sanguma*. The white man had brought medicine saving the lives of many villagers, struck down by a strain of swine influenza introduced deliberately by Indonesian forces.

Isolated from the outside world there were no transmission towers, cell-phones, television sets or radio receivers. Nor had the Indonesian language penetrated this far into the mountains. Hidden by extreme jungle conditions, the Mek Mek culture remained intact. The men wore penis gourds, and were extremely proficient hunter-gatherers. The women remained bare-breasted; their bodies adorned with charms, their position within their family structures, submissive to all.

Witchcraft and sorcery prevailed as the Mek Mek believed their world was occupied with all kinds of spirits, ancestor worship being bedrock to their belief in reincarnation. Essential to the continuity of life was their acceptance that those who passed could return at any moment in time to the land of the living, reincarnated in a newly born child of their blood line. The tribal witch doctor remained subservient to the Mek Mek chief; the *Khakhua–Kumu* always cautious not to exceed the limitations his position held. The villagers practiced ritual cannibalism and were thought to devour the souls of their victims, such as interlopers who transgressed into Mek Mek tribal territory.

There were no rival clans. Few ventured into the isolated domain for the Mek Mek's fearsome reputation amongst the Eipo People had been evident since the beginning of time. Tales of Mek Mek brutality had circulated widely, occasionally evidenced by the discovery of mutilated, headless corpses of those who foolishly ventured to far.

Because of the distance to the nearest community, the village could only be located after days of trekking along occasional trails that criss-crossed rivers twisting and turning, occasionally spilling into thunderous falls. Vertical-steep gorges embraced the primitive community challenging all who would venture there, the only access to the unique near-Neolithic environment being via a swinging twine bridge.

One of the village men had unwittingly introduced swine flu into the Mek Mek community. Within days most of the villagers had fallen mysteriously ill, stricken with fever and diarrhea.

*   *   *   *

More than a decade had passed since Stephen Coleman first came into contact with the Mek Mek people. The financially-rewarding relationship established with Bennie Tabuni and Jules Heynneman had required establishing supply routes along the PNG-West Papua border. Coleman knew the territory intimately, the scars from his clandestine activities across SE Asia over fifty years evidence of this. Now in his seventies, the exhausting, mountain-crossings demanded all he could give, the frequency of such undertakings diminishing with time.

Coleman sat in silent company with the older man observing a number of native men returning with a slaughtered pig carcass. He had witnessed such preparations many times, the sacrificing of the sacred animal a custom usually conducted to signify the settlement of tribal disputes. However, on this occasion, the chief had ordered the ceremony to sanctify the natural cave site located high upon the slope, overlooking the village. It was *Lapun Buna* who had suggested the site, now a natural vault filled with ordnance.

Coleman continued to idly observe, women now wrapping portions of meat that had been butchered to size, with large leaves, ready to be placed on heated stones. The scene evoked a memory of how he had come to know the Mek Mek people and the hermit figure who sat quietly alongside.

The outbreak had been first detected amidst villages close to Jayapura. Within weeks the swine flu had spread widely across low-lying communities decimating the pig population, the intention being to deprive the indigenous inhabitants of their main source of food. When the disease mutated and infected humans, vaccines promised by Jakarta never appeared, the ampoules mysteriously disappearing in transit permitting the disease to spread unabated. When Coleman learned that this form of N1H1was in every way similar to the deadly pandemic that had swept Europe one hundred years before, killing upwards of one hundred million people, he was inclined to postpone the journey. Convinced that the anti-viral agent administered by his doctor would prevent infection he decided to go.

During that time, Coleman had been endeavouring to establish relationships with a number of isolated mountain communities close to the PNG border. The epidemic event occurred during the embryonic commencement of his relationship with Bennie and Jules. Having conferred with medical sources and anticipating the outbreak would not yet have spread into the isolated highland areas, Jules arranged for a supply of prophylactic antibiotics to be delivered from Singapore by air to Jayapura. From there the medicine was carried to a prearranged point amongst the sparsely-populated mid-levels pending Coleman's arrival.

Expecting news of the outbreak would have reached the mountain tribes he had taken advantage of their predicament to cultivate ties via the medicinal supplies. When word carried even further up into the highlands and reached the village in which *Lapun Buna* resided, the eccentric had quickly conferred with the tribal chief.

Subsequently, the *Khakhua–Kumu* was sent to locate and escort Coleman to their community.

The punishing climb required several days through leech-infested forest thick with seemingly impenetrable walls of vegetation in order to reach the rickety-twine bridge. When the first sighting of skulls atop poles positioned along the trail came into view, Coleman had great difficulty convincing his bearers not to bolt. Suddenly and without warning, a group of Mek Mek warriors appeared, their appearance threatening, and Coleman's already terrified bearers abandoned their boss man with screams as they turned and fled, leaving everything they had carried behind. The tribesman swooped upon the load and disappeared across the wobbly bridge leaving Coleman with no choice but to follow.

With gnawing concern that the structure would collapse at any time Coleman had crept his way across the gorge to where a strange fellow stood, arms crossed in a challenging stance.

The first encounter with *Lapun Buna* was, for Coleman, a "Stanley and Livingstone" moment. Taken aback when sighting the tall, gaunt figure that appeared to have been abandoned by time, Coleman regained his composure and extended his hand in greeting. 'Stephen Coleman,' he waited, annoyed when his gesture was ignored, 'I've brought medical supplies.'

Tense moments lapsed before the weathered figure grunted, issued instructions in the Mek Mek dialect then turned to retrace his steps back to the main village. Coleman followed, his curiosity enormously aroused, tales and rumours relating to sightings of a white hermit living amongst the natives returning, as he struggled to keep pace from behind.

Entering the community compound Coleman was struck by the height of stilt huts, some standing as high as twenty metres, dominating the surrounds.

'The Mek Mek call me *Lapun Buna*,' were the only words the old man offered. He then pointed to the tribal leader standing proud, complete with black, animal-skin headdress and rows of bone trinkets slung across his chest.

'Chief', he announced, then in a loud, clipped, guttural tone he entered into conversation with the leader and his entourage. As the villagers looked upon Coleman with an obvious mixture of curiosity and anxiety having never seen a white person other than *Lapun Buna* before, the chief's eyes never left the newcomer. Coleman, conscious of the challenge, responded with a smile then lowered his head in respect. '*Amakane*,' he said, hoping the common Moni Tribe greeting that was generally used in most West Papuan dialects would be understood.

The chief's eyes widened in surprise. '*Amakane*,' he reciprocated, touching open palms to his chest.

Moments passed until the precious cargo that had earlier been seized appeared and placed on the ground for all to see. Coleman stepped forward and, without thinking, extracted his Glauca B1 custom blade from its sheath to open the cartons, freezing in that moment when spears flashed to within inches of his face. Wisely, he surrendered the knife to the *Khakhua–Kumu* who then cut open the cargo for all to see.

Coleman recalled his one-sided conversation with *Lapun Buna*, explaining that the drugs he brought were to be used prophylactically, to protect the villagers against any swine flu infection. With each attempt to engage the elderly hermit, Coleman was greeted with grunts, shakes of the head or just simply ignored. Having endured this frustration by the end of the first day, Coleman reverted to using sign language, concluding that this belligerent soul had either lost the full use of his vocal chords or the ability to recall his native tongue.

Throughout the day he had administered the oral vaccine, his every movement monitored closely by the *Khakhua–Kumu*.

There had been a ceremonial slaying of a pig also at that time to celebrate the gift Coleman had brought. The festivities had continued into the clear, rainless night, and Coleman lay on his back gazing at the sky, mesmerised by the infinite number of stars, oblivious to time.

Rising to relieve himself, his unsteady legs a consequence of the brew he had consumed throughout the celebrations, Coleman lost balance and tumbled. He remembered *Lapun Buna's* deep belly-laugh when the *Khakhua–Kumu* stepped up and caught him by the arm, saving Coleman from falling on his face. Uncontrollably drunk he had opened his trousers and urinated where he stood. A village woman giggled loudly. He turned, giddily, and found himself face to face with a bare-breasted woman with betel nut-coloured teeth and a glint in her eyes. Startled, he lurched away, but the woman was not to be deterred, leading him by the arm as she marched him away.

Stephen Coleman reminded himself of the regrettable moment when he awoke the following day. With pounding village drums reverberating inside his head, he crawled to his knees and, willing his stomach not to throw up, had dragged his body to the open doorway and looked out. The rush of fear from the dizzying height propelled him backwards away from the precarious drop. A hand reached out and pulled him down, Coleman was repulsed by the native woman's overwhelming, pungent, musky scent and, realising he was naked, he threw up.

He remembered the agonising hours that followed and the terrifying climb back down to the village floor, amazed that he had no recollection of how he had climbed tens of metres up the shaky ladder whilst drunk. Curious children had followed his path down to a running stream where he had ignored their unintelligible banter, crouching and relieving himself in full view.

Returning to the village, he was surprised to find the aged European waiting, and for the first time since his arrival, responsive.

Indicating that Coleman should sit, the old man squinted. 'You have done a good thing bringing the vaccine here.' He offered his hand and Coleman accepted the gesture. 'We were aware of the spreading disease. The Mek Mek will always be indebted.' Coleman recollected how the other man's features had suddenly hardened with the question, '...but as life has caused me to be naturally distrustful I want to know your real purpose in coming here?'

Coleman sat cross-legged, facing the hermit figure for several hours in deep conversation, engrossed, listening to the elderly man relate the events which had led him into his self-imposed exile. Towards the close of his revelation, he insisted that Coleman only refer to him as *Lapun Buna*, that he respect his right to anonymity, and asked that he pledge not to reveal his existence to others.

Stephen Coleman agreed.

It became clear that, although this remote Mek Mek community appeared completely cut-off from the outside world, they were very well informed regarding the struggle other tribes endured against the Javanese. Coleman had expected resistance to his solicitations to establish a secure location where weapons could be stored far from the Indonesian military presence. *Lapun Buna* remained adamant that in no way would he or the Mek Mek permit their existence to be compromised. However, because Coleman had been instrumental in providing the community with the vaccine, the Mek Mek would always offer him sanctuary.

Rhythmic, soft but discernible tapping on a hollow, log drum drew Coleman back from the past. A woman approached with a wooden pitcher and leaned forward to offer water, her necklace made from animal teeth dangling between full breasts. Both he and *Lapun Buna* watched the slender figure walk away, the two elderly men glancing at each other smiling knowingly, reminded of pleasures lost.

\* \* \* \*

# Autonomous Region of Bougainville

Prior to the referendum which provided Bougainville with the opportunity to secure independence from Papua New Guinea (PNG), foreign nationalities were prohibited from travelling to the island, significantly reducing the risk of discovery by outsiders of the West Papuan underground training facility. With the cessation of internal hostilities, Bennie had engaged remnants of the BRA, the Bougainville Revolutionary Army, to participate in training his recruits. These were experienced men who had actively fought against the Papua New Guinea Force during the violent ten-year conflict.

Bennie had been concerned that, with independence, there would be a wave of foreign interests establishing a presence in the new nation of the Republic of West Papua, increasing the risk of discovery. However, appreciating that human nature operates on the same premise across all societies, funds channelled through Jules extensive business network greased appropriate palms, and their facility remained undisturbed.

The possibility of any collusion between Indonesia and the fledging nation vaporised when Bougainville applied, and was accepted, into the Melanesian Spearhead Group that supported West Papuan independence. And, although reconciliation between the BRA and PNG was progressing, Bennie was not overly concerned with this rapprochement.

Over a period of five years, along with shuttling weapons for Bennie's fighters, Stephen Coleman had facilitated the movement of select members of the West Papuan resistance to the island. There they remained, to undertake rigorous basic training, before returning to their respective villages.

\*  \*  \*  \*

# PAPUA NEW GUINEA

## UNITED NATIONS PEACEKEEPER OBSERVATION POST

Shrill screams punctured the morning when brawling women fought for advantage over the meagre water ration.

'Shall we break it up?' the Ethiopian soldier asked anxiously, uncomfortable with the knowledge the UN post was severely undermanned.

'What, and get trampled for the trouble?' his lieutenant responded impassively. 'Just sit tight and watch. They'll run out of steam soon enough.' He had seen it all before.

Pandemonium regularly erupted in the overcrowded refugee camp housing fifteen-thousand West Papuans who had fled across the border to escape the brutal Indonesian Special Forces. Designed to accommodate a third of that population, many of the refugees lived in squalid conditions, some even in uncovered ditches exposed to the tropical elements.

New arrivals have swelled to uncontrollable numbers, disease and starvation now common throughout the camp. As neither the

United Nations High Commission for Refugees (UNHCR) nor the Papua New Guinea government recognised the inhabitants as refugees, medical treatment and food supplies were not provided.

Indonesian troop infiltration into Papua New Guinea territory in pursuit of West Papuan rebels had overwhelmed PNG, and with the Melanesian Spearhead Group openly voicing support for an independent West Papua, relations had soured between Port Moresby and Jakarta.

With Papua New Guinea's dysfunctional and inadequate defence force totalling less than five thousand, the Prime Minister felt obliged to seek a United Nations peacekeeper-presence. UN soldiers had been deployed to the seven-hundred kilometre border the year prior, maintaining posts in the most vulnerable areas where clashes between Indonesian troops and West Papuan rebels were frequent. Uniquely positioned to monitor the demarcation line, their complement consisted predominantly of African soldiers seconded to the UN.

Bennie Tabuni and Jules Heynneman were realists. They understood that the rebel movement was no match for Indonesia's superior numbers and, although the Free Papua Movement fighters constantly engaged Jakarta's military with their strike-and-retreat tactics, these leaders accepted that any prolonged conflict would be unsustainable from their perspective. The deployment of foreign troops in PNG was an integral component to their strategy to drag a multi-national force into conflict with the Indonesians to protect PNG's sovereignty, and to drive Third-World sentiment in support of their cause. Bennie had expected that the UN contingent would be primarily African in makeup and, with any such conflict, Bennie and Jules counted on the Australians sending troops under a mutual defence pact that virtually guaranteed such support.

The Ethiopian soldier glanced questioningly at his lieutenant when a group of women turned on one of their own, stomping her into the ground. The officer sighed resignedly, straightened his blue beret and felt for the weapon strapped to his side. 'Inform the other posts we are going in,' he ordered, at precisely the moment the area was sprayed by Indonesian soldiers, with automatic fire.

The heart of the UN force's mandate was the protection of refugees and monitoring the PNG/West Papua border, providing security across the conflict zone. The parameters determining when they could use their weapons was clearly defined, foremost being the right to return fire when attacked. But the soldiers' small arms weapons were no match against the intense bursts of rapid fire that had been unleashed against their position.

The attack lasted but moments before the cacophony of gunfire ceased, leaving the air surrounding the post hollow with surprise. The UN officer stood embarrassingly motionless in his tracks, his weapon still holstered, aware that he had fouled himself.

Alongside, the Ethiopian private lay dead.

Over the following days, recriminations were in abundance. The PNG accused Indonesian forces of the attack. The Indonesians were adamant their forces were nowhere near that border crossing which placed the blame with the rebels. The United Nations could not determine which party was responsible and immediately increased its presence along the border, by adding a further one hundred peacekeepers; precisely what Bennie Tabuni had hoped for.

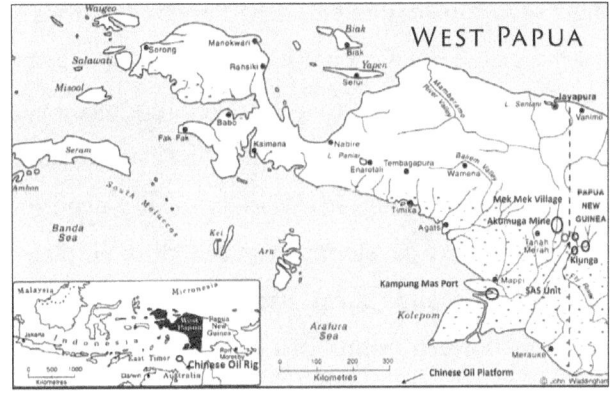

\*　　\*　　\*　　\*

# WEST PAPUA

## KAMPUNG MAS PORT CITY

As Alice Heynneman's Jeep followed the snaking road down the mountain, intermittent views of the Akumuga people camped along the river's path came into sight. She knew from reports that many thousands lived off the mine tailings along the river. When the operation had first commenced decades before, the local population had envisaged that employment opportunities would lift their community's impoverished status but this was not to eventuate.

Alice was uncomfortably aware that less than five percent of her company's employees were sourced from the Akumuga tribes. This produced a community of informal miners, who worked the dumps of material left over following the mining process along the river's reaches. These river banks were once lined with sago forests but now with their natural resource so polluted, they could not drink from the mountain flow. With their sago forests depleted and deprived of this natural food source, children scoured the river banks in search of snails to trade.

Alice always felt disheartened making this overland journey to Kampung Mas Port City, gateway to the Akumuga Mine. She had witnessed how these river mining environments produced a new class of displaced youth who had drifted to the massive port development in search of employment. Often she had observed small groups of early-age teens who, when not gainfully engaged working as porters around bus stations and other transit points, sat around smoking a brand of glue known as *aibonm,* which contained trichloroethylene, a chemical that sent the user into a hallucinogenic state. The jeep entered the last stretch and Alice sensed the driver's impatience when he increased their speed, as they approached Kampung Mas Port City. Alice unconsciously shook her head at the incredible pace the newly created special zone had developed, under the Indonesian-Chinese lease arrangements.

When Jakarta signed over the existing fifty-thousand hectare Kampung Mas port to a Chinese Government state-owned enterprise (SOE) eighteen months before, not even the Indonesians had expected such a rapid change to what was previously an operating port gateway terminal, for the massive Akumuga Mine. The Chinese had committed $35 billion to developing the port and its surrounds, the project similar in many ways to what Beijing had accomplished in African destinations.

Under the terms of the ninety-nine-year investment agreement, the SOE had absolute control of all development within the confines of the allocated area, including the administration of the project. Within weeks of executing the agreement, heavy equipment arriving by sea was immediately engaged in the accelerated infrastructure expansion of existing facilities. Chinese labour arrived in waves, displacing both indigenous and Indonesian labour, which were sidelined and offered only the most menial tasks.

Six months following the commencement of the SOE's ambitious programme multi-high-rise accommodation blocks housing only foreign employees appeared, creating a mini-city of twenty-thousand Chinese. Amongst these were more than five hundred People's Liberation Army specialist soldiers, who maintained security in the autonomous destination.

Kampung Mas had become a Chinese satellite city.

Alice's Jeep approached the outskirts and she was dismayed to find a sign declaring that from the point entering the special zone, the path had been renamed "Beijing Road". Passing through the first checkpoint where a row of high-rise apartments had been constructed immediately inside the zone's permitter, the signage changed to Mandarin characters. The special economic zone was now basically a separate city with separate rules inside a locked border, boasting its own electric power grid, harbour, airport and security force. The coal-fired power station that had been built to service the Akumuga Mine now lay under the control of Chinese hands.

Arriving at the heavily-guarded airport entrance Alice displayed her identification and was permitted through to the terminal. Having checked in, and with time on her hands until the flight departed, Alice entered the facility's duty-free store discovering a dearth of English Language reading material. With the exception of a two-week-old edition of the New York Times and an English version of the *China Daily*, everything else on offer was in Chinese.

Bored, Alice sat alone in the terminal staring out into space across the tarmac, wishing for a power failure to deaden the overly-loud Beijing satellite broadcasts, dominating airport television screens.

By mid-afternoon, Alice Heynneman was airborne heading for Darwin in Australia's Northern Territory where she would carry out pre-shipping checks on replacement equipment, destined for the Akumuga Mine. Airborne and with seatbelts loosened, the flight path took her aircraft directly over an offshore jack-up drilling rig being tugged further out to sea.

Unbeknown to Alice, when the Chinese extended their reach from the Special Autonomous Zone out to sea within the Akimeugah Foredeep area, the Australian Government challenged the proximity of the discovery well, in relation to the Indonesian-West Papua-Australian ocean border. The gas discovery was located along the Merauke Ridge adjoining the Arafura Basin. Decades of negotiations between the two countries had yet to define with any accuracy, the common maritime boundaries between West Papua and Australia. This had occurred when previous agreements had to be revisited due to East Timor becoming independent and sea boundaries changed.

The few Australians amongst the mine's expatriate community believed their government would challenge the Chinese expansionist move, into what might be perceived as Australian waters.

*   *   *   *

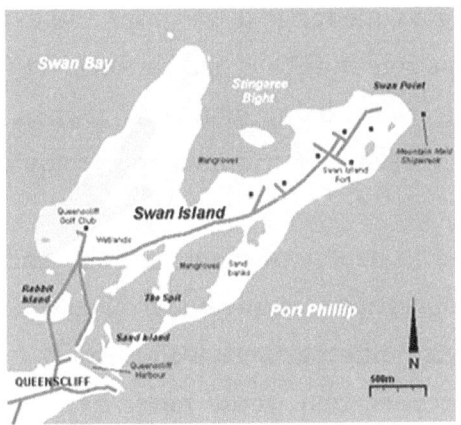

# Victoria — Australia

## Swan Island Military Base

Lieutenant Colonel Brent Shepherd remained in his quarters preparing for the final session before departing the Swan Island Military Base, off Queenscliff, in Victoria. The course was less physical than what he had experienced with the Special Air Service Regiment (SAS), the focus being primarily updating the officer regarding highly sensitive intelligence, in preparation for his posting to Port Moresby as the Assistant Defence Attachè.

Earlier in his career as a member of SAS 4, Shepherd had attended the ultra-secret clandestine warfare centre's special warfare school on the one-square kilometre island; a facility so secret the Department of Defence never revealed what went on at Swan Island, and information on the base was not found on any government website.

During that time he had met and become familiar with agents from Australia's key intelligence agencies, who were also learning

97

the skills in using a wide range of weapons and explosives. He was reminded how his role in SAS 4 had seriously curtailed his social and family connections, being unable to discuss, let alone reveal, the existence of the relatively unknown fourth squadron, within the SAS structure.

Often required to deploy overseas, secretly and out of uniform, and conducting operations usually undertaken by Australian Secret Intelligence Service officers, there were heavily redacted sections of his personal papers, that would never be revealed. These missions involved gathering intelligence on terrorism and scoping rescue strategies for high-profile entities, and as such often placed his actions questionably at the outer reaches of International law.

Brent Shepherd's mind wandered to his future posting to Papua New Guinea. Ostensibly, the position he would occupy was designated Assistant Defence Attachè to the Australian High Commission. However, in reality he would be working hand in hand with ASIS, the Australian Secret Intelligence Service.

Confident that he would be in his element, the absence of hubris in his self-appraisal as being perfectly suited for the role reflected his appreciation of the professionals, who had prepared him for service. He excelled at the Perth-based SAS training course at Campbell Barracks with its mock-up area of "embassy" buildings and sniper towers. He also attended the *Bahasa Indonesia* language course. He served with the SAS Regiment that spearheaded many of the operations conducted by the international force, during the early days of the East Timor intervention. For his role in the combined air insertion of Black Hawk helicopters into the Oecusse Enclave, to secure a beachhead in preparation of the amphibious assault by the main force, Lieutenant Colonel Brent Shepherd's star enjoyed a meteoric ascent.

Shepherd accepted also that had it not been for the guidance his uncle had provided then he might never have considered a military career. His mother's brother had served in the Australian Army and, prior to retirement, had completed a two-year posting to Jakarta as Army Attachè towards the close of the 1960s. It was his uncle's influence that had led him to seek a career in the military.

The distinctive sound of army boots slapping the passageway alerted Shepherd to the final briefing that was about to commence. He would leave the Swan Island facility the following morning and, before the weekend, would observe the final days of the joint Indonesian-Australian military exercise, close to Darwin.

*   *   *   *

# CANBERRA

## OFFICE OF NATIONAL ASSESSMENTS (ONA)

'The Prime Minister has been briefed.' The ONA Director General muttered to the gathered heads of Australia's spy agencies. 'And he is understandably concerned…' continuing as he pointedly addressed the ASIS chief. 'And demands to know how our most secret intelligence agency could not prevent being hacked?'

A group calling itself the Indonesian Security Down Team (ISD) had hacked ASIS the evening before by launching a successful "distributed denial of service" attack, which crashed the security and intelligence website. ISD was linked to the global cyber-activist network *Anonymous* and was known to operate in conjunction with the Indonesian Cyber Army and the Java Cyber Army. The ONA was responsible for providing all-source assessments relating to international political and strategic developments. Before doing so, the director-general would need the nation's six intelligence groups to provide the most current data available. Once the information was received, the ONA South Asia and Middle East Branch would evaluate the data, as this section was responsible for analyses and assessment of all-source intelligence products from the six intelligence authorities. Once the Director had examined the vital information, he would personally brief the Prime Minister and the National Security Committee of Cabinet.

'The PM is incensed that such seriously sensitive intelligence is now in the public domain!' He paused to inhale, aware that his high-blood pressure issues had not resolved from lack of sleep. 'He's demanding assurances that we won't have a repeat of the "Snowden" disaster.'

The ONA head was referring to the leaks back in November 2013, when the United States whistle-blower leaked documents revealing activities of Australian spy facilities program code-named STATE-ROOM, an electronic spying effort by the Australian Embassy in Jakarta. 'Do we know what the damage might be?'

'Unfortunately we don't know what, precisely, the hackers have harvested until our IT department has completed their investigation,' the ASIS director replied, the current pandemonium evoking unpleasant memories of the many recriminations that had flowed downhill following the disastrous leaks. He had been the section head when the event occurred; his entire team flabbergasted when information as to how Australia had accessed "bulk call data" off the Indonesian satellites, without their knowledge, had been revealed.

When Wikileaks picked up the story and added that the Australians had acquired almost two million encrypted master keys, which were supposed to protect the privacy of calls on the Indonesian telecommunications, at that time he had considered making a career change. Reminded that such revelations had set the scene for the collapse in Australian-Indonesian relations then, he anticipated some hostility in retaliation from the northern neighbour.

'The Indonesians are going to make a meal of this, again,' the Department of Foreign Affairs Minister moaned.

The Chief of Defence retorted. 'It's ridiculous to imagine the Indonesian government would be surprised by the news Australian intelligence agencies intercept some of their phone calls, and digital communications. They are aware of our surveillance activities, and for them to come out and condemn us again, would simply be expressing faux concern at the disclosures, as ... '

'I agree,' the ASIO spy chief interjected. 'Our media mostly ignored the time when Indonesia bugged our embassy in Jakarta during the East Timor crisis.'

'Nevertheless, it's an unnecessary distraction, and one which we can't afford to permit to overshadow the more pressing concerns, with the United Nations PNG-West Papua border attack. The PM wants an update on what proposals each of your departments consider appropriate action, and if the situation requires discussing further Australian troops on the ground.'

With the meeting closed the Director General sat alone, morosely contemplating the onerous position of later having to submit a recommendation to the Prime Minister, one that would again place Australian troops in direct confrontation with Indonesia.

*   *   *   *

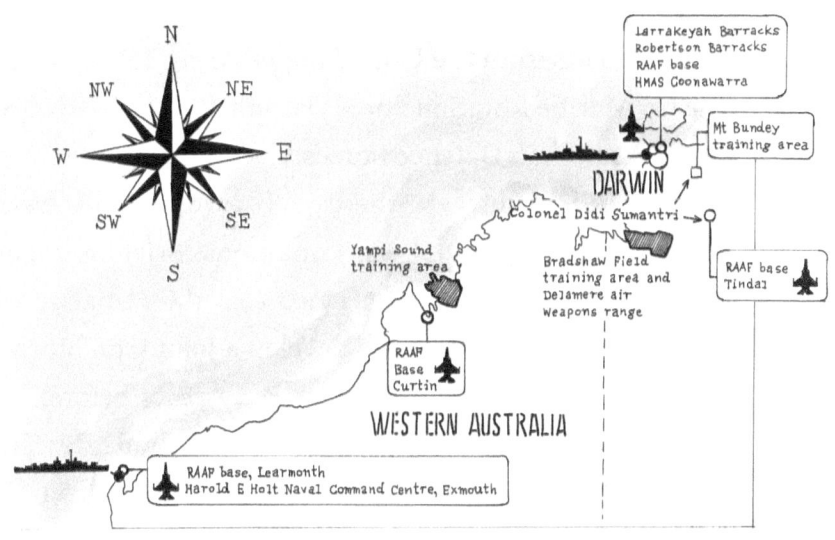

# AUSTRALIA

## NORTHERN TERRITORY

This was the Indonesian colonel's first visit to the Bradshaw Field Training Range, a defence property in the Northern Territory set aside for use by Australian, US and on occasion when invited, SE Asian military. Within this vast area, a substantial chunk of land had been allocated to the Delamere Air Weapons Range. Whilst there, he observed infantry and armoured formation manoeuvres, live ground, and air bombing practice. Under his command, elements of the Indonesian Special Forces, *KOPASSUS* had participated in the land and air deployment exercises, the live firing of artillery, operations in urban terrain warfare, and defensive training against nuclear, biological and chemical warfare.

The "Quokka" Joint Military Exercises were the trilateral exercise with elements from the United States Army 25th Infantry Division, the US Marine Rotation Force Darwin, the Indonesian Special Forces and Australian Defence Forces.

Colonel Didi Sumantri was there to observe the USA-Australian relationship under simulated war conditions. Briefing documents had been informative. He had learned that the initial agreement between the two allied nations to develop a Joint Combined Training Centre had been signed almost twenty years before. He also knew that the overall plan stretched from the Bradshaw Training Area and the Delamere Air Weapons Range far across from Central Australia to Northern Queensland to the Shoalwater Bay Training area.

The colonel's expectations of what he would find in the heart of Australia's Outback had not prepared his *KOPASSUS* contingent for the isolation of the Bradshaw Field Training Area, surprised when informed that few Australians would be aware of the Delamere Air Weapons Range. When they arrived and discovered their camp would be one hundred kilometres from the desert town of Katherine, and another three-hundred kilometres to Darwin's watering holes, morale slumped. Their temporary camp was erected surrounding a dusty-red soil airstrip, and their tents filled with suffocating desert dust, whenever the American C-17 Globemaster transport arrived with supplies.

Colonel Sumantri's troops were overawed when the first American bombers flew over their camp on their practice bombing runs over the Delamere range. Later, during exchanges with the US and Australian ground support units, they would learn that the Americans had been conducting regular bombing runs over this area for twenty years, without the knowledge of the Australian public. Flying from the Andersen Air Force Base in distant Guam, US B-52 pilots accompanied by KC-135 Stratotankers would undertake the twelve-hour round flight to demonstrate the US strike force capabilities, dropping their payloads over the Delamere range.

When the *KOPASSUS* contingent's participation in the "Quokka" exercise was completed, Colonel Sumantri's soldiers were flown directly to Darwin, and ensconced at the Robertson Barracks. Having opted to take the opportunity to fly via the RAAF Tindal Air Force Base, he was given passage on a US Marine helicopter.

Arriving at the Tindal Air Force Base, Colonel Didi Sumantri exited along with the American marines down the wide loading ramp, at the rear of the Chinook MH-47G chopper. Dry heat, emblematic of the Outback, sucked the air from his throat as he shouldered a carryall, and dragged his remaining kit, managing a path to the unflattering, terminal building.

'Colonel Sumantri?' An RAAF sergeant saluted as he approached. Didi nodded. 'You're on the Beechcraft King Air, sir,' he continued, pointing to a twin-engine turbo prop passenger aircraft preparing for departure. 'Would you follow me please sir?'

Didi strutted after the NCO who was now carrying his gear.

Seated in the cramped setting, Didi observed an F-18 Hornet land then taxi towards the RAAF 75 Squadron hangers, a twitch of contempt pinching his face with the knowledge that this was the home of the Australian Air Force's fighter squadron that had supported the INTERFET peacekeeping deployment to East Timor.

He made another mental note counting the number of aircraft

lined along the hard standing area as Didi's defence intelligence briefing required he do so. Jakarta sought an in-depth update on the Tindal base, since the Australians had long moved their fast jet base from Darwin to Tindal, in keeping with a revised strategic policy of defence.

As the King Air flew across an endless expanse of red earth below on its hour long journey to Darwin, Didi Sumantri's mind wandered, considering his promising career prospects, and what else might lay ahead.

∗   ∗   ∗   ∗

# DARWIN

'You will be joining us at the farewell party?' the senior liaison officer wanted to know.

Lieutenant Colonel Brent Shepherd grinned widely. 'SKYCITY Casino, 1900 hours. I was given the invite by the 5th Battalion CO yesterday.'

'Need transport organised for later?'

'No, thanks, I've already booked a room there for the night.'

'What, Robertson Barracks not up to RAAF standards?'

'Somewhat overrun, wouldn't you agree?' Again Shepherd smiled.

Robertson Barracks was the major Australian Army base located fifteen kilometres from Darwin's CBD. Home to key, front-line fighting units including the 1st Brigade, the 1st Armoured Regiment with its Abram tanks, and the 1st Aviation Regiment with Tiger armed reconnaissance helicopters, it was now also the site for three thousand US marines operating under the United States Pacific Command.

Brent Shepherd completed his rounds as he finalised a two-day briefing regarding the joint exercise, prior to taking up his position in Port Moresby. Arriving at the seaside resort hotel he was astonished to find Alice Heynneman exiting the lobby.

'Brent?' Alice stalled in her tracks and removed her sunglasses. 'My God, what are you doing in Darwin?'

'I could ask the same of you!' They embraced then stood holding each other. 'Where are you heading?'

'I was sent over from the mine to check on some equipment problems. Been here for days already. And you?'

'Doing the rounds before returning to Canberra for a few more weeks then off to Port Moresby.'

'Really?' Alice pulled away in mock surprise. 'What did you do to deserve that?' She challenged him playfully.

'Assistant Defence Attachè, no less.' He moved a hand to Alice's waist. 'Were you heading out?'

'I was, but it can wait until tomorrow. I have another shipment arriving by air that requires inspection over the next few days.' She turned on her heels and slipped her arm into Brent's. 'Are you still on duty?'

'No, I'm done for the day except a farewell cocktail party tonight.'

'Then let's go and sit by the pool and catch up.'

'Great idea,' Brent agreed. 'Give me ten to check in and change then I'll meet you poolside.'

'Done,' she squeezed his arm, 'I'll change as well.'

Brent Shepherd watched Alice Heynneman move through the lobby, the shift she wore disguising the shapely body he remembered. Moving from reception to his room Brent momentarily reminisced, delighted to have this opportunity to resurrect a relationship from the past.

They had met and become close when Alice attended Sydney University. Brent's uncle, having long since retired from the army, had occasionally been engaged by Australian mining companies, during their dealings with Indonesia. He had met Jules Heynneman on a number of occasions and developed a rapport. When Jules visited Sydney on one occasion, he was accompanied by his "daughter" Alice, who met Brent at the uncle's home on the North Shore. A relationship soon developed, interrupted when Brent was accepted into the Royal Military College, Duntroon, in Canberra. Towards the final stages of the eighteen-month course, Brent already sensed they would have no future when Alice returned to Indonesia, the long-distance relationship evaporating within a very short time.

\* \* \* \*

Together they lazed around the lagoon swimming pool, each conscious of the relationship they once enjoyed. By mid-afternoon, Darwin's muggy weather brought thunderous skies; the spectacular lightning display driving Brent and Alice inside where an unguarded moment, took them back in time.

Still bathing in the afterglow of their earlier intimacy, Brent sighed heavily. 'Never thought I would again see the day … '

Alice placed a finger to Brent's lips to silence him, then leaned her naked body against his, encouraging another erection. Brushing her lips softly across each of his nipples, she slid her tongue slowly, tantalisingly, caressing and teasing a path down to his now hardened phallus.

Brent responded as he traced the line from the shaved mound between her thighs gently caressing the moist vaginal lips his fingers found. Alice then took his shaft into the warmth of her mouth. Together they held each other, each lost in their own, mindless ecstasy. As their urgency grew, Alice deftly manipulated his manhood into her warm pouch, her shuddering cry when she climaxed sent her lover's warmth pumping into her body.

\* \* \* \*

'If I'd knew I'd be socialising I would have brought something more appropriate,' Alice stood alongside Brent, drink in hand.

'Don't worry you look great as you are.'

'Anything in a sack would look appealing to this crowd. Where are all the women?' she asked, observing but a small number of females present.

'It's an outpost, Alice. Wives and girlfriends are mostly back in their hometowns.'

Alice Heynneman surveyed the room. 'Must be more than a hundred guests,' she suggested, then, when her eyes settled on a solitary figure in dress uniform across the room, she nudged her partner and asked, 'The Indonesians were invited?'

Brent lifted his chin and immediately recognised the figure. 'I know that chap. We met when he attended one of our SAS training courses in Perth. He caused quite a furore at the time, almost single-handedly causing a rift between our governments over some childish comments, that one of ours texted in error.'

Catching their eye, Colonel Didi Sumantri made his way over

to their side of the room and introduced himself. 'I believe we've crossed paths before?' he asked as Brent Shepherd nodded in the affirmative.

'Campbell Barracks, SAS.'

'Ah, yes, that would be it.' His forced smile was received with a blank response from Alice.

'And you would be?' he asked without extending his hand in her direction.

'Alice Heynneman,' she answered, her expressionless face not revealing her distaste for the embroidered insignia the officer wore. Alice had witnessed what the cruel *KOPASSUS* could deliver.

'Australian?' he pressed.

'West Papuan,' Alice responded proudly, the minute muscles in her face tensing.

'You mean, Indonesian,' Didi Sumantri insisted. His eyes narrowed evaluating the woman's mixed features.

'I would never think of myself in that term,' Alice replied, immediately wishing she could be somewhere else.

'You should celebrate being part of our great nation,' Didi did not attempt to hide a growing smirk.

'And what do we West Papuans have to celebrate?' Alice countered, her anger now evident, several other guests turning heads in her direction. 'Hundreds of thousands of Papuans have been killed and thousands raped, tortured and imprisoned by *your* Indonesian forces,' she continued. 'So please do not refer to me as Indonesian!'

Brent reached for her arm. 'Let it go, Alice.' Then, addressing Sumantri, 'You'll excuse us, Colonel?' He steered Alice away and towards the bar, her arms trembling as he did so. 'What brought that on?' he lowered his voice.

'Members of my family were murdered by soldiers wearing the same uniform.' She defended.

'I'm sorry, Alice, I wasn't aware,' he replied awkwardly. He lifted a glass of wine from a passing waiter and handed it to her. 'Drink this.' He paused. 'It might help.'

'No, Brent, I just want to leave.' Refusing the wine, she placed a hand on his arm. 'You stay, you need to be here.'

'I'll come to your room later?'

Alice hesitated. 'If you don't mind, Brent, let's call it a night.' She glanced in the Indonesian colonel's direction. 'Best I go now before I get you into trouble.'

'Breakfast, then?' He held her hand questioningly.

Alice failed in an attempt to smile. 'Call me in the morning. We can have something in the room.'

Brent nodded. 'Okay, get some rest. I'll buzz you first thing tomorrow.'

Alice reached up and kissed Brent lightly on the cheek then made her way through the gathering, avoiding a path that would place her anywhere near Didi Sumantri.

The Indonesian colonel monitored Alice's exit with disdainful eyes, incensed at the woman's insolence.

\*     \*     \*     \*

Alice closed the curtains, undressed, and showered. Having washed away her anger, she lay naked on the bed under dimmed lights thinking about that afternoon's tryst with her former lover. Her hand moved to the crease between her thighs while visualising Brent's touch, the slow stroking movements suddenly interrupted by her room doorbell. With a wide grin already in place, she jumped from the bed and hurried to welcome Brent with open arms, shocked to find Didi Sumantri standing there.

The colonel muscled forward knocking Alice backwards, kicking the door closed from behind. Before she could scream, he lunged and punched her twice in the stomach. Alice gasped for air as she collapsed to the floor.

Sumantri undressed and dropped his full body weight on his victim, forcing her legs apart. Alice was pinned down, unable to move with her attacker's forearm across her neck in a choking, military hold.

The rape lasted but minutes.

By the time she recovered from unconsciousness the vicious assault had been consummated. As her eyes refocused she could see Didi Sumantri standing over her, his face covered with a malicious grin. Dazed, she stared up at his nakedness, filled with disgust and apoplexy that she had been so humiliated, by such an inadequate appendage.

Didi Sumantri left without uttering so much as a word.

Alice ran a bath and immersed herself, remaining in the tub until she was confident that any traces of the *KOPASSUS* colonel had been scrubbed into oblivion.

The following morning when Brent Shepherd's calls to Alice's room remained unresponsive, he wrote a short note apologising for not saying goodbye, then left to catch his flight to Canberra.

The message was never delivered; Alice Heynneman had paid her account and vacated her room the night before, and moved into more nondescript accommodation out of concern that Didi Sumantri might attack again.

\*   \*   \*   \*

# Den Hague

The assembly closed with a recording of the anthem, *Maluku My Homeland* filling the surrounds. The annual event was closely observed by BIN agents, the Indonesian Intelligence Agency. They, in turn, were monitored by Ambonese recruited by the Algemene Inlichtingen en Veiligheidsdienst, the General Intelligence and Security Office of the Netherlands.

Bennie Tabuni exited the hall accompanied by Frans Soumokil, the Republic of South Maluku President in Exile, together with his trusted associate Obet Manusomo, a serving Member of the Dutch Parliament. Entering a taxi, the trio remained silent until arriving at their destination, a modest dwelling in an Ambonese-Dutch neighbourhood.

With Java coffee served and permitted the privacy this meeting dictated, the conversation immediately turned to the purpose of the discreet gathering.

'Support continues to gather momentum,' Soumokil commenced. 'Although I must concede that the current generation has lost much of their parents' appetite to participate.' The President in Exile for the self-proclaimed Republic of the South Moluccas, a group of islands in eastern Indonesia which included Ambon, Seram and Buru, lit a *kretek* cigarette, and filled his lungs with clove-scented smoke. 'Since our people arrived here in Holland it has been difficult to sustain support for the movement through the generations.'

'They will follow when called upon,' Obet Manusomo assured. In his heart he felt differently. However, the politician was not overly concerned because whatever outcome was achieved would be derived from a parliamentary committee, and not the voting public.

'We should do more to remind our youth of the sacrifices made by their forebears,' Frans Soumokil muttered. 'They have little appreciation of what we and our parents suffered.' He addressed Bennie as Obet had heard the story many times before. 'When the Dutch government finally decided to transport our families to the Netherlands, my grandparents were amongst those who disembarked from the ship *Kota Inten*, in Rotterdam in 1951.' Pausing to accommodate a coughing attack he looked at the clove cigarette then digressed. 'Did you know that the Moluccan Islands were the only place across the globe that grew clove and nutmeg?'

'Frans…' Obet reminded, and Frans recognised he had strayed off point.

'Sorry. Where was I?'

'You were telling us about your grandparents and when they arrived by ship,' Bennie prompted.

'Ah, yes. When my family arrived like all the other Moluccans, they were considered to be only temporary residents who, in the future, would be repatriated back to Indonesia when the political situation permitted.' He looked directly at Bennie. 'My family were housed in camps. Ironically, they were sent to the former Nazi transit camp Westerbork.'

'Those were tough times,' Bennie acknowledged moving to direct the conversation. *Au fait* with the deep animosities that existed between Moluccans and Indonesians, Bennie had specifically targeted the Moluccan Community in Holland, as this group had parallel independence expectations for their native homeland; the indigenous people, like Papuans, were also Melanesian, by origin. The South Moluccan people being predominantly Christian also shared the Papuans' distaste for the Moslem migrants being transported to their islands.

Bennie identified the similarities between how disastrously history had treated both the Moluccans and West Papuans. Following the Indonesian-Netherlands independence conflict, in 1949 the Dutch Government ordered the re-formed Royal Netherlands East Indies Army to accept Moluccan soldiers as part of the rebuilt force. The Moluccan community was, in consequence, regarded by the Dutch as allies, this position reciprocated by the Moluccans.

In return for this commitment, the Netherlands promised the Moluccans that they would have their own free state. Powerful international, anti-colonial forces, led by the Americans, prevented the Dutch from maintaining its colonial position, both in the Moluccas as well as West Papua, resulting in the Netherlands being obliged to renege on its commitments.

Indonesians, the new colonials who then displaced the Dutch considered the Moluccan Army as collaborators and, under the threat of total annihilation, engineered the mass exodus of almost thirteen thousand Moluccans, to the Netherlands.

Since that time, the Dutch-based Moluccans remained restive and disruptive, maintaining their claim for a free Republic of South Maluku, continuously reminding the Dutch Government of their failed promise to guarantee their freedom. Demonstrations were a regular feature along Amsterdam's streets. When their voice was not heard they changed tactics, engineering violent hijackings of trains, buses and attacking banks.

It was the Dutch-Moluccan deep-rooted-desire to have the international community support their claim for an independent state which Bennie intended to exploit, as his Wooden Horse into the nation's powerful parliament; the quid pro quo, an independent West Papua would recognise a Moluccan sovereign state in return for The Netherlands support in the United Nations.

Bennie had built the relationship through intermediaries, the Papuan resistance often secretly meeting with members of the Maluku Sovereignty Front in the pursuit of their common aims. He was anxious to have confirmation that the Dutch Government would indeed be a main driver towards having the United Nations conduct another plebiscite, to determine West Papuan independence. Bennie had believed from the very beginning that past historical events, which had deprived West Papuans of their independence, would be the foundation for the international community to revisit the issue.

Prior to the Indonesian annexation, the Netherlands had prepared the Papuan people for self-government, educating thousands to administer the former territory, building a political structure, only to have the colony's right to self-rule manipulated into the hands of the Indonesians. The loss of the rich, resource territory remained a contentious issue amongst Dutch entrepreneurs and politicians, some openly supportive whilst others, such as Obet Manusomo, built momentum behind closed doors.

Once his stratagem was set in motion Bennie envisaged the simultaneous endeavours would take time to coalesce, his deepest concern being that of managing the timing of each event to bring about the desired result.

Now, almost ten years since forming an alliance with Frans and Obet, Bennie was on the cusp of reaching the penultimate step towards achieving West Papuan independence. First of all, gaining the Netherlands' support as a member of the European Community, in proposing a vote in the United Nations to invalidate the flawed plebiscite Act of Free Choice of 1969, and initiate a referendum to provide a path towards full independence for the West Papuan people.

He was confident that the Pacific Island nations and African states that had already indicated they would support such a vote would encourage other countries to follow.

With the arrival of a new dawn, Bennie would work with his Papuan colleagues to establish a Council of Tribal Elders initially with a view to hold elections as quickly as feasible. Bennie would lead from the shadows. He would offer his "brother" Marcus' services to the people as President, should they accept. Jules would be appointed to restructure the economy and in doing so, assume all existing foreign investment from forestry to mining, to infrastructure development and finance.

The change would bring many opportunities and Bennie would ensure that those who had supported the movement would be remembered when West Papua emerged under new management. And to further encourage any within the Dutch Government that might vacillate and waver in support, Bennie had committed to inviting Royal Dutch Shell to return to their former colony, to assume joint management of all oil and gas ventures, once independence became a reality, virtually the same arrangement he planned to offer the British.

'When the time comes, the Indonesians will not go quietly,' Obet postulated.

'Not without a fight,' Frans agreed. 'We were all surprised they let East Timor go without any real resistance.'

'They had little choice once their own president opened the door and the international community supported the UN's involvement.' Bennie used the opportunity to remind the others of their own vested interests.

'Yes, but East Timor does not have the wealth of resources West Papua has to offer,' again Frans voiced his concern. This had been one of the predominant issues relating to the Moluccan cause for independence. The group of islands constituting the proposed state had proven gas reserves, the Abadi Gas Field, which was well into production, delivering close to three million tonnes of LNG annually together with a daily tally of nine thousand barrels of condensate. The natural owners were yet to enjoy any downstream benefits from the field.

'The same could be said of the Moluccas,' Bennie reminded.

Obet stretched his legs outwards from under his chair. Leaning back with hands supporting the back of his neck he peered at the ceiling, then sighed. 'The possibility of Independent Mollucas will be greatly enhanced should West Papua succeed in parting ways with Jakarta.' Obet moved his hands forward and clasp them together as if in prayer. 'Then we should endeavour to ensure such an outcome.'

Frans nodded sagely while Bennie offered no response.

Frans Soumokil and Obet Manusomo carried the conversation for several hours. Before terminating their meeting, Bennie passed envelopes containing cashier cheques amounting to one hundred thousand Euros, to both men. Bennie was satisfied that the Dutch Parliament would vote with their pockets when the time arrived, and he departed the following morning, for Bougainville.

*   *   *   *

# WEST PAPUA

### JAYAPURA

Many of Jayapura's buildings were burning; the cacophonous sounds of rapid gunfire like some high-powered chainsaw shattering the air.

Jules Heynneman focussed his binoculars on the KFC billboard atop the supermarket as it collapsed in flames, with sections falling four-stories to the street. From his vantage point on City Hill dwarfed by communication towers he could see across the provincial capital and Yos Sudarso Bay. Fifty kilometres to his right, the distant mountains that delineated the border between Indonesia and Papua New Guinea remained covered in low-lying cloud providing cover for rebel troops.

Below, as if oblivious to the danger Papuans rode their motorcycles in defiance, with pillion passengers carrying the *Morning Star* flag by their side. Thumbing their noses at the many anti-riot troops guarding the police station across from the Jayapura Mall, they weaved their way around military vehicles summoned to address the unrest that had attracted tens of thousands onto the streets.

Demonstrations had erupted simultaneously across the two

provinces of West Papua. In the more populated towns of Sentani, Serui, Manokwari, Nabire, Merauke, Biak, and Sorong gatherings had exceeded expectations, Jules attributing the success of the collective show of Papuan unity, to Bennie Tabuni's patient planning.

The week before, Mobile Brigade troops attacked a large gathering in Timika, a city on the south coast. The flag-raising ceremony had been organised at the Three Kings Parish Catholic Church where daily speeches were recited by Free Papua representatives. When Indonesian officials demanded the flag be lowered, several thousand Papuans assembled in the churchyard to prevent the *The Morning Star* from being taken down. A *BRIMOB* police unit attempted to enter the churchyard, where several hundred women formed a human gate to block their passage, singing *"Hai Tanahku Papua"*. Angered by their resistance, the soldiers released tear gas and attacked them, killing twenty-four and injuring dozens more within minutes. Striking viciously at anyone within reach using rifle butts and nightsticks, their numbers were reinforced, when an army helicopter arrived with additional troops.

When news of the slaughter reached Bennie in Bougainville, he was incensed, immediately determined to send a message to the Indonesians that Papuans would no longer tolerate such brutality.

With military precision, coordinated attacks on unguarded Indonesian civil servants' homes, several mosques and other designated targets were executed by Bennie's commanders, who had received their training in Bougainville. The Indonesian forces were stunned with the appearance of Bennie's ten-thousand-strong, black-clad, *Satgas Papua* pro-independence militia, commanded by surrogates under Bennie's leadership and funded secretly by Jules.

With the arrival of armoured vehicles and transports ferry-ing additional troops from Sentani to the provincial capital, Jules decided to return to his well-fortified villa on the city's outskirts. He texted his movements to the senior *Satgas Papua* commander to ensure his safe passage then waited for armed escorts to arrive.

The violence continued for ten days, during which time more than eight hundred Papuans and three hundred and twenty Indo-nesian soldiers were killed. Curfew was implemented across both Papuan provinces. Convinced that the rebel *Satgas Papua* units had crossed from secret camps across the PNG border, the Indonesian military command in Jakarta deployed a further eighteen hundred troops, divided into four battalions, from Jayapura to Merauke. The battalions guarding the border at Keerom and Pegunungan Bintang Regencies were drawn from the 726 Tamalate Infantry Battalion and 141 Palembang Infantry Battalion Task Force Units respec-tively. The Battalions guarding the Jayawijaya and Merauke Regen-cies originated from the 310 Siliwangi Infantry Battalion and 631 Palangkaraya Infantry Battalion Task Force units.

United Nations peacekeepers across the border monitored the Indonesian military's increased level of communication traffic and raised their own level of alert. Upon receiving the update, the Papua New Guinea Prime Minister made a frantic call to Canberra to seek reassurance from the Australian Government that they would inter-vene, should the threat escalate.

Momentum was growing; Bennie Tabuni's strategy was now well into play.

*   *   *   *

# JAKARTA

## OFFICE OF THE PRESIDENT

President Abul Moewardi cogitated for several minutes before deleting sections of the announcement he was composing. Troubled, he rose from the stylish leather Chesterfield sofa and returned to the work desk installed following his election as President. He had chosen *Puri Bhakti Renatama* as his official office which, for practical reasons, was located in the courtyard between the Merdeka Palace and the State Palace where office functions took place.

In the presidential race, Abdul Moewardi's reformist agenda had been widely supported by the country's younger generation. Having served less than a year in office, he had already learned the Machiavellian path to balancing power between the many vested interest political groups, and the forever-challenging, high-handed military establishment.

National unity as expressed in the constitution had always occupied a preeminent position in Moewardi's mind. A realist, he understood the fractious nature of the diverse population that represented the Republic, his position evolving having studied the nature of other nations' constitutional structures.

Moewardi's judgment was that the limited autonomy granted to some of the more rebellious provinces had failed.

The president discreetly harboured the belief that Indonesia as a nation would be less divisive under a commonwealth model as opposed to the current system of government. He understood that as long as the majority of non-Javanese felt disenchanted with what they perceived to be another form of colonisation, calls for separation from the Republic would persist. Moewardi was convinced that a commonwealth of Indonesian states, in which each territory would have their own constitutions, retain the power to make their own laws as well as a structure of legislature, executive and judiciary, would bond the nation's indigenous groups and dissuade the notion of separation. However appreciating the depth of resistance any suggestion of amending the constitution would bring, President Moewardi was selective with whom he discussed this conviction knowing the military would be against such change.

The issue of West Papua remained paramount in his thoughts. The implementation of autonomy had been disastrous there, with the central government again contributing more than a billion dollars annually to the overall territory without achieving any significant economic progress. Moewardi was firm in his belief that if a commonwealth model of government had been introduced when East Timor was annexed in 1975, independence might not now be the troublesome issue that it was.

The president returned to his notes. Facing mounting international condemnation Moewardi was preparing a proposal that might circumvent any United Nations intervention in West Papua. He anticipated total resistance from the military establishment, as the generals still retained a substantial flow of benefits from the eastern provinces. They would also argue that by providing the Papuans with quasi-independence, suggested in his commonwealth model of government, other recalcitrant provinces would make similar demands, creating a domino effect.

He agreed; that was the conundrum.

'*Maaf Bapak,*' the Palace personal assistant tapped quietly at the doorway, apologizing for the interruption. 'Your daughter, Pipi apologises for the interruption and asks if she may speak to you?'

Pipi Hedi Moewardi swept into the chamber, sat demurely on the sofa, then feigned wiping tears from her eyes.

Abdul Moewardi steeled himself for what he expected would follow. Jakarta's whispering class enjoyed the gossip surrounding his daughter's turbulent relationships.

'Didi is sleeping with that actress, Angelina again.'

'You must learn to ignore such rumours,' the president comforted.

'It's true, *Bapak,*' Pipi insisted. 'They were seen driving into her home together.'

Moewardi was aware of his son-in-law's penchant for models and actresses. 'You knew who you were marrying,' was all he could muster.

Didi's father, General Sumantri, was an adversary with whom he did not wish to become embroiled in any domestic dispute.

'Just give him time. It will pass. Bring my granddaughter over tonight and you can spend some time with your mother.'

Pipi understood she was being dismissed, leaving her father with lingering misgivings about her relationship with the sociopath who had married his daughter. The president had not been keen on the union. Culturally, and socially, they were not a great match. Pipi and her siblings had been raised in a traditional Javanese manner. Moewardi's family were cultured and educated. Didi Sumantri was brash and had an obvious appetite for power, radiating an arrogance often found amongst military elite.

His son-in-law had already acquired a reputation amongst his peers. Having graduated from the military academy in Magelang, Didi had then served with *KOPASSUS* and was assigned Commander of a *Sandhi Yudha* group. With the support of his father, General Sumantri the most senior officer in the country's military, Didi's star enjoyed a rapid ascent. Moewardi was aware that the Americans had their eyes on Didi, ever since his actions involving the rescue attempt of several foreigners who had been taken hostage by rebels in West Papua. The young officer had attracted severe international criticism for using the Red Cross emblem on a white helicopter to deceive the rebels. When the helicopter landed in the remote highlands, innocent villagers, who had no involvement in the kidnappings, ran towards the aircraft believing it was their friends from the Red Cross. Instead, *KOPASSUS* soldiers rolled out of the machine and shot the villagers dead.

Moewardi had long been cognizant of the Sumantri family's position in the vast agricultural program that was being developed in the Papuan districts not far from Kampung Mas. Approval for the acquisition of more than a million hectares of land had been granted by the previous administration, the beneficiaries, an Agus Winarko-consortium that fronted for the army's commercial operations. The project was to meet Java's increasing demand for rice, and so, government-sponsored trans-migrants, and other settlers from elsewhere in Indonesia, were transported to the site. Although the program required the cancellation of traditional rights to lands and forests in the allocation of those resources to the consortium, there was no mention of the development in the national press. As a result of this program the resource tenure rights of local people were extinguished.

Such was the power of the military establishment he faced.

Dwelling on the inevitable power-play, a sudden shortness of breath, followed by a sense of lightheadedness, caught him by surprise. Alone in his office, the president clutched his chest and grimaced, the attack lasting but moments before he could again breathe with ease. He called the First Lady and asked her to invite her own doctor to visit their residence later in the day.

*    *    *    *

# USA — Phoenix — Arizona

'Apart from the potential public relations hit we'll take, our share-holders will be banging on the doors demanding what impact the report will have on future revenue streams.' David Shackleton had been president of the Summit Gold Mining conglomerate for less than a year, though his rapidly receding hairline aged the Yale graduate well before his time.

'The information was not released by our office,' he insisted. 'And we had planned on including reference to the uranium ore in an internal report to the shareholders, once the Secretary had been updated.' He remained silent listening to the voice at the other end of the call. 'No. The Indonesians had insisted that we sit on the information. They just don't want the world knowing about this development.' Again he listened, nodding in agreement with what was being suggested. 'That is the course I intend taking. Okay, fine.' Shackleton dropped the news release onto his desk and drew a deep breath.

He expected the article would be widely read and would require an explanation to the other government agencies that he had, until now, avoided. The Secretary of State had been apprised when commercial grade quantities of the ore had been discovered in the West Papuan mine.

He grimaced, knowing that the media would distort the information that for most of the past year, uranium ore was being mined at the Akumuga Mine site. He could only hope that they would not be aware that this was a breach of the original agreement with the

Indonesians. The media would undoubtedly associate this development with the production of nuclear weapons, and that could derail
current negotiations in Jakarta, to prevent the dilution of Summit's
shareholding in the Akumuga Mine from its current holding of fifty-
one percent. This was of deep concern, as Indonesia's rising economic nationalism had already manifested itself in proposed new
laws and regulations that eroded investor value, with the require-
ment to divest equity shares to local stakeholders.

Shackleton suspected that there was a correlation between the
media release of their covert mining of the uranium ore and the
executive summary he had received earlier in the day. There had
been mention of uranium tailings in the document, and obviously
this had been leaked by staff inside the environmental group, prior
to forwarding the final brief to his office.

Retrieving the news release, he read the pertinent paragraph
again.

*"Uranium mining leaves behind huge amounts of radioactive waste tail-*
*ings. These tailings contain approximately 80% of the original radio-*
*activity of the ore and have a half life of up to two hundred and forty*
*thousand years; dangerous forever, in human terms. These tailings are*
*in most cases left in the open, exposed to wind and rain, and radioactive*
*and poisonous materials are contaminating the surface water, ground-*
*water aquifers, soil, air, plants and produce, livestock and wild animals,*
*and will continue to do so for thousands of years into the future. The*
*highly-sought uranium-bearing minerals are removed by heap leaching.*
*As yet, the industry has not developed any means of safe disposal of the*
*tailings which at the Akumuga Mine, are left out in the open exposed*
*to the elements. The poisonous material then contaminates surface and*

*groundwater, affecting all forms of flora and fauna and the air the Papuans breathe, for thousands of years to come."*

Shackleton crunched the news clipping in the palm of his hand and dropped the paper ball into a bin as if deeming the matter closed. He then turned his attention to the executive summary titled, "The Environmental impacts of the Summit Gold Mining Operation in Indonesia" sitting challengingly on his desk, and pushed the document across the table to his personal assistant.

'Guess the Indonesians would have already seen the report.' Rubbing an invisible mark on his forehead he frowned, facing the inevitable. 'Set up a call with Winarko in Jakarta,' he asked quietly. 'After that, contact the Secretary for State's office and ask for a meeting if he is available, anytime this week.'

Alone with his thoughts, Shackleton considered the environmental report, and grudgingly admitted that most of what it contained, was an accurate account of the Akumuga Mine's operation. He was deeply troubled by the most damaging claims which related to accusations that the mine operation had contaminated the river, to estuary, food chain. The report had stated that there were significantly higher concentrations of toxic metals evident in the system, and Shackleton expected the Indonesians would use this to increase their levies.

Recently, Summit had narrowly avoided serious charges in relation to the fifteen million dollars paid annually into military coffers in Jakarta, to ensure the mine's security. This had been the product of the United Steelworkers union writing to the US Department of Justice, asking it to investigate whether Summit Gold payments amounted to bribing a foreign government, in violation of the US

Foreign Corrupt Practices Act. Relieved that the US Securities and Exchange Commission, having received similar allegations, decided there was no case to answer, Shackleton facilitated future payments from a Cayman Islands account, rerouted via Hong Kong to Jakarta.

Agitated by the accumulation of worrisome events, the Summit Gold Mining president unconsciously raised a hand to his head and scratched an irritation on his scalp, pensively waiting for his call to Jakarta.

\*   \*   \*   \*

# JAKARTA

'Thank you for your guidance, *Bapak Agus*.' Herman Alomang respectfully addressed Agus Winarko understanding the billion-aire's position and influence in the Akumuga Mine in Papua, the eastern province carved out of West Papua of which he was now governor. 'I shall discuss your suggestions with the regional legisla-ture and the Papuan People's Council upon my return.'

The conversation was in the national language *Bahasa Indonesia*. The governor was also fluent in English and, of course, many of the local Papuan dialects.

Agus was not impressed with the suggestion that the council, known locally as the *Dewan Perwakilan Rakyat Papua*, a coalition of Papuan tribal chiefs, should be consulted. 'You do appreciate the urgency of having the local regulations promulgated quickly?'

In a retrograde step from a foreign investment perspective, the central government had amended foreign investment regulations, providing provincial authorities the right to set their own regulatory requirements on mining companies. The Akumuga Mine already paid these additional levies, however Agus had managed to convince the governor to initiate action against the company, citing that the mining of uranium ore had caused environmental damage and therefore had to cease. That would become another bargaining chip with the American shareholders.

'Of course, *Bapak*,' Alomang smiled and Agus was intrigued by the Papuan's solid gold incisor. 'As we will be the beneficiaries my office will act swiftly.'

'More funds would mean more schools, Governor,' Agus reminded, somewhat pompously. 'And less interference from those insurrectionists who don't appreciate the status quo.' The governor had been given a substantial amount of rupiah as additional encouragement.

Governor Herman Alomang had been directly elected governor by the Papuan people. Although his activities were strictly monitored by Jakarta-regime agents, he still managed to elude their suspicious eyes and provide a direct line of communication with Bennie Tabuni, and his growing army of freedom fighters.

Agus Winarko's next meeting was with the chairman of the nation's Investment Coordinating Board, another government official whose fingers were constantly in others' pockets. The official was greeted warmly by Agus, as the pair had worked together manipulating other government departments, to accommodate their pursuits.

'The draft has been approved in principle by Jono.' The chairman referred to the Minister of Mines as he passed a set of documents to Agus. 'The proposed new Laws on Mining will, of course, have to be approved by the House Committee, but that won't be an issue.'

Agus skimmed through the thick bundle then exhaled deeply. 'I'll read the draft later.' Preparation of the draft had taken many months of deliberation with the military, government department heads and of course, the president's closest advisers. The revised mining regulations would provide Agus with the means to achieve control over the Akumuga Mine's vast wealth. In a typical Indonesian power-play, the entrepreneur endeavoured to seize assets from his foreign counterparts by using updated government directives that would make the mine's profitability almost unachievable. Agus' objective was to legally squeeze the American Summit Gold partners into relinquishing their shareholding in the operation.

Agus had outlined what was required of the new mining regulations. All ore exports of unrefined tin, gold silver, chromium, and uranium would cease within two years; mining operations must commit to the construction of local smelter/refinery operations within that time frame. Although these requirements would, in his mind, be sufficient to achieve strengthening his position and deliver the operation into his hands, the most important component of the new directive would be the final hammer blow to Summit Gold. The regulation also required that all mining companies must comply with a maximum foreign ownership of nineteen percent within the stipulated two-year period, irrespective of whether they had their own processing or refining facilities.

He envisaged having the Chinese finance, and build, the smelter plant within the Special Autonomous Zone of Kampung Mas.

He accepted that foreign mining investors, especially his Summit Gold partners, would be apoplectic upon receiving news of the new regulations. They would, of course, be offered the opportunity to litigate through the Indonesian judicial system. The thought of the foreign party challenging through the local courts brought a self-satisfied chuckle. The dispute resolution process in Indonesian civil proceedings followed the Dutch civil law tradition, and normally took more than three years to finalise. Agus was fortunate that his foreign partners did not have the provision in the original agreements to take any dispute to a foreign jurisdiction. In short, with the new mining regulations becoming law, Agus' acquisition of Summit Gold's shareholding could be considered *fait accompli*.

'Then we can expect the new regulations to come into law before *Ramadan*?' Agus Winarko was near salivating at the prospect of the new mining regulations becoming law within the next months.

'*Insha Allah,*' the chairman invoked.

*   *   *   *

# LONDON

The British Foreign Secretary remained deeply immersed in thought contemplating the recommendations contained in the report. The substance of the counsel was indeed a tempting proposition; *"Prepare a draft memorandum of understanding with the future, Papuan transitional government to provide a committed British presence by developing four joint naval facilities at Sorong, Biak, Jayapura and Port Kampung Mas.".* In consideration of such an arrangement, the future West Papuan authority would offer British Petroleum a thirty-year monopoly on all offshore oil and gas developments within its territorial waters. This would include any existing operations that had been allocated by the Indonesian Government in the Tangguh LNG gas fields.

The British were not aware that a similar offer had been suggested to the Dutch.

The Secretary had repeatedly reiterated the significance of having the British Navy re-establish a naval presence in SE Asia, as contemporary developments provided a timely opportunity for the United Kingdom to act. It was clear that the Papuans were troubled by China's growing presence, fearful that Beijing would continue to utilise its military prowess to establish a Chinese hegemony in their territory.

The Foreign Secretary had always felt that since the 1967 withdrawal from Singapore and Malaysia, with Maggie Thatcher's insane decision to surrender Hong Kong to Mainland China, Britain had lost the last vestiges of empire. He and others of similar ilk appreciated the many trade opportunities that could flow to the United Kingdom with the rise of the Asian Century. However, they also understood that as SE Asia and China became more strategically important, in order to maintain its position within those economies, the UK would need to commit to a renewed military presence.

The UK was currently linked militarily with a number of South Asia Commonwealth nations through the Five Powers Defence Arrangements. This relationship reflected a layer of multi-lateral agreements between the UK, Australia, New Zealand, Malaysia and Singapore that provided an immediate response in the event of any threat or armed attack on its members. However, the Foreign Secretary was dissatisfied with the absence of any British naval bases within those domains, and Britain's only real naval access to the Far East was through Diego Garcia in the Indian Ocean. He was resolved to remedy by supporting the recommendations contained in the dossier on his desk. Intrigued by the genesis of the submission, the Secretary had summoned Anne Whitehead to his office to learn more.

The Principal Secretary of State for Foreign and Commonwealth Affairs had first become acquainted with Anglo American Aerospace Defence Technologies (AAADT) as a junior cabinet minister. At that time his knowledge of the relationship between the British Government and the multi-national was in relation to arms shipments to Saudi Arabia. With his appointment as Foreign Secretary came the revelation that AAADT was much more than he had previously known. The conglomerate's executives were, without exception, either senior government civil servants, ex-military chiefs, or a combination of both. As Foreign Minister, he had ministerial oversight for the Secret Intelligence Service MI6. As a result, the intelligence dossier covering an AAADT senior executive's relationship with West Papuan rebel leadership had been hand-delivered directly to his person.

It was known to the Secretary that the British Government had been indirectly supplying arms to the West Papuan rebels. What he had not envisaged was the speed the Free Papua Movement had developed its militia. He never questioned why his government would supply weapons to the rebels when the very enemy that confronted the insurgents was, in fact, a significant client for British armament sales. Selling weapons to the West Papuan independence movement was not, in his mind, a philosophical issue. The existing 'Five Eyes' arrangement, where the British drew on shared intelligence provided by the US, Australia, New Zealand and Canada, had provided compelling evidence that the tide was changing in the rebels' favour, as the independence movement gained further international support.

Now, with the real possibility of an independent West Papua the opportunity for the United Kingdom to reinstate its place in Asia could be achieved. The Secretary had conferred with the Prime Minister and Home Secretary, and both had agreed to pursue further discussion with the rebel movement's intermediaries. After all, had not the British Government been a signatory to the Westminster Declaration?

The report also included a hypothetical projection of what revenues might flow as a result of arms sales to a democratic West Papua state. AAADT suggested that although initial sales would require

British Aid support, the estimated value of military sales from UK manufacturers would exceed one billion pounds over ten years and hundreds of millions in revenues generated from services and other British manufactured product.

A tap on the chamber's door drew the politician's attention. 'Your appointment with Miss Anne Whitehead,' his private secretary announced.

Anne Whitehead appeared as summoned, to provide a first-hand account of her long association with the West Papuan, rebel leadership.

'Sit down, my dear.' The Secretary moved from behind his desk. 'I am keen to hear your story.'

\*    \*    \*    \*

Returning to the corridors of AAADT power, Anne Whitehead reported to her chairman, discussed her meeting with the Foreign Secretary, then retired to her own spacious surroundings, situated on the senior executive level.

She felt she had acquitted herself satisfactorily and was relieved that the Secretary had complimented Anne on her refreshing candour following her disclosure as to the past personal nature of her relationship with Jules Heynneman. Having provided an assurance that the substance of the information contained in the report was in no way influenced by her association with the Papuan cabal, Anne presumed the integrity of the proposed memorandum would not be challenged.

When Bennie and Jules had outlined their strategy, it was evident that the proposition needed to be advocated by the most subtle and plausible means. Although Jules had established credentials with AAADT and enjoyed their trust, neither he nor Bennie had access to British halls of power. It had been Anne who had suggested that she take the concept initially to the AAADT chairman and see where it might go from there. Over a period of weeks, and guided by her superiors Anne had convinced Bennie and Jules that by offering the United Kingdom a future naval presence, their proposal would be given serious consideration. When they reconvened and committed to negotiating with British Petroleum to manage all West Papua oil and gas resources once the territory became an independent state, a draft memorandum had taken shape.

Anne was not surprised to learn that the concept of having the British establish a naval presence appealed to Bennie, considering his deep dislike of the growing Chinese presence in Papua. However, she understood that to dislodge them and the Indonesians, when they were now so ensconced, would be a formidable task.

The sovereignty of a future independent West Papua would be guaranteed not only by the presence of UK naval assets, but indirectly through the British Commonwealth defence agreements that would have Singapore to the north, and Australia to the south, committed to ensuring a free Papua.

Deep folds creased Anne's brow when reminded of Jakarta's military dominance, a sense of despair supplanting any earlier euphoria derived from the success of the day.

*       *       *       *

# United Nations

Bennie Tabuni waited for silence before commencing his address at the 44th session of the Human Rights Council.

'Today, I have the honour of speaking on behalf of Ecuador, Venezuela, Peru and seven other nations of our Pacific region: Vanuatu, the Solomon Islands, Nauru, Palau, Tuvalu, the Marshall Islands, and Tonga.

Mr. President, these nations have offered their voice together today to draw the attention of the respected members of the UN Human Rights Council to the gravity of the situation in what is known as Indonesian-occupied West Papua. Indonesian military cruelty has been invisible to the world due to the curtain of secrecy that has been drawn around the territory, burying the systematic killings that have been underway, even prior to the previous UN-sponsored referendum.

Mr. President, since the flawed plebiscite deemed to be an Act of Free Choice the indigenous people of Papua have been displaced by a tidal wave of transmigrants under an Indonesian program instituted to dilute the Papuan people. The land has been appropriated without adequate compensation and rightful owners are now refugees in their own habitat. This amounts to colonisation, introduced to disguise the thousands of retired Indonesian soldiers transported to native land who, upon arrival, act as agents for Jakarta business interests. Indonesians now control the majority of all wealth in Papua where the indigenous population is now treated as an underclass, relegated to selling betel nuts on the roadside whilst the towns' enterprises are dominated by outsiders. Foreign mining companies destroy our food sources and contaminate the water supplies. Logging enterprises cut swathes through the land destroying the very lungs of our forests.

Mr. President, the brutal Indonesian *KOPASSUS* Special Forces can be found in every village across Papua on their path of slow-motion genocide. These soldiers kill and arrest with impunity, conduct extrajudicial executions of activists, and rape Papuan women. We will never know precisely how many Papuans have been killed by the Indonesian military that protect Jakarta's elites and their investments in Papua. We see the wealth of our resource-rich land stripped of its timber, minerals, oil, and gas ripped from our hands only to be delivered to non-Papuans.

Mr. President, even though for most of the past sixty years the international press has been denied access to Papua, evidence of these atrocities and other issues cannot be denied. There is a powerful current of solidarity building across the globe and on behalf of the people of West Papua, I appeal to the honourable members present, to join us in support of West Papua's right to self-determination.

Thank you.'

Present at the UN session in an unofficial capacity was the Indonesian *chargé d'affaires,* who immediately returned to the embassy, and reported by phone to General Sumantri in Jakarta. The disgruntled Armed Forces chief then called the BIN director to challenge why Bennie Tabuni had not already been removed from the international stage.

\*    \*    \*    \*

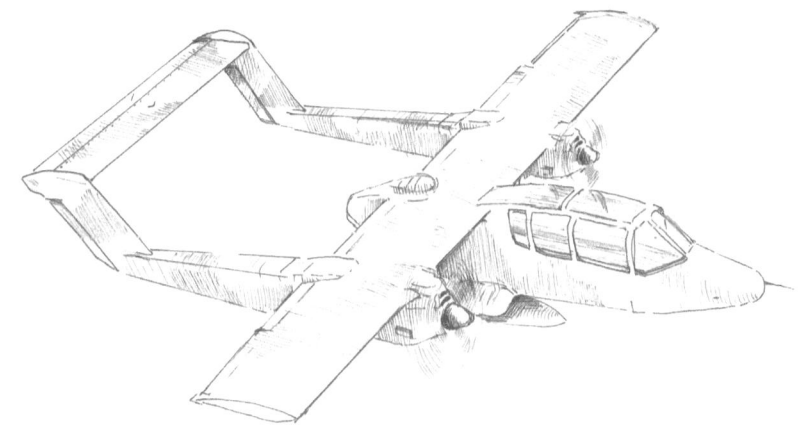

# PAPUA

Papua's early morning village tranquillity was abruptly ruptured when machine-pistol fire punctured the surrounds. A contingent of fifty *KOPASSUS* red-beret and Army Strategic Command green-beret Indonesian soldiers carried out their merciless attack. Terrified Papuans fled screaming into the forest and those unfortunate enough to be caught in the cross-fire crumbled in their tracks.

The troops had been ordered to attack the Asmat villages suspected of harbouring rebel sympathisers. The soldiers forced survivors into an open space between the two villages and killed the men, sixty-five in total, in front of the remaining women and children. A pregnant girl, still in her teens, was shot dead in view of weeping women and children. The soldiers then callously cut the foetus out of her body and dissected the baby.

The next day, the ruthless soldiers arrested forty men from neighbouring villages. They manhandled the captives into boats, tied stones around their necks, and threw them into the river.

Further inland, other elements of the Indonesian army executed operations in the Jayawijaya Mountains. Supported by US-supplied OV-10 Bronco aircraft, strafing and bombing missions killed hundreds of Papuans, causing thousands to flee their impoverished villages in search of safety in the jungle. Daisy Cluster bombs rained down on rebel soldiers who remained hopelessly incapable of preventing the onslaught.

In a village overlooking the Akumuga Mine, Indonesian Special Forces continued their massive and indiscriminate action sweeping the area, burning huts and slaughtering pigs and chickens before continuing their barbarous and relentless attack on men, women and children. Ruthless soldiers used bayonets to pierce women through the vagina, tearing them open to the chest. Females found to be bearing children were ripped open and their unborn babies sliced into halves. An elderly tribesman was butchered, his blood used to fill a bucket. At gunpoint, the soldiers then forced the tribal leaders to drink the blood.

When the massacres were over leaving the countryside filled only with the sound of women and children wailing, the rivers were so full of corpses that for months to come, Papuans could not bring themselves to eat fish from these waters.

\*    \*    \*    \*

Devastated by news of the inhumane attacks, Bennie Tabuni sat ruminating on his collective rebel forces that now numbered more than ten thousand.

Jakarta's attempt to undermine the independence movement by

previously dividing West Papua into two provinces, West Papua and Papua, did nothing to deter his rebels, who continued to build their underground training camps in the near-inaccessible mountain hideaways.

The freedom-fighter-machine was managed via a complex hierarchy down to the village level. Those who had not undergone basic training fell back on tactics that combined traditional native fighting techniques such as bamboo-arrow archery attacks, together with long-established village, guerrilla tactics.

Unlike back in time when the rebels were obliged to drill with spears and arrows and M16s stripped from dead Indonesian soldiers, now the main body of his troops were armed with West German Heckler & Koch carbines, and the Indonesian-produced SS2 assault rifle, which was standard issue of the Indonesian military and police forces. As the SS2 was produced under a licensing agreement with the Belgium Fabrique Nationale arms manufacturer, five thousand units had been accessed in Europe by an AAADT affiliate and shipped to Vanuatu for onward delivery into rebel Papuan sanctuaries.

Although wholesale retribution would be deservedly appropriate, Bennie remained determined to avoid directly engaging Indonesia's overwhelming military numbers, preferring to execute attacks against posts manned by smaller numbers.

Throughout the day, he formulated a strategy that would send an adequate response to Indonesia's Papuan-based forces. And, in doing so, inflame the simmering animosities against Jakarta that were steadily building across the PNG border.

He opened a drawer and withdrew a postcard from a supporter in

Chile. The inscription quoted the deceased activist who died under a hail of bullets when robbing a bank. It read:

> *"Throw yourself into freedom; that is my proposal. Loot, rob, burn, assault the one who exploits you, and destroy authority, which conditions and imprisons us. Do not seek leaders, aspire to your freedom. Break with the logic of power and with those who sustain it."*
>
> — *Sebastian Oversluij Seguel*

\*   \*   \*   \*

In 1986, Indonesia and Papua New Guinea signed the *Treaty of Mutual Respect, Cooperation, and Friendship.* The treaty was, in effect, a bilateral nonaggression pact in which the two sides agreed to "avoid, reduce, and contain disputes or conflicts between their nations and settle any differences that may arise only by peaceful means".

Bennie Tabuni was committed to creating an environment which would compel the PNG government to abandon the treaty. In determining an appropriate target for his rebel attack Bennie wished to identify a border post where he knew that the target, Papua New Guinea Defence Force personnel (PNGDF) would be in close proximity on the other side. Intelligence had reported the presence of a company-strength-PNGDF base at Kiunga, located twenty-five kilometres from the border.

Manned by less than one hundred soldiers that belonged to the Long Range Reconnaissance Unit, Bennie expected any surprise attack would be met with limited resistance, as the PNG forces were poorly trained and inadequately equipped. The PNGDF were not only chronically short of weapons, but also did not possess any armour or artillery and were bereft of skilled leadership. Being aware of the necessity to eliminate the target's communication facility, Bennie advised his commander to prioritise destruction of the mobile, digital satellite communications network station, that enabled real-time reporting to any of the seven fixed ground stations across the country.

Bennie's bold and ambitious plan required taking control of the Boven Digoel border post. Rebel elements regularly reconnoitred the site which was supported by a platoon of *KOPPASSUS* regulars. The unit could not easily depend on rapid support from the Tanah Merah garrison, as the remote site was often cut off by perilous, unsealed road access whenever rain fell.

Bennie's rebel commanders were briefed and the first action commenced three weeks later.

The Boven Digoel *KOPASSUS* post was taken with ease and without any significant rebel losses. Dressed in Indonesian Special Forces attire, fifty of Bennie's Bougainville-trained fighters simply marched into the border post and assumed control. Of the twenty Indonesian troops all but two were executed and their weapons seized. The prisoners were bound and taken on the arduous trail across the border through almost impenetrable jungle, taking three more days to cover the short distance to Kiunga.

The port town built on the Fly River was the terminus of the Kiunga-Tabubil Highway and, apart from selecting this target due to the presence of the PNGDF base, Bennie was counting on international condemnation of the attack, because of its relationship with the massive Ok Tedi Mine.

When the surprise pre-dawn offensive commenced, the main body of PNG forces were caught in their barracks. Half of the Papuan force dressed in *KOPASSUS* uniforms entered the buildings and emptied a hail of bullets into the sleeping soldiers' bodies. The remaining rebels dragged the two Indonesian prisoners to the police station, killed the local police officers then executed the Indonesian soldiers leaving their weapons in evidence.

An enraged community would identify the perpetrators as members of the brutal, Indonesian Special Forces.

Bennie's rebels then roamed the town until identifying the small backpacker boarding house where foreigners were known to reside. Finding a pair of Norwegian women hiding in their room both were immediately dispatched, their crumpled half-naked bodies, evidence of the callous act.

Less than an hour after the strike commenced, the rebels had withdrawn. But not before the bodies of six of their comrades were stripped, and cast into the Fly River.

The group then followed an alternate route back into West Papua, crossing the frontier border into the safety of their own, natural surroundings. Weapons and uniforms were stored in a secluded mountain repository, and the team then dispersed, the men returning to their respective villages.

Over the following days, Bennie's commanders sent another armed group of freedom fighters dressed in bush attire to attack small pockets of Indonesian troops. Immediately following their brief exchange, the Papuan force withdrew, drawing the *KOPAS-*

*SUS* into the chase. The heavily-armed soldiers followed the rebels, illegally crossing the PNG border, and penetrated thirty kilometres into foreign territory, terrorising villagers along the Torasi River.

In what was a clear violation of PNG sovereignty the Indonesian troops mounted machine guns pointed towards the Bensbach Lodge, then swept the communities of Bondobol, Bala-muk, Korombo and Wando in search of Papuan rebels. They were unsuccessful; Bennie's freedom fighters had already left the area and returned to the Papuan side of the border.

As was expected, international outrage condemning the brutal attacks resulted in calls for those responsible to be brought before the International Court of Justice in The Hague.

Norway recalled its ambassador and the Government of Papua New Guinea immediately closed its border with Indonesia and referred the matter to the United Nations. Port Moresby called upon Canberra to send troops, citing the 1991 agreement which committed Australia to support PNG in the event of any external armed attack that threatened PNG's national sovereignty.

In the Netherlands, Obet Manusomo introduced a private Member's Bill into Parliament seeking government support for the West Papuan Independence movement.

In Jakarta, mob demonstrations outside the Papua New Guinea, Australian, and United States embassies were orchestrated by military factions associated with Agus Winarko. Whilst the Indonesian Foreign Office issued a statement accusing foreign elements of fabricating the story of the Kiunga attack, the Ministry of Defence moved secretly to conceal the annihilation of the *KOPASSUS* platoon, deploying a further fifty *BRIMOB* police to the Boven Digoel outpost.

*   *   *   *

# WASHINGTON

'Jack, we need to exert some political pressure on those bastards in Jakarta,' David Shackleton explained.

The Secretary of State had been apprised when commercial grade quantities of uranium ore had been discovered in the West Papuan mine.

'Jakarta won't back down from new rules,' he muttered, his grievance taken before the US Secretary for State seeking government support.

The Indonesian Government had promulgated new laws ordering foreign shareholdings in a number of fields to divest majority stakes in local Energy and Mineral holdings.

'We've brought in billions of dollars of investment to West Papua and employed thousands,' he complained.

Concentrate exports from the Akumuga Mine have been at a standstill for the past month following the announcement. The new rules demanded Summit divest its majority holding in its Indonesian unit, pay more taxes, and commence building a smelter.

'Summit Gold has been there for fifty years,' David Shackleton continued. 'They want us to sell our stake to that asshole, Agus Winarko.'

'And you believe he's behind the grab?' The Secretary wanted to know.

'Sure look that way.' Shackleton paced slowly around the government office. 'This move is nothing short of expropriation.'

'Why don't you take it to arbitration?'

'What, go before the corrupt courts in Indonesia?' Shackleton shook his head.

'It's a commercial matter, Dave,' the Secretary reminded. 'And as such, there's not a great deal the State Department can do to assist.'

Shackleton raised an eyebrow. 'Summit's major shareholder anticipated you would say that, and suggested I remind you of his substantial support last time around …' he said, leaving the rest hanging.

The politician accepted the nudge. 'I'll have our ambassador talk to the Indonesian military. They have their hands out for the next tranche of aid money so let's see if we can use that as leverage.'

'The military is part of the problem. We allocate millions in protection payments and yet the entire countryside remains unsafe.' The Summit executive drew a deep breath then exhaled slowly, gathering his thoughts. 'It's obvious they intend on taking it all.' Looking resignedly he then suggested, 'If I thought there was any chance in hell of the Free Papuan Movement actually succeeding in kicking the Indonesians out, then I would be suggesting a different approach to the problem.'

'Langley believes any direct large-scale confrontation between the Papuan rebels and Indonesia's forces would settle the issue once and for all.' The Secretary paused when an aide knocked politely, apologised and mentioned the next appointment. 'I'll do what I can, Dave,' he promised, slow-walking the Summit CEO to the door. 'Keep in touch,' he smiled insincerely. 'And give my regards to you know who.'

Immediately upon Shackleton's departure the powerful Secretary for State returned to his desk, followed almost on his heels by the aide. 'The file you requested, Mr. Secretary. The NSA Director will arrive in fifteen minutes.'

The fourth in line to the US Presidency opened the sensitive document and commenced reading. When he came to the personal note appended to the general summary section originating with the US ambassador to Indonesia, his curiosity was piqued with the recurring sightings again being mentioned.

An hour passed. As the National Security Adviser was preparing to leave, the secretary asked him to wait and read the summary from their ambassador in Jakarta.

Bemused by the report, the NSA director placed his hand on the Secretary's shoulder and chuckled. 'We've commenced drone reconnaissance flights around the Chinese fleet which has got the Aussies rattled. I'll have the lads in Guam run a few drone passes over the Papuan landscape. If they can come up with something definitive then the question of Michael Rockefeller's whereabouts will be finally put to rest.'

\*   \*   \*   \*

# PNG — PORT MORESBY

Lieutenant Colonel Brent Shepherd left the United Nations Resident Coordinator's building and returned to the Australian High Commission, where he uploaded photographs taken by locals of the carnage they witnessed, in the river-port town of Kiunga. The images had been passed to the United Nations peacekeepers that had been called to the scene before being forwarded to Port Moresby.

As a serving military officer, Shepherd could not publically condemn the Indonesian attack which, he expected, would have profound consequences. He was pessimistic that the outcome would be the same, should history repeat itself, with Australia and Indonesia once again engaged in hostilities similar to the undeclared war which continued from 1963 to 1966. Shepherd's uncle had often reminisced about the violent conflict that brought Singapore-based, British RAF Vulcan bombers into Indonesian airspace to protect Australia and other SE Asia Commonwealth nations, stunning his nephew with the revelation that the aircraft were armed with atomic bombs and were ready to drop them on Indonesian airfields should the threat increase.

Indonesia, at that time, was a pro-communist state heavily armed with modern Soviet fighters, bombers and missiles. In those years, Australian troops fought a covert war inside Indonesian territory. The Australian public was not informed about the cross-border operations; they were kept so secret that only a handful of cabinet ministers knew of their existence. Even the soldiers were under strict instruction to tell no one, not even their wives, keeping their secret for more than thirty years.

The Assistant Defence Attaché accepted that the current Indonesian Order of Battle would make for a formidable enemy, with four hundred thousand troops at their disposal. Shepherd was under no illusion as to the size of the threat that the predominantly-Moslem-nation offered. He acknowledged that for decades, Canberra had provided extensive economic and military aid to Jakarta, directly supporting the government's efforts to militarise Indonesian society which, paradoxically, aggravated rather than reduced their potential, military threat.

Often during peer-group discussions, when hypothesising a scenario of a war between Australia and Indonesia, most were in agreement that, although Australia did not have the sheer size of its Indonesian counterpart in technical aspects, Australia's military was more advanced and more potent. He found that such a debate always concluded that it would be inconceivable Indonesia would mount an invasion on continental Australia. The key vulnerability would be their supply lines, which would be attacked and destroyed by aircraft, ships and submarines. Nevertheless, should Australian ground troops be deployed to Papua in the defence of PNG, the lieutenant colonel expected Australian forces would be substantially outnumbered with devastating effect.

Conscious of Papua New Guinea's inability to defend itself against its powerful neighbour, Shepherd knew that Australia would be obliged to come to the country's defence, in the event of any external threat.

Grossly underfunded, PNG's military shamefully consisted of only a handful of frequently-grounded light aircraft, half a dozen patrol boats and landing craft and less than four thousand personnel. This prompted a return to matters at hand; his instructions from Defence HQ involved evaluating the carnage at Kiunga first hand, visiting and familiarising himself with the UN peacekeeping border posts, returning to Port Moresby and submitting his report.

Having instructed the office sergeant to make the necessary arrangements involving seeking passage on dubious, light-aircraft and helicopter flights, Brent Shepherd addressed the growing mountain of correspondence neglected over past days. Amongst the incoming post, he discovered a letter from Alice Heynneman, explaining her sudden departure in Darwin.

With mounting anger, he read and re-read Alice's revelation of her encounter with Didi Sumantri, his rage turning to self-recrimination for having encouraged her to attend the event that provided the Special Forces officer, that brutal opportunity.

\*   \*   \*   \*

# Papua Highlands

## Mek Mek Village

*Lapun Buna* struggled for balance, placing each foot carefully ahead on the slippery path leading up to the main village centre. He slipped and fell to one knee; the excruciating shock to already swollen knees bringing a string of curses in a language unintelligible to the young tribesman, who faithfully guarded the old hermit's every move.

Accustomed to such outbursts, the youngster immediately came to the revered *Lapun Buna*'s aid, and was rebuked angrily, for his trouble. Ignoring the verbal abuse, he persevered until the old man was steady back on his feet, then took his place behind, and followed.

Resting at the forest's edge where a fallen log had been hewn with axes into some semblance of a bench seat, the octogenarian caught his breath and waved, cantankerously, for his minder to leave him alone with his thoughts.

The sun was hidden behind low-hanging clouds, the air heavy with the threat of rain but it did not bother him. He glanced down at his knees and frowned at the fresh wound, the blood slowly congealing under the onslaught of flies. Angrily brushing at insects and losing the battle, he spat on the gashed leg and gently cleaned the immediate area around the cut. He expected swelling and considered calling *Khakhua–Kumu* for one of his suspicious, traditional concoctions.

When he had first arrived in the Mek Mek community and had hungrily devoured whatever was offered, within hours he was struck down with a debilitating dose of diarrhoea. The *Khakhua–Kumu* had squeezed young leaves of an *atepulopulo* plant into captured rain-water, the solution soon remedying his complaint.

Reminded of the occasion he inhaled deeply and sighed, memories of his past intruding, evoking a time when life was vastly different to the one he had finally chosen; one of self-imposed exile.

With events blurred by meandering time, it was difficult for him to state precisely when he felt the desire to abandon civilisation. Perhaps the genesis could be found in his accidental discovery, prior to his departure for Papua's shores. This had occurred during a solitary moment studying the German philosopher, Maximilian Karl Emil

Weber. He clearly recalled the quote which embedded itself in his thoughts, eventually influencing his decision to abandon all material things, and leave civilisation, as he had known it, behind.

*"Wealth is thus bad ethically only in so far as it is a temptation to idleness and sinful enjoyment of life; and its acquisition is bad only when it is with the purpose of later living merrily and without care."*

As a young man, he had been raised with a keen appreciation of the value of money. As an adult, having survived a life-and-death moment, he had been struck by the futility of the material world and in one moment of clarity, decided to opt out of civilisation. In the early morning hours before the break of day, he had set out in the direction of the mountains, his goal, to lose himself from civilisation.

By nightfall on the first day, he had reached a point of exhaustion and realised that his trek had been undertaken with a complete lack of forethought. Foraging for food, he came across an abandoned garden left behind by native dwellers that, unbeknown to him, had been chased from their isolated village by the arrival of the first elements of invading, Indonesian soldiers. He continued his journey upwards into the higher mountain reaches, eating wild air potato plucked from lengthy vines, sugar cane, and young bamboo shoots.

Losing track of time, and unaccustomed to the altitude, an attack of dizziness had sent him tumbling down an embankment. There he was discovered by the Mek Mek and, believing they had captured a Dutch man and could trade him for a prize, the natives had taken him to their village.

It was there that he encountered the Mek Mek chief. Face painted in red and yellow ochre with a cassowary quill pierced through his nasal septa, the intimidating figure had stood transfixed, examining his prize.

A moment in nostalgia brought a smile. In the days following his arrival into the community, he had recovered some semblance of his former self and taken to the stream to bathe. He was standing naked in the flow when a plump, pubescent-breasted village girl descended, stripped to bare buttocks, and plunged into the water.

Although unable to communicate, she deliberately brushed her body against his then stroked his genitals, her natural scent triggering memories of unguarded moments of lust that had almost cost his life, in the Asmat village. Resisting the temptation, he gently pushed the girl away.

By that action, his destiny had been sealed. The teenage girl was the chief's youngest daughter. Subsequently he became part of the village mosaic, meticulously observing their habits and customs.

Thus began his life of abstinence.

From the outset, communication had been frustratingly impossible. A year would pass before he could manage any semblance of the Mek Mek language's distinctive rising and falling pitches when they spoke.

In his efforts to embrace tribal ways, he frequently found the wrath of the elders. On one occasion he was chased by a machete-wielding elder for grasping a sacred artefact. In time he would appreciate the blunder, discovering the significance placed in the artefacts; they believed the symbols referred back to the original creation of their culture and society.

Many years would pass before he would be invited into the special hut where ancestor worship was practised only by chosen elders.

With the progression of time, his hair and beard grew longer, and he spent long periods in self-absorption. Isolated from the outside world, he had not recognised the gradual transition from his earlier self into near-hermit, shocked when the village was visited by another white man. Stephen Coleman's visit had caught him off guard, the initial contact leaving him mortified, unable to find his former tongue.

Deeply annoyed with the intrusion of another into his domain, he was instantly suspicious of Coleman's presence, questioning the sincerity of the man's mission to assist in preventing the deadly swine-flu amongst the Mek Mek.

Reminded how the relationship had developed through the years, he confessed that he now missed the man's company. This revelation disturbed him deeply; the prospect that he retained feelings for the life he had abandoned played with his mind.

Through this relationship, a bond of trust had matured, and then tested when Stephen Coleman had attempted to convince the village elders of their vulnerability against attack by encroaching Indonesian military forces. Although the remote Mek Mek community appeared protected by its isolation from the outside world, evidence regarding the troubles other tribes endured had filtered through to their realm. He had been fiercely against compromising the community.

Eventually though, even he had acquiesced and permitted Coleman to store weapons and other supplies in the tribal mountain caves.

Smoke drifted casually in his direction and he shuffled to his feet. Then, stooping somewhat, he slow-gaited his way through the village to his hut which, unlike many of the others in the village, was built low to the ground.

Thirty-five thousand feet above the thick jungle, even heavily clouded landscape could not prevent the Northrop Grumman MQ-4C Triton's sensors from capturing everything across the landscape. At the very moment he turned and peered skywards into the surrounding canopy identifying the singing call of a bird of paradise, the passing drone captured the entire village's imagery.

*   *   *   *

# NEW YORK — UNITED NATIONS

'West Papuans greatest hope is that New Zealand and Australia review current foreign policy and look at West Papua through our eyes…' Bennie Tabuni's visit to New Zealand was rewarded with surprising support.

When a significant number of New Zealand's Parliament openly validated the right to self-determination for West Papua, groundswell for an initiative demanding the United Nations provide the mechanism to achieve such an outcome, spread around the globe.

New Zealand's support for the action immediately created a diplomatic furor in Australia where sentiment remained supportive of Jakarta's occupation of West Papua. Embarrassed at being caught in diplomatic crossfire, the Australian Government felt obliged to issue a statement explaining its position, declaring unconditional support and respect for Indonesia's sovereignty. Although an unstable independent, West Papua located only one hundred and fifty kilometres from Australia's northern coast would be untenable; being dragged into conflict with Indonesia would be far more challenging.

When the United Nations General Assembly convened, the debate for a free and autonomous West Papua was included in discussions and the Netherlands' ambassador stunned the assembly when seeking a resolution supporting a Free West Papua.

'Human rights violations in West Papua and the inherent right for self-determination of West Papua should no longer be ignored. Indonesian occupation through the flawed 1969 plebiscite must be ended now. It is clear that the UN must act without further delay to provide the people of West Papua with the opportunity to rectify the great injustices they continue to suffer. The UN must act on this issue and find a workable solution to give autonomy to the indigenous peoples of West Papua.

'Therefore, the Government of the Netherlands requests that members support a resolution that deems Indonesia's annexation of West Papua to be a violation of Indonesia's obligations under the UN Charter, and a threat to international peace and security. Additionally, the resolution requests Member States cease trading all weapons and arms with Indonesia.

'Furthermore, the Netherlands requests that the resolution demands the people of Indonesia to:-

Release Papuan political prisoners arrested for acts of peaceful political activism, including raising flags;

Commit to addressing cases of serious crimes against the Papuan people;

Accept the distinct rights to self-governance afforded to the West Papuan community by the United Nations Declaration on the Rights of Indigenous Peoples and in doing so, agree to a referendum conducted by the United Nations and have it carried out within one year.'

In response, the Indonesian Ambassador to the UN accused the Netherlands of hypocrisy, and warned the Assembly that any attempt to deny Indonesia's sovereignty, would be addressed with every resource his country could muster.

When it became apparent that the majority of Third World countries had shifted position endorsing such a resolution, the Indonesian government immediately conferred privately with the Chinese delegation. As any UN General Assembly Resolution usually required a simple majority to pass, China's connivance in having the motion considered an "important question" was essential. This would then require a two-third majority as such questions deal significantly with maintenance of international peace and security.

As decisions were mulled over, the plight of the Papuans continued to germinate in the global consciousness.

* * * *

# DARWIN

### SYDNEY

'You must leave Darwin today.' Bennie Tabuni's mouth appeared out of sync with the Skype computer exchange. 'Leave everything. We can have someone pack up later.'

Marcus Tabuni nodded at the screen. 'I'll book the first flight.'

Bennie was emphatic. 'If you are going to fly, it's best to travel to Sydney first then hire a car and drive to the address in Melbourne. Don't leave any trail. We need you to become invisible for the next few months.'

'It's moving fast now, brother,' Marcus' voice echoed across space.

'Much faster than *they* expect,' Bennie responded referring to the Indonesians.

'I was really surprised when their announcement came out of the blue,' Marcus referred to a block of independent Members of

Parliament who had declared their support for a UN-sponsored, West Papuan referendum to be held as soon as practical.

'We can also now add Uganda, Guinea-Bissau, Cameroon and Nigeria to the list. In all we have more than enough votes to achieve a simple majority.'

'Fifty years...' Marcus' voice trailed away.

'Just keep you mind on the future. We'll have time to reflect on the past.'

'Will you come to Melbourne?'

'Not at this time. Would be too tempting for the Australians to refuse entry then shove me on a flight to Jakarta.'

Marcus thought about this. 'They're unlikely to do that now we have such international support.'

'Wouldn't wish to take that chance,' Bennie insisted. 'Canberra and Jakarta are still tied at the hip.'

'They'll come around.'

'I'm not counting on it,' the weariness in his voice evident.

'Okay, I'll get moving now. Travel safe, brother.'

'You too, Marcus.'

Bennie waved and terminated the Skype session, unaware that within minutes the substance of their conversation would be relayed to the Indonesian Ministry of Defence's Strategic Intelligence Agency, *BAIS*, via a decoy server in Sydney. The Indonesian government had installed a server collecting information via monitoring spyware acquired from Germany. West Papuan activists were amongst those targeted in Australia, and Marcus Tabuni had been allocated the highest priority by Jakarta.

BIN operatives in Sydney were alerted and incoming flights from

Darwin were monitored, Marcus' arrival and movements observed until he departed by car for Melbourne. Indonesia's spy agency BIN, were not alone in tracking his movements. Australia's domestic spy agency ASIO had a copy of the car-hire contract even before the Papuan activist had left the car rental parking lot.

\*    \*    \*    \*

# PHOENIX ARIZONA

## SUMMIT GOLD

David Shackleton had sought counsel before agreeing to the meeting with Bennie Tabuni. In view of Summit Gold's precarious relationship with Agus Winarko and the Indonesian Mines Department, he had agreed to the contact conditional that their discussion remain concealed.

The Summit Gold president was surprised when coming face to face with Bennie, quietly disarmed by the man's candour.

'It is obvious to all that Summit is on the brink of losing its holding in the Akumuga Mine. The longer the operation remains in limbo, the weaker your position will be. When Papua becomes independent, subject to whatever support you can generate to assist our efforts, then I am in a position to guarantee that the new government would negotiate a fair compromise with Summit so you can retain an interest.' Bennie relied on this offer to generate further support from American investment circles. Summit Gold could be a powerful ally in seeking congressional support. The "Black Caucus" had already declared in favour of a UN resolution, and Bennie believed that by proving a willingness to treat foreign investors fairly in the future, the numbers would improve with oil and gas lobbyists' backing them.

'If you had something more concrete for me to take to the stake holders then I would be confident of garnishing their support,' Shackleton suggested.

'We appreciate that Summit has the expertise to continue operating the mine. What we would expect is that within six months all non-indigenous labour would be replaced with Papuans, and that training programs would be introduced so that within two years, there would be a skilled Papuan labour force as well.'

'That is feasible,' Shackleton agreed. 'This might have already been achieved if the Indonesians had not monopolised the labour supply.'

Bennie ignored the comment. 'We will come to a profit-sharing arrangement that will compensate Summit Gold for funding the smelter requirements currently being imposed by Jakarta.' He glanced at the American executive. 'We will treat you and other investors fairly…and in return would expect the same consideration.'

'How do you propose addressing the problem of the Chinese control of Kampung Mas? Will the new government also negotiate with them over the port and their other facilities?'

'We had considered meeting with the Chinese about Kampung Mas but decided it would not be in our interest to have them continue under the current arrangements. It wouldn't make commercial sense to leave them in charge of the port area.'

'They aren't likely to give it up easily,' Shackleton surmised.

'Neither are the Indonesians,' Bennie's response came with a twisted smile. 'But that is for another day.'

Their meeting concluded with David Shackleton committing to take the discussion to another level then communicate further. Their frank exchange offered sufficient substance for Shackleton to consider the real possibility that Summit Gold's investment in West Papua would still have a future. Unlike other US mining giants, Summit Gold had only the Akumuga Mine holdings to consider. He knew it would be unlikely that the other companies would be supportive, concerned that in doing so would certainly jeopardise their operations elsewhere in Indonesia. Nevertheless, Shackleton felt that the offer deserved further consideration and this would require Washington's support.

\*    \*    \*    \*

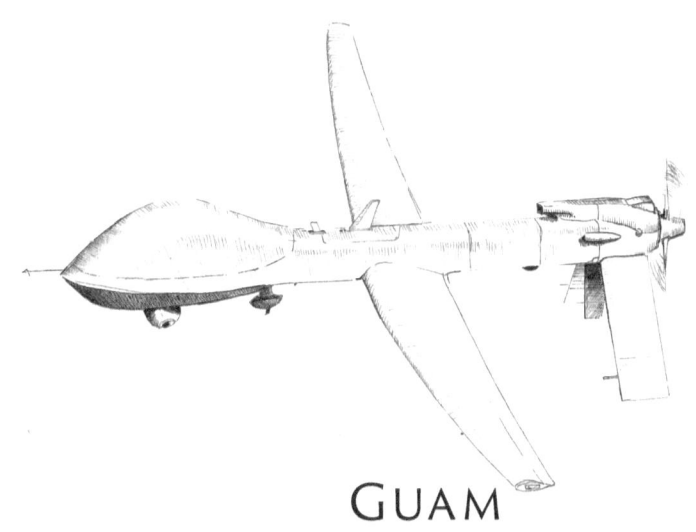

# GUAM

The evening skies were clear when crew members who had been flying the mission saw their screens go blank. The advanced *MX-8K Thalassa* unmanned aircraft had been capturing aerial images and electronic data from an altitude of only five thousand metres over the Papua New Guinea-Indonesian border when it simply disappeared from the pilot's screen. Equipped with transponders to broadcast its last known location, when it was established that the unmanned aircraft had crashed somewhere inside Indonesian territory, Washington rapidly unraveled at the thought of such sensitive technology falling into Jakarta's hands.

When further surveillance flights and satellite reconnaissance failed to identify the missing drone's precise location and, as the self-destruct mechanism had failed, an immediate mission to recover or destroy the downed vehicle was imperative.

'We have appropriate assets in the general area.' The briefing officer referred to elements of the elite Delta Force which were in the Philippines, mopping up remnants of the *Abu Sayyaf,* under the Enhanced Defence Cooperation Agreement. The EDCA allowed the rotational deployment of US ships, aircraft, and troops at five bases in the Philippines.

'No.' The general shook his head. The image of a huge Chinook clattering its way into the Papuan highlands did not appeal. Adding with exasperation, 'We can't send in a recovery team without knowing precisely where the drone came down. It's impenetrable jungle and if we were to deploy assets without knowing the exact location, the unit could disappear, forever, just like Rockefeller's son did when he went in there.'

The National Security Adviser's ear pricked up immediately, recent aerial intelligence coming to mind.

When the President was briefed, the Defense Secretary advised that mounting any ground mission from the PNG side of the border would be ill-advised, due to heightened activity following recent cross-border incursions. There was concern that the Chinese-controlled Kampung Mas Port facility might have detected the drone's presence when it passed over the area, and this galvanised the White House into action.

The NSA director attended the meeting, well prepared. The United States had no assets on the ground in West Papua, and it was most unlikely that the Indonesian Government would permit USA citizens into the area until the mining dispute had been settled.

Upon departing the Oval Office, the NSA director communicated via CIA channels with the British Government. The chairman of

Anglo American Aerospace Defence Technologies Inc (AAADT) was summoned by the Foreign Secretary. The British and United States' governments enjoyed oversight positions within the company's structure due to the sensitivity of military equipment frequently supplied by the group. AAADT had provided the Tactical Signals Intelligence Payload sensors for the advanced *MX-8K Thalassa* unmanned aircraft. In consequence, these organisations frequently shared operational information.

By mid-afternoon, Anne Whitehead had been fully briefed and was on her way to Indonesia.

*       *       *       *

On board the Singapore Airlines Boeing 777-300, Anne Whitehead pressed the night light button when the cabin dimmed, and returned to reading the downloaded references she had hastily compiled before departure. Having only a brief knowledge of the wealthy young American explorer Anne was determined to be fully acquainted with his story before arriving in Singapore to meet with Jules Heynneman.

Anne read that the 23-year old son of New York Governor Nelson Rockefeller had mysteriously disappeared whilst on an anthropology expedition in the Asmat territory of Dutch New Guinea. When Anne delved deeper into the young American's background and discovered that the 1961 expedition had been undertaken immediately after the young Rockefeller had discovered his parents were divorcing, she considered whether this might have been a contributing factor in his desire to disappear.

She set the sheets of paper aside and leaned back on the leather-upholstered seat then gently massaged her eyes.

Anne's relationship with Jules, both personal and commercial, had existed since Jules' company became involved with the AAADT subsidiary, when supplying mining equipment to the Akumuga Mine. A generation had passed since they first met and enjoyed a passing, amatory liaison. Although the nature of their relationship had evolved forsaking all physical intimacy, now their bond of secrets tied them even closer together.

Anne was Bennie's conduit into the British Government and Jules his adopted brother's financier. She accepted that Jules had his eye on reaping whatever he could once West Papuan independence had been achieved. Contrary to Bennie, Jules was materialistic, vain and uncompromising, and she had little doubt that he was the architect behind the proposed draft memorandum offered to the British Government.

A ripple of concern came then passed. Anne had never misled Jules before, and in appealing for his support for her to visit the isolated Papuan highlands she knew that she had, for the first time, crossed that line.

When called to the AAADT chairman's office, Anne could not have envisaged what would be asked of her. When sighting her personal file open on the chairman's desk and the presence of unfamiliar faces, Anne's composure belied the uneasiness she felt building in her stomach.

'We expect you will find what we have to say as somewhat unusual, Miss Whitehead,' the chairman commenced. 'But whatever transpires in this meeting remains covered under the Official Secrets Act.'

He looked directly at Anne. 'You already enjoy a high-level clearance, and have what is considered the appropriate background for assisting the Americans in a somewhat delicate intelligence recovery matter.'

'How may I be of service, Sir Anthony?' she asked the AAADT chairman.

'AAADT has a vested interest in recovering a lost asset. I'll pass you over to our American friends to explain.' He nodded at the US-Embassy official.

'Anne…is it okay for me to call you Anne?' he started, continuing without waiting for her response. 'We have lost a state-of-the-art unmanned aircraft on the Indonesian side of the Papua New Guinea border.'

'That's a long border,' Anne quipped.

'We know precisely, well, almost precisely where the drone came to rest.' The American looked around the room then back to Anne. 'We believe the aircraft is within an isolated area north of the Akumuga Mine.

'Why not have someone from there, assist with the recovery?' she asked.

'The entire operation is in shutdown with virtually all expatriates removed from the site. Apart from that, we don't wish to show our hand. If the Indonesians get wind of the wreckage they will be all over it, ripping out some of the most sensitive reconnaissance equipment ever developed.'

'My activities have always been confined to administrative duties. How can I help?'

'Your file mentions you have a graduate degree in anthropology. Correct?'

'Yes, that's accurate. I studied at the University of Edinburg. But I've never worked in that field.'

'That's okay, Anne. We want to use it as a cover.'

'Cover?'

'Yes. If you agree to help us out then George here will brief you on the drone and what we would like you to do for us.' He pointed to an associate who had been sitting silently nursing a briefcase on his lap.

A worrying thought came to Anne. 'Was the drone armed?'

'No,' the American assured. 'This type of vehicle is purely for reconnaissance. I have prepared a file for you to study within the confines of this office if you agree to assist in the recovery. This aircraft contains the most advanced technology, and with its miniature parts is substantially smaller than other systems in use.' He showed a photograph of a technician standing alongside a prototype *MX-8K Thalassa*. 'As you can see, the vehicle is less than five metres in length and weighs less than 400 kilos. It's powered by a hybrid solar and battery system.'

Although her acceptance was tempered with some reservations, at the conclusion of the briefing, Anne agreed to undertake the journey. She would fly to Singapore and meet with Jules Heynneman as prearranged. His office would book her seat on the daily charter flight to Kampung Mas. Jules would arrange for Alice to be driven to the Akumuga Mine where she would organise the trek into the highlands, ostensibly to attempt contact with the hermit figure Washington believed to be Michael Rockefeller. If challenged by the Indonesian authorities, Anne was prepared to explain her expedition into the isolated mountain region as a way to learn more of the primitive tribes; research she needed for her dissertation to complete a doctorate degree in anthropology. Her pursuit of the recluse Michael Rockefeller, would not be mentioned to any other than Jules and Alice Heynneman.

Anne's passion for hiking over the years placed her in good stead for the difficult trek into the Papuan mountains. Having completed the Three Peaks Challenge climbing Scafell Pike, Snowdon, and Ben Nevis all within twenty-four hours, she was not daunted by what the Papuan highlands might offer.

Anne was directed not to reveal the existence of the downed aircraft to anyone, including Jules, as it was assumed he would mount his own attempt to recover the drone and use it to his own advantage. Neither the British, nor the Americans wished to have their sensitive technology compromised. Anne was therefore encouraged to convince Jules of the authenticity of her motives to study the relatively unknown mountain tribes, as she was considering leaving her current position with AAADT in favour of academia. She expected Jules would accept the deception, as she had raised her retirement expectations in the past.

Aerial imagery of what was perceived to be Michael Rockefeller was included in the dossier Anne studied before departing. She carried a company-manufactured GPS *Troodon* receiver that had been preloaded with the latitude and longitude GPS coordinates pinpointing Rockefeller's village hideaway. The in-house company receiver could track both GPS and the Russian, GLONASS satellites simultaneously, providing Anne with the ability to determine any position quickly and precisely, and maintains a location even in heavy cover and deep canyons. As the lithium battery life was limited to thirty hours she carried a backup supply in her backpack.

If successful, and contact with Rockefeller eventuated Anne's task was then to appeal for assistance in searching for the missing drone. The aircraft's last known position placed the crash area within reach of the recluse's sighting and the Americans believed the local tribesmen might already be aware of the wreckage. If the vehicle was located then Anne was to photo whatever remained of the wreckage and upload the information immediately. She knew that would provide the Americans with the opportunity to determine whatever subsequent action might be attempted. They assumed the damage would be extreme and in that circumstance, Anne would retrieve the advance sensor and pass the unit to US Embassy officers upon departing Papua, leaving the remaining wreckage for the jungle to assume. If, however, the aircraft was substantially intact then the decision might require destroying the remnants from the air.

Anne had called ahead to alert Alice Heynneman of her pending arrival, without imparting more than a suggestion that she would be carrying her walking boots and a backpack.

*   *   *   *

# Papuan Highlands

## Akumuga Mine

Alice Heynneman shivered. Moving slowly, she stretched up from her bunk and closed the only window in her quarters. Although acclimatised, often when the cloud ceiling dropped below the mountain peaks adding to the sense of extreme isolation, Alice had to remind herself of the financial advantages of remaining there. At three-thousand metres where a prefabricated city had grown to accommodate the many thousands of mine employees, the ambient temperature fell to five degrees Celsius at night; and even colder out on the higher peaks, where light glacier flowed and patches of snow were evident.

Alice was restless. With an eerie lack of sound permeating the mountain surrounds, overhead street lighting presented a spectral quality to the outdoor ambience.

The mine, and consequently the entire settlement, including its bars and brothels, was in shutdown. Most of the fifteen-thousand employees were now idle. Apart from the three Australian teachers who remained at their post running the local, church-sponsored primary school, the town was devoid of expatriates.

The open pit mine, with its kilometre-wide crater together, with all underground operations, crushers, and grinding units that would normally process a quarter of a million metric tonnes daily, remained ghostly still.

Alice understood the conundrum that had stifled the mining

operation. Summit Gold Mining was being manipulated out of its holding in the Akumuga Mine, which had abruptly stopped production and laid off most of its foreign and domestic workers. Senior management was aware of the wealthy Jakarta entrepreneur's machinations to acquire full ownership of the extensive multi-billion-dollar operation.

When Jakarta announced it had held discussions with the duplicitous billionaire Agus Winarko, who already controlled a substantial stake in the mine, the gloves came off. Summit Gold issued an ultimatum to the Indonesian government to rescind its new demands, or face US Government intervention and the possibility of sanctions.

She was deeply concerned that the stoppage would result in violence now that the labourers were left without income. Akumuga, she knew, was the *Wild Wild West* of Papua and she doubted that even the thousands of security officers employed would be capable of preventing hordes of disgruntled employees attacking with picks and axes.

Although her light-coloured skin and fairish hair often had Alice mistaken as Caucasian, she was adamantly Papuan, and deeply empathised with the indigenous people and shared their dream of enjoying their own land without the presence of the oppressive Indonesians. Sharing Bennie's deep animosity for everything Indonesian, Alice kept her own counsel and avoided political discussion during these volatile times.

Alice was not normally prone to introspection but the night's uncustomary silence placed her in this mood. Her thoughts shifted to her father, Bennie Tabuni and "Uncle" Jules. Alice cherished her relationship with Jules, deeply grateful for his guardianship and love. She accepted the necessity for the shrouded relationship imposed since early childhood, and appreciated the implications, should it become known, that it was *her* father who led the international movement to free Papua from Indonesian subjugation. Had they been aware, the Indonesian authorities would have long placed her in custody, the life she now enjoyed being an impossible dream.

The lingering threat of discovery precluded any public contact with Bennie. On the rare occasion when they did communicate, such conversations were conducted incognito. Jules, however, called frequently and often arranged for her to fly from Kampung Mas to Jayapura where his business interests were headquartered. Following her most recent visit, Jules had indicated that within a few months she would be asked to join him for an undetermined period, in Singapore. Jules was taciturn when pressed as to why, so Alice had returned to the Akumuga operation with the growing expectation that something significant would soon eventuate.

A failing exterior security lamp blinked, signalling the end of its service, the momentary distraction offering Alice the opportunity to consider the call she had received from Anne Whitehead earlier in the day. With those thoughts in mind she yawned widely then slipped under the bunk's warm blankets, immediately willing away everything that had been discussed.

\* \* \* \*

# MEK MEK VILLAGE

*Lapun Buna* sat mesmerised examining a shattered piece of the

*MX-8K Thalassa's* fuselage. Frenzied villagers returning from hunting the high slopes less than a kilometre from the main community had carried the wrecked piece and laid it on the ground. Sensing danger, villagers climbed down from their huts and assembled, eyes cast upwards, faces filled with dread, the *Khakhua–Kumu* chanting as he danced in an attempt to dispel their fear.

Once the commotion had settled, *Lapun Buna* questioned the men who had discovered the find. He understood that whatever the light material belonged to, it was part of a larger discovery less than a kilometre from the main village, buried deep below the thick forest canopy.

Unable to ascertain what it was the men were attempting to describe, and having asked in as many ways the simple language could offer, he decided to attempt the exacting climb. Coaxing weary legs up the steep track past the cave where Stephen *Sanguma* Coleman's cache of weapons was hidden, three hours passed before *Lapun Buna* could examine the find for himself. His initial impression was that the wreckage was part of some type of glider. Wrestling with the drone's frame, he was fascinated by the light-weight material with which the structure was made. The carbon fibre-reinforced polymers used in the construction of the small aircraft perplexed him, as he had never seen material in this form before.

The wings, propeller, and V-shaped tail were all shattered to pieces. A round apparatus shaped similar to a robot's head hung loose from its housing terrifying the natives. Unbeknown to all present, this sensor, when operational, was the eye to the highest-resolution surveillance camera ever developed, and the target of Anne Whitehead's recovery expedition.

A worrying knot gripped his stomach when he realized there would be a search for the wreckage.

'We hide and give to Sanguma.' *Lapun Buna* declared then insisted the villagers cover the remaining wreckage with jungle vegetation.

\* \* \* \*

# JAKARTA

President Abul Moewardi again cleared his throat before continuing his address to the select group summoned to the historic venue. His preamble had revisited the country's sixty-year involvement with the far-eastern Papuan provinces; what he would now present representing the most audacious gambit in his short political life.

'Friends and colleagues,' Moewardi paused, inhaled deeply then plunged ahead. 'Our nation is facing perhaps the most critical time since international opinion brought about our withdrawal from the former province of East Timor. As some of you have known of my position with respect to how we govern the Republic, it will come as no great surprise that I have arrived at a decision to address the issue of growing separatism that has become increasingly burdensome for the people of our great nation. It is therefore my wish that in considering the welfare, security and future of our nation that you support the passage of my presidential decree through Parliament.'

Moewardi's circle of confidants glanced at each other apprehensively. They represented the core of the reformist movement within the parliament and, although closely allied with the President, some

within their number were critical of his openly, confrontational atti-
tude towards the powerful military elite.

'It is my intention to offer a compromise to the people of West
Papua, one which I deeply believe will provide the basis for achieving a peaceful solution that would also be endorsed by the international community.

Friends and colleagues, we, as a democratic people must acknowl-
edge that in the pursuit of our nation's security and prosperity have,
on occasion, marched hastily into situations without appreciating
the consequences of our actions. It is therefore imperative that we
accept that the implementation of the 1969 referendum known as
the Act of Free Choice was indeed flawed.'

Gasps of disbelief greeted the President's statement.

'The presidential decree I offer for your consideration today pro-
vides us all the opportunity to strengthen our relationship with the
people of Papua by proposing a system of self-government by, and for,
indigenous Papuans. Subject to a bill being passed by Parliament, the
decree will provide that within one year, West Papua and Papua will
again be amalgamated into one entity to be known as the Commonwealth of West Papua, a state within the Republic of Indonesia, with
its own constitution and laws in accordance with those of the Republic. Finally, the people of West Papua will have their own parliament,
executive and judiciary.'

The President accepted there was no way to discern which way
the Parliament would vote. He did, however, anticipate resistance
from the military block. Moewardi needed to curtail their power
and hoped the democratic process would enable him to do so.

The politicians present were stunned to their core believing

Abdul Moerwardi had just committed political suicide. Exiting the palace they activated their cell phones and broke the news widely.

At Department of Defence HQ, General Sumantri's mood was contemplative as he reviewed what options might be available, to prevent the President from achieving his objective.

The General understood the need to move expeditiously.

Powers accorded to the President entitled Moewardi to propose the Bill. However, laws could only be approved by the People's Representative Council. Should the legislation be passed by the House, and the President sign his acceptance, the Bill would automatically become law within thirty days.

Upon learning of the proposed legislation, the Chinese Ambassador requested an immediate hearing with the Minister for Foreign Affairs, to determine how the Special Autonomous Zone of Kampung Mas might be impacted. Receiving nothing less than an ambiguous response, the ambassador offered Beijing his interpretation of what outcome might be expected, which resulted in an additional one thousand marines being transported to Kampung Mas.

Early the following morning President Abdul Moerwardi suffered another mild heart attack.

\*     \*     \*     \*

# PAPUA

## AKUMUGA MINE

Constantly restless with the inactivity of her predicament, Anne Whitehead uncrossed arms and placed both hands on her hips. 'I need to leave soon, Alice. Can you talk to the senior officer again as I'm running out of time to complete my mission and return to the UK?'

'I can give it a try. The captain seems more approachable now, than when his unit first arrived.'

Three weeks had passed since Anne visited the mining town only to find that travel restrictions had been introduced, immediately following the substantial increase of military numbers across the landscape.

'Thanks Alice. While you're doing that I'll be over at the school.'

There was a chill in the air with the sun's rays impeded by low-hanging cloud as Anne approached the prefabricated school building. Outside village children waited impatiently, while the teachers registered their attendance before permitting the youngsters entry.

'I'm not here for the lessons,' Anne joked good-heartedly, ruffling the curly hair of a child that had sided up to her.

'Just as well, you'd be bored. Haven't had any new material for the best part of a month,' one of the teachers complained.

Anne admired the team of three Australians who had left most creature comforts behind to provide elementary schooling to the local village children. She understood the contribution the three had already made, evidenced by the number of children who now enjoyed some semblance of literacy. Two of the teachers were accompanied by their wives, the small group of five now the only other white expatriates left from the original expatriate community. Anne had been invited to join in what had despairingly become a daily ritual; filling in time together and playing cards with the women.

Anne had communicated her dilemma to London in an oblique message to her superiors expecting to be recalled. Instead, she was instructed to pursue the designated objective. With no clear indication when travel permission might be given, Anne remained in limbo. Her original expectations of allowing three to four weeks to trek into the designated area, attempt contact with Michael Rockefeller, locate the drone wreckage, and return to the mining town was now impossibly stretched. On top of that, there was now the threat of deteriorating weather on the horizon.

\*   \*   \*   \*

# JAKARTA

### OFFICE OF THE VICE PRESIDENT

General Sumantri greeted the news that the President had departed for Hanover, Germany, to undertake an annuloplasty procedure. Sumantri had pressed the Palace's senior medical adviser for further information.

'The heart valve repair operation will be conducted within forty-eight hours of the President's arrival in Germany'.

'Will he require further rest following the procedure?'

'Yes General. Considering his age I would suggest a minimum post-operative recovery hospitalisation period of at least ten days.'

Sumantri knew he had to move swiftly. He called the Vice President, a former fellow officer who had served with him and was now a close confident. 'This is our opportunity, Hamid,' Sumantri coerced the Vice President. 'You have the authority to sanction the orders and suspend the presidential decree before it passes through parliament.'

'The constitution is vague. There are no specific powers mentioned, and in the past the convention has always been for the Vice President to seek approval, for any decisions of this magnitude.'

Sumantri came prepared. Reading from an extract of the Amendment to the 1945 Constitution he quoted, "*The Amended 1945 Constitution: The Vice President replaces the President in the event that the President dies, resigns, or is unable to perform his/her duties for any reason. If the President and the Vice-President dies, resigns, or is unable to perform his/her duties for any reason, the government will be taken over together by Minister of Foreign Affairs, Minister of Internal Affairs and Minister of Defence.*"

'The President will not be happy,' the Vice President predicted.

'Can't argue with the democratic process,' Sumantri chortled sarcastically.

Within the hour General Sumantri triggered the largest mobilisation undertaken by the Indonesian military since General Suharto toppled President Sukarno in 1965. With communications filling the airwaves, foreign listening stations collected the data as four hundred thousand Indonesia troops were placed on alert. The Chiefs of the Army (TNI-AD), Navy (TNI-AL including the Indonesian Marine Corps), and the Air Force (TNI-AU) were given copies of the Vice President's authorisation and immediately initiated already established procedures to marshal their military assets.

The recently created Army Strategic Reserve 3$^{rd}$ Division together with the 2$^{nd}$ Division were ordered immediately to the far eastern provinces.

Before the Indonesian President recovered consciousness from his operation in Germany, the mobilisation was in motion. The legislation legitimising the presidential decree to change the political status of West Papua was suspended.

*   *   *   *

# CANBERRA

'Time's run out. We must decide now on what position we'll take if the United Nations supports another referendum in West Papua,' the Foreign Affairs Minister suggested. The Prime Minister's Cabinet had been summoned to address the rising crisis on Australia's northern doorstep. For months the diplomatic rhetoric between the two countries had been high, as Indonesian separatist groups across the archipelago took advantage of the political instability. Violence against Javanese transmigrants erupted across Kalimantan, Sulawesi, Nusa Tenggara, and even Riau threatened to break away from the Republic.

Orchestrated demonstrations occurred on a daily basis against the Australian, Dutch and US embassies. The representative offices of African, Pacific and South American nations that supported the motion for an immediate UN referendum were attacked, with some razed to the ground.

The mood was tense. No one wished to raise the possibility of a military conflict with Indonesia. It was a taboo subject. In anticipation of Canberra vacillating as to where its loyalties should lie, Jakarta sent its navy provocatively close to Christmas Island. When the Jindalee over-the-horizon radar system reported a number of Indonesian, Russian-built Su-35 Russian fighters violating Australian airspace, the message was clear.

'Indonesia has an inflated view of its military capability and even their suggesting conflict with Australia is insane.'

'I don't believe it will come to that,' the Prime Minister offered, while mentally crossing his fingers.

'If it does, they wouldn't get a shot off before the RAAF turned Jakarta to rubble,' a muffled voice from their number muttered, nudging the member alongside.

'We won't see a land war on our shores. They don't have the capacity to transport sufficient numbers of combatants by sea, to offer any real threat. I still believe they'll continue to bluff. They might try disrupting shipping lanes and that could cripple our exports. But, apart from any direct land confrontation across the PNG-West Papua border, I am of the opinion that at the end of the day they will grudgingly withdraw from West Papua, trashing the place as they did in East Timor.' The Foreign Affairs Minister said with conviction.

'Slash and burn,' the Attorney General reminded. 'The Indonesian military would systematically burn villages, shops, buildings and destroy infrastructure if they are forced to withdraw.'

'I don't agree,' the Defence Minister argued. 'Losing all of Papua would be a powerful precedent for other provinces to follow. Both the East Timor and West Papua independence movements have overshadowed other fractious ethnic groups such as the Acehnese, Moluccans and Dayaks. And for that very reason I don't envisage Jakarta ceding independence to the Papuans without a fight.'

The Prime Minister was deeply anxious. Australia was tied to defending Papua New Guinea by treaty and the Indonesians should understand that commitment. But, should Australia join a United Nations Peacekeeping Force in Papua New Guinea, Indonesian-Australian relationships would surely rupture.

A hostile neighbour would cause chaos with Australian shipping, not to mention the impact damaged relations would have on the four hundred Australian companies' investments, across the archipelago.

'On the bright side we would save just under a billion dollars in Aid annually,' a junior member suggested. 'And ...'

'Sure...' the Foreign Affairs Minister interrupted. 'And the fifteen billion dollar, two-way-trade both countries enjoy would be crippled.'

'How can we justify supporting the UN vote in favour of another plebiscite, when we already recognised Indonesia's sovereignty over all of West Papua under the 2006 Lombok Treaty?' the Attorney General argued.

'A plebiscite would nullify that agreement,' the hawkish Deputy Leader took the floor. 'And that would leave West Papua floundering politically and economically. If they achieve independence they would burn their only connection with ASEAN and most likely Asia. That's precisely what happened to East Timor. Most Asian states would not consider an independent West Papua as a part of Asia so they would be excluded from trade blocs. If we need proof of what an independent West Papua will look like in ten, twenty years, just consider Papua New Guinea. Like its neighbour, the PNG has enormous resources yet we still dump more than $400 million in Aid there annually. Their government is corrupt and the majority of its people still live in the Stone Age. My position is that we support Jakarta and leave the status quo as it is.'

The Defence Minister stepped in. 'Let's be honest. We have an unfortunate history to consider. For decades we have excessively pandered to the Indonesians. We provide billions in Aid, train their military, kowtow, and apologise whenever they feel offended by our Press; all of this whilst choosing to turn a blind eye to atrocious human rights abuses and the re-colonisation of the archipelago by a handful of corrupt elites. Do I believe West Papua is another East Timor? The answer must be yes. Jakarta cannot ignore the substantial, international support for an UN-sponsored referendum to pave the way for an independent West Papua.' His jowls fell short of a growl as he slowly glared his way around the lengthy table. 'This is the moment that will ameliorate the misfortunate outcome that we, as Australians, supported over fifty years ago.' He paused for breath. 'The Indonesians won't leave West Papua peacefully and that will demand Australian troops on the ground.'

'Then do we have consensus?' The Prime Minister needed to know.

A show of hands gave the leader their support, the import of the decision lost in the silence as the Cabinet then retired to prepare for the two o'clock parliamentary session.

\*   \*   \*   \*

The Defence Minister summoned the chiefs of all defence departments to be present at the Office of National Assessments where a solemn air of inevitability permeated the meeting.

The Minister's commenced the briefing.

'The following is an overview of what pre-emptive action is being taken in anticipation of an outbreak of hostilities with Indonesia. Department of Foreign Affairs and Trade (DFAT) has today updated its Travel Advisory site to reflect a change from "High Degree of Caution" to "Do Not Travel — due to the developing situation in many provinces. Protests and demonstrations are expected to continue and these will most likely be violent. If you are in Indonesia you should consider leaving immediately."

'DFAT's Crisis Action Plan will be initiated and the four-thousand Australians registered across the country will be informed. Unfortunately, with more than ten thousand unregistered, many of whom are in Bali, the dissemination of the update will not be efficient. Embassy and Consulate offices in Jakarta, Bali, Makassar, and Surabaya have been advised to prepare contingency plans for a full evacuation. Additional Australian Federal Police personnel have been deployed to those locations.

'The RAAF will place 35, 36 and 37 Squadrons on notice to prepare for evacuations from Bali and Jakarta only. The Australian business community across Indonesia will also be contacted to enable management make arrangements regarding their investments prior to departure.

'Our Intelligence sources have confirmed that Jakarta has commenced the deployment of its Army Strategic Reserve Infantry Division 3, to Jayapura, on the northern West Papua-PNG border, and also ordered the Division 2, from Malang in East Java, to Merauke on the southern PNG-West Papua border. We also believe that the 1st Marine Corp is to relocate from East Java to Sorong. This substantial increase of sixty-thousand troops is consistent with the strategy of preparing to reinforce Indonesia's claim on the territory should the UN vote, as we expect, not be in Jakarta's favour. As we know *KOSTRAD's* three divisions all include airborne and cavalry brigades.

'It is therefore our opinion that Indonesia is preparing to repel any attempt to dislodge their presence in the Papuan territories. The consolidation of forces along the common border with PNG repre-sents a significant threat to Papua New Guinea.

'In view of the unexpected marshalling of their military assets, the Prime Minister has ordered all defence personnel leave can-celled, and both components of the Army Reserve mobilised. The Prime Minister will make the announcement in Parliament during the afternoon session.'

*   *   *   *

# Australian Prime Minister's Address to Parliament

'…and, Mr. Speaker, our intelligence services confirm that, within the next days, some eighty-thousand additional Indonesian troops will be deployed to the eastern provinces of West Papua. I now report to the parliament that it is our defence and intelligence agencies understanding that the main body of this force will be positioned along the border with neighbouring Papua New Guinea.

'It is important as we analyse this move by the Indonesian Gov-ernment, in light of the imminent United Nations vote to determine whether a referendum be undertaken.

'The House must be clear. In view of the unexpected deployment of massive numbers of military assets to West Papua, Indonesia has clearly signalled total opposition to any outcome which would cre-ate a sovereign independent state in that territory. In consequence, the likelihood of a direct confrontation between Indonesian troops and any multinational force placed in Papua New Guinea to defend the integrity of the common border, although not inevitable, should be regarded as highly possible.

'As the House would be aware, in past days the United Nations Security Council has commenced debating the establishment of a multinational force to restore peace and security in Papua New Guinea.

'As members will know, the conflict between Indonesian and West Papuan independence forces continues to escalate. I have communicated to the Indonesian leadership, encouraging them to prepare for a peaceful response, when the United Nations votes on the West Papuan independence issue.

'I appealed to the Vice President that the Indonesian Government negotiate directly with the West Papuan parties to avoid any military conflict. I regret to advise the House that my conclusion, as a result of that conversation, is that Indonesia would prefer to withdraw from the United Nations, before they relinquish West Papua.

'Mr. Speaker, I believe that it is time we address our complicity in ignoring the West Papuan independence issue over the past fifty years. Both our mainstream political parties have acquiesced in addressing the reality of the flawed 1969 plebiscite, due primarily to the fact that Australian governments favoured our relationship with Indonesia, over that of humanitarian considerations.

'I accept that today represents a major shift in policy in terms of our relationship with Indonesia, the path we will now follow based on our values as a democratic people, and not one based on special relationships that exist primarily to serve commercial interests.

'Mr Speaker, Australia enjoys strong defence links through the

ANZUS Treaty and the Five Power Defence Agreement. I advise the House that over the past few hours I have communicated in depth with our allies, and wish to relay that we continue to have full support for the position we now take.

'The Australian community must know that we, as a nation, can expect considerable disruption to our Asian relationships over coming months. This is unfortunate as Australia has no quarrel with the Indonesian people. However, we need to consider the likely transition of West Papua from the current status of an occupied province to an independent sovereign state and in doing so, endeavour to resolve our differences with Indonesia.

'Our relationship with Indonesia is now in jeopardy, given the mobilisation of its military and its confrontational rhetoric. Clearly, Australian citizens living in Indonesia may come under threat, and it is within this context I have also asked the Indonesian people to ensure their safety, and that Indonesians refrain from violence against Australians and their commercial enterprises there.

'Mr. Speaker, I advise the House that I have ordered all Australian Defence personnel leave cancelled and components of our Army Reserve, mobilised.'

Interjections filled the chamber with calls for the Prime Minister to resign.

'The Prime Minister still has the floor,' the House Speaker directed having brought the assembly back to order. 'Prime Minister ... '

'Thank you, Mr. Speaker. Mr Speaker, Australia cannot stand by and permit a repeat of the East Timorese disaster in which a third of its population were killed before we interceded. Therefore I ask that the Opposition set aside partisan differences and support the following motion.

'I move that this House,

One: Notes the overwhelming international support from seventy-eight nations for a declaration as a state, for an independent West Papua and supports a United Nations resolution for a referendum to be held at the earliest opportunity;

Two: Supports a United Nations Security Council resolution authorising an increase in the existing multinational force currently deployed to maintain security in Papua New Guinea; and

Three: Supports an Australian military contribution to this multinational force.

I commend the motion to the House. Thank you, Mr. Speaker.'

With only a few exceptions from hard-line left-wing socialists, and members of the Green Party, the members voiced their approval in support of the call.

Three hours following news of Australia's major policy shift in relations with Indonesia, elements of the *KOPASSUS* Group 3 Sandi Yudha fire-bombed the Australian Consulate in Surabaya, killing all in residence.

\*  \*  \*  \*

# JAKARTA

'*Bangsat!*' General Sumantri glared at the photo of his president hanging on the wall. 'I can't believe he is actually ordering the withdrawal!' General Sumantri was demonstrably angry with the President's demands to recall the divisions from West Papua.

Recovering from his operation in Germany, the President had vented and ranted upon learning of the relocation of military assets to West Papua. Declaring his position had been usurped, the President spent the following week in recovery communicating his displeasure to all.

Upon his return to Jakarta, their one-on-one exchange had been acrimonious; the President's innuendo that his position as Chief of Army might be reviewed sooner, rather than later, a challenge the General could not ignore.

'He's openly challenging your position, *Bapak*.' Colonel Didi Sumantri was equally resentful. 'Pipi caught sight of Agus Winarko and a delegation from the House of Representatives in another closed discussion with the President, just prior to his meeting with you.'

'I've never trusted Winarko. He comes to us with cap in hand whenever it suits.' He looked sternly at his son. 'Be careful of Pipi. She might be your wife but don't forget her first loyalty will always be to her father.'

'Pipi will do whatever I ask,' Didi said, overly confident of his relationship with the President's daughter.

The General lowered his voice. 'It is paramount that the international community believes we'll never withdraw from West Papua. We can't send a message that the President refuses to support his own military.'

'So, where does that leave us?'

'We believe he's maneuvering with his parliamentary allies to replace our leadership with those who support his position on West Papua.'

'A coup against his own military?' Didi was genuinely aghast at the suggestion.

'I've already conferred with Subroto, Nuryadin, Sudomo and Putu Nusten,' the Chief of Army lowered his voice even further when mentioning each of the chiefs of staff. 'And they concur.' He tapped his son on the shoulder. 'As of now, you will carry the rank of Brigadier General. You will replace Major General Sutarmin and assume command of *KOPASSUS.*

Genuinely surprised Didi rose and stood erect. 'What will become of Sutarmin?'

'He will be overseeing the security of our President,' the seasoned officer replied with trademark smugness.

\*   \*   \*   \*

Mosques across the archipelago broke dawn's imminent arrival with the call to *Subuh* prayer. Having already completed his ablutions, the Indonesian President gently lowered his forehead to the marble floor in a posture of submission to God. Completing the final movement with feet folded under his body, the *Bapak* recited *'Peace be upon you and God's blessing,'* then slowly rose and exited the prayer room at the rear of his private residence.

Surprised when his servants had not appeared as was their routine the President frowned and returned to his chambers. There he found the First Lady in shock, tears streaming down her cheeks as a guard of Special Forces stood menacingly waving machine pistols in the air. In the grey moonless night Indonesia's Presidential Guard stood aside, as the president was unceremoniously whisked away to a military training camp, overlooking the mountain city of Sukabumi. Shrouded in secrecy, Pipi and the President's family were rounded up and transported to military destinations outside the capital.

As sunrise peeled grey light into day, the city's residents awoke to learn that their President had been rushed to hospital, his condition related to the recent medical procedure undertaken in Germany. In view of the mounting threat to the country's sovereignty the Vice President had asked General Sumantri to assume military control over the nation.

Within twenty-four hours, Indonesia was in the midst of a political crisis as the upper echelon of *Tentara Nasional Indonesia*, the country's military machine effectively initiated a *coup d'état*. *KOPASSUS* and *BRIMOB* units swept across Jakarta and arrested high-profile reformists, members of parliament, and pro-government sympathisers. Military officers who were suspected of supporting the president's agenda were hauled before their superiors and suspended from their duties.

The headquarters of *Badan Intelijen Negara*, the State Intelligence Agency produced a list of more than seven hundred names of those suspected of supporting the Free Papuan Movement. Within days most had been located, arrested and 'disappeared', the Indonesian vernacular for murdered and, amongst those who would be arrested and detained was Jules Heynneman.

Agus Winarko was escorted to *KOPASSUS* HQ in Cijantung, where he was placed under protective custody as Brigadier General Didi Sumantri's guest.

Gangs supported by the Islamic Defenders Group swept across the capital plundering supermarkets, restaurants, and bars. The United Nations Resident Coordinator's Mercedes was intercepted immediately upon leaving the Menara Thamrin office, the Resident dragged from the rear seat and stomped to death. International schools were closed and the mass exodus of expatriates commenced.

General Sumantri declared martial law, suspended parliament and assumed the position of Caretaker President. The military immediately imposed a midnight to dawn curfew across the country. From Sabang to Merauke deep racial and religious resentments flared, villages turned against villages and transmigration camps were torched as history again repeated itself.

\*   \*   \*   \*

# NEW YORK

Deeply troubled, Bennie stared out over the Manhattan skyline across the East River, oblivious to his prestigious surrounds. When CNN first announced news of the *coup d'état* he was astonished. With the information flow then confirming the massive Indonesian troop build-up in West Papua, he was crushed.

Bennie had positioned himself in New York maintaining a constant round of meetings with vacillating UN delegates, soliciting support in favour of the imminent vote on West Papua independence.

The turn of events was not the outcome he expected. He now believed that by positioning such disproportionate military numbers across West Papua, many potential supporters of the proposed UN resolution might now waiver, in view of Indonesia's superior strength. A peacekeeper force would not wish to be confronted with the threat of an all out confrontation against one of the world's largest militaries.

He desperately needed a catalyst to drive support in the desired direction. He called Jules and, in their customary oblique manner whenever communicating, made arrangements to meet urgently, selecting a destination that would ensure Bennie's presence remained recondite and out of Indonesian reach.

Before night fell over Jayapura, Jules would be in custody.

\*     \*     \*     \*

# New York — United Nations

## Declaration Adopted by
## General Assembly resolution 1288

*"The General Assembly,*

*In consideration that the right of people to self-determination is a cardinal principle in modern international law and that all peoples, based on respect for the principle of equal rights and fair equality of opportunity, have the right to freely choose their sovereignty and international political status with no interference.*

*Declares that:*

1. *The subjection of peoples to alien subjugation, domination and exploitation constitutes a denial of fundamental human rights, is contrary to the Charter of the United Nations and is an impediment to the promotion of world peace and co-operation.*

2. *All peoples have the right to self-determination; by virtue of that right they freely determine their political status and freely pursue their economic, social and cultural development.*

3. *All armed action or repressive measures of all kinds directed against dependent peoples shall cease in order to enable them to exercise peacefully and freely their right to complete independence and the integrity of their national territory shall be respected.*

5. *Immediate steps shall be taken, to implement a referendum in the territory known as West Papua for the natural people (indigenous) of that territory to determine whether to accept the Republic of Indonesia proposed special commonwealth, status for West Papua within the unitary state of the Republic of Indonesia or, reject the proposed*

*special commonwealth status for West Papua, leading to West Pap-*
*ua's separation from Indonesia."*

The implementation of the Resolution required that the referendum be initiated within a period of twelve months.

Although Indonesia rejected the resolution, Jakarta reluctantly
accepted that the referendum would take place, immediately executing steps to not only delay the event, but coerce the Papuan population with whatever means to influence the outcome. A total media
ban was imposed. A disinformation campaign, spreading false
information to deceive the Papuans commenced, with the intent
to convince the native population that separation from Indonesia
would leave them destitute.

Brigadier General Didi Sumantri set in motion *Operasi Sapu Ber-*
*sih,* "Operation Clean Sweep", with the arrest, followed by the disappearance of fifteen hundred university and high school students,
suspected of collaborating with the rebel movement.

Notwithstanding the total media blackout, reports revealing
the atrocities were successfully leaked by missionaries to the world
press. Activists in the Netherlands, Pacific Island nations, the USA,
and Australia commenced applying pressure on their respective
governments to take action.

Australia and the Netherlands conferred with the United Nations
Secretary General and lobbied the US President, to prepare an international peace keeper force to enter West Papua, and end the intimidation and associated violence.

Anticipating a call to provide troops and support services, the
Australian Government prepared legislation to reintroduce National

Service for citizens and residents, between the ages of eighteen and thirty-five years of age.

Indonesia's Caretaker President General Sumantri warned that any attempt to impose a UN Peacekeeper occupation of Indonesian territory would be met with the full force of his nation. In contradiction of international treaties, the Indonesian Navy then commenced sea exercises intimidating vessels transiting the three declared archipelago's shipping lanes. In response, Canberra ordered six of the navy's eleven frigates, and ten Armidale-class patrol boats to increase surveillance patrols along the northern economic exclusion zone.

An imminent outbreak of hostilities between Indonesia and Australia was suddenly very real.

\*   \*   \*   \*

# Papuan Highlands

## Mek Mek Village

'That's the last one,' Alice held a leech for Anne to see. 'You can get dressed now.'

Anne looked at the slimy parasites now doubled in size since attaching to her body. 'In all my years of mountain trekking and travels I have never even seen one of these damn creatures before.' Disgusted, she shivered involuntarily then scratched. 'Any chance these bites will become infected?'

'Unlikely. I wouldn't worry about it.'

Weary to the bone, Anne was tempted to sit on the damp ground but resisted. It had taken eight days to reach this point close to the satellite reference grid. She glanced over at Alice, acknowledging that without her the journey might not have been undertaken; the consequences for Alice had she not followed, were unspeakable.

During another attempt to secure a travel permit for Anne, Alice had learned that the ego-maniacal Brigadier General Didi Sumantri was scheduled to arrive, and reconnoitre the territory from Kampung Mas to the Akumuga Mine.

Alarmed, Alice recounted the circumstances of her encounter with the Special Forces officer to Anne. They discussed their situation and agreed to travel together, crossing into Papua New Guinea once Anne had encountered the Mek Mek people. Both understood that returning to the Akumuga mining town would not be an intelligent option. They decided to leave without travel approval and, having informed the Australian teachers of their intentions, slipped unnoticed into the night.

Anne and Alice's final passage through the seemingly impenetrable mountain jungle terrain had been monitored from afar by the Mek Mek community. Confronted by the daunting task of continuing their journey, having frequently sighted human skulls placed conspicuously to scare, the women had camped within sight of a suspended river crossing. It was then that Anne had discovered a leech attached to her breast. Panicked, she shed her clothes and pleaded for Alice to examine her back.

'I can feel we're being watched,' Anne whispered.

'Me too,' Alice responded, her eyes searching the walls of green.

When the Mek Mek appeared on the other side of the stream the women were surprised, and somewhat relieved, to discover a white man in their midst. Anne rose and started across the bridge.

'Stop,' Stephen Coleman called. 'Wait there!' He stepped onto the rickety structure and approached.

'Are you lost?' he asked. 'What are you doing here?' Coleman's authoritative voice demanded.

Anne crossed her arms defiantly then squinted at Stephen. 'And you are...?'

'It doesn't matter who I am.' His face hardened. 'You're intruding here.' He pointed back along the path from where they had emerged. 'You must go back. It's dangerous here.' He paused. 'Especially for women.'

'Is this you?' Anne refused to be bullied. She extracted the enlarged aerial imagery of what was thought to be Michael Rockefeller. Stephen Coleman examined the print and instantly became concerned. 'Not me,' he denied. 'That could be anyone.'

Exhausted from their journey, Anne's shoulders slumped. 'We're not here to cause any trouble.' She produced her *Troodon GPS* receiver and activated the display. 'These coordinates represent a location nearby. If the person in the frame is not you then it must be someone else.' She extended her hand. 'I'm Anne Whitehead and this is my friend Alice Heynneman.'

Upon hearing the name Stephen Coleman's eyes narrowed as he examined the younger woman. 'The villagers call me *Sanguma*.' He continued viewing Alice as if she were a landscape painting. Reluctantly, he relented. 'Grab your backpacks and follow me.'

The interlopers followed, crossing over the fast-flowing stream, up an embankment and through several hundred metres of thick growth, before emerging at the perimeter of the main Mek Mek village.

Coleman led the women into the village where, after a brief exchange with the chief, Anne and Alice were offered food and water. Coleman observed the visitors closely, experience dictating that their ill-timed arrival was suspicious; the woman, Anne, with the aerial photograph, was an ominous sign of further, unwanted attention.

Coleman had arrived the day before Anne and Alice were spotted approaching the isolated community. Bennie Tabuni, distraught with the news of Jules' arrest had contacted him to discuss freeing his brother, by mounting an attack on the heavily-guarded Jayapura residence. Coleman argued that, without knowing the precise location in the residence where Jules was being held, an open fire fight should be avoided at all costs. Instead, he convinced Bennie to have his men use the smoke and stun grenades currently secreted away in the cache stored above the Mek Mek compound. Coleman returned to the village, again travelling familiar passages of the Fly River upstream through western PNG, towards the outpost Erekta, leaving the river where it formed the boundary between Indonesian Papua and New Guinea.

Coleman had just returned from the mountain cave when he learned that Anne and Alice were almost on the Mek Mek community's doorstep.

'They must be kept out of the village,' *Lapun Buna* insisted. 'You need to discourage them from remaining in the area.'

Coleman nodded. 'I'll find out more. If they are lost or need help then it would be wise not to leave them wandering around as that could bring others looking for them.'

'I'll make myself scarce until they're gone.' The elderly American recluse had then retreated angrily up to the mountain cave, to hide.

Coleman had been taken aback when confronted by Anne Whitehead. Suspicious by nature, when the woman referred to satellite coordinates, he became unsettled and wanted to know more.

\* \* \* \*

Anne Whitehead sat hunched forward on a log alongside her companion, deliberately casting a shadow over the *Troodon GPS* receiver's screen display. Her reserve battery had died, and Anne needed to advise London that she had finally arrived at the designated coordinates. Raising her head Anne noticed Stephen Coleman closely observing them both and she cocked her head and stared back enquiringly. Ignored, she sighed, stretched then rested her chin on open palms, and slowly absorbed the village's stone-age environment.

Laughing children fell silent when an aloof-strutting tribesman passed near to where they played in the dirt, the feared *Khakhua–Kumu* not so much as casting a glance in the visitor's direction. Mek Mek warriors armed with bows and arrows, returning from their hunt, adjusted their *koteka,* penis gourds when they spotted Alice and fell into laughter when one pointed at Anne and uttered something alien to her ears.

* * * *

Alice Heynneman scratched at the dirt with a stick. Having lived most of her life in West Papua and having had travelled the land extensively, she had been exposed to such villages before, saddened that so many of her people still lived in a world that had been left behind. She knew that many of the children in this village would never survive their parents due to malnutrition and disease, the simplicity of village life the only barometer they would ever know.

Alice glimpsed at Anne out of the corner of her eye, and was again troubled by her determination to make such an onerous journey into this remote part of the highlands, where danger presented at every turn.

'Anne, when you arrived at Akumuga you never mentioned anything about looking for someone. I thought your expedition was to complete work for your studies?'

'I'm sorry, Alice. That slipped my mind. When I was preparing for the journey, one of the university professors gave me the reference points where he believed I would find isolated communities to study.'

'And the person in the picture…?'

Anne struggled to answer. She looked her young friend directly in the eye. 'Again, I'm sorry. One day I'll explain. For now, you'll just have to trust me.'

'So, really, you're here looking for someone?' she persisted.

'Yes and no.' Anne responded, evasively.

'If they don't chase us away, how long do you intend staying here?' Alice probed.

'To tell the truth, if there is nothing here then there is no reason to stay.'

Alice was relieved. 'Then you'd be okay if we leave for the border as soon as we can arrange a guide?'

'Let me try to talk to him first.' Anne glanced in Coleman's direction.

'He seems distant, even aloof.'

'Probably spent too much time alone,' Anne suggested. 'I've met his type before.'

'He looks a little old to be wandering around mountain tribes.' Alice raised her eyes in Coleman's direction. 'He must have spent a great deal of time here for the villagers to give him the name *Sanguma*.'

'Why couldn't he just have an ordinary name like everyone else?' Anne suggested rhetorically. 'Why *Sanguma*?'

'Sounds similar to what I've come across in other dialects. Could mean someone who heals...but I can't be sure.' Alice explained. 'Let's see if we can get him to talk.'

*   *   *   *

Coleman had his back to the hut's entrance when the women approached. Caught by surprise, he immediately terminated the conversation and placed the Iridium 966 satellite phone back in its aluminium case, and retrieved the solar charger. This was his only means of remaining in contact with Bennie Tabuni whilst travelling isolated destinations, as this phone could work on the remotest locations on the planet, having access to more than sixty low orbit satellites.

'We want to thank you for having the villagers feed us,' Anne called inside. 'Guess we should explain what we are doing so far from civilization?'

'That would help.' Coleman moved into the open doorway to prevent their entry. This hut was in fact, *Lapun Buna's* simple home situated on the ground due to his age and infirmity, which he shared with Coleman during his infrequent visits.

'Can we commence by asking your real name?' Anne tried.

Coleman brushed the question aside. 'Why not start with explaining what you're really doing here?'

'Well, it started out partly to study isolated tribal communities but the plan was interrupted by the Indonesian military.'

'Why didn't you just return home?'

Alice gave her companion an inquiring look as she, too, was keen for an answer.

'Okay,' Anne looked apologetically at Anne. She realised nothing more could be achieved unless she risked revealing more. 'I have a background in anthropology. For some time I planned on completing a doctoral degree and with my long-service leave had decided it was time to do so.' Again she hesitated, feeling her way through the explanation. 'There had been rumours floating around for some time regarding sightings of a European living amongst the mountain tribes. One school of thought suggested it could even be the missing heir, Michael Rockefeller.' Anne continued manufacturing the story, attempting to offer a credible explanation. 'I approached one of the British media groups and they agreed to fund my journey. The satellite photograph I showed you was from an older file sourced from one of their American affiliates. They provided the GPS phone, not that it's of much use now as even the backup battery is dead.'

'And that's it?' Coleman lifted an eyebrow.

'Just about,' she continued. 'A few days before I left London the British Historical Society contacted me. They had heard through the grapevine of my intention to go into the Papuan highlands, and asked me to keep my ears and eyes open for any World War II aircraft wreckage that the villagers may have found. Did you know there are at least a dozen aircraft from that period that were never located?' Anne then offered her most innocent face and asked, 'Don't suppose these villagers have ever come across anything fitting that description?'

Coleman immediately saw through the deception and suspected the true purpose of her visit must have something to do with the downed drone. Earlier, *Labun Buna* had organized for several of the village men to take him to the wrecked drone. The moment Coleman sighted the pilotless plane he guessed it belonged to the Americans and that they would want it back.

'Nothing like that around here,' he lied convincingly. 'So, what do you intend on doing now?' Coleman needed to leave with the weapon supplies. Bennic had ordered one of his rebel units to a staging point, a full-day's journey from the Mek Mek where Coleman would offload the ordnance. The women's appearance complicated his movements.

Anne had already accepted that the probability of finding the missing wreckage was next to none. She was drained physically, and wished only to be home in England soaking in a warm bath with everything associated with Papua, far from her mind.

'We want to know if you can arrange a guide to take us over the border into New Guinea.' Anne wrapped an arm around Alice's waist. 'It's too dangerous to go back to the Akumuga area. It's crawling with Indonesian troops and I, for one, don't have a travel permit.'

Coleman thought quickly. 'The Indonesian military is spread right across the territory and camped along most border crossings. I can ask the chief to provide a guide, but it's best they go out and test the route to ensure it's safe before attempting any crossing.'

'How long will that be?'

Coleman needed time. 'I'll check it out myself and be back in four to five days. You'll be safe here provided you don't leave the compound.'

Anne forced a smile. 'Guess we can survive a few more days.' She leaned and peeked inside the hut. 'They will be worried about me back in London. My phone is dead. Any chance I can use yours?'

Coleman considered refusing, but if by giving her access prevented third party concerns for her well-being then he had little choice. 'Okay, one call. But keep it brief.' He opened the aluminium case and Anne dialled the designated London number and spoke for less than thirty seconds. The message, albeit cryptic, was clearly understood.

*    *    *    *

Across the border in Papua New Guinea, a "stringer" journalist adjusted the antenna connected to his laptop which was used to facilitate monitoring communication traffic between UN peace-keeper posts. In doing so he inadvertently intercepted Anne's call, his curiosity instantly piqued when he heard reference to the name, Rockefeller. Unperturbed as he was out of reach of US Federal Communications Commission authorities, and could not be targeted for violating wiretapping laws, the journalist filed his story.

Within the hour, Fox, CNN, CNBC, the BBC, and even RT were running the headline that the missing heir, Michael Rockefeller, had been discovered living in the Papuan highlands. Alongside, a photo taken of the young man in 1961 was an artist's impression of how the explorer might appear today. The lifelike, gaunt, long-grey-haired illustration was copied, posted, and reposted across electronic media registering multi-million "likes".

Meanwhile, the central figure to the growing brouhaha remained ignorant of it all. Incensed at having to remain out of sight, the American hermit remained in the cave, cursing the two women for creating his predicament.

*    *    *    *

# WASHINGTON

When David Shackleton learned of Agus Winarko's detention his immediate reaction was one of satisfaction that the conniving associate deserved his downfall. Unfortunately this sentiment was almost immediately displaced with the conclusion that any potential relationship with the prospective Federal Republic of West Papua might now be doomed. Shackleton had flown to Washington to meet with the Secretary of State once again, to solicit guidance as how best to proceed in view of mounting hostilities that would impact on the Akumuga Mine.

'We just don't know which direction to follow. Should we consolidate with the Papuan entities who may be the beneficiaries of the UN vote, or do we approach the new Indonesian military leadership to negotiate a new arrangement?' Shackleton shook his head aimlessly. 'What happens if the Indonesians dig in and refuse to withdraw? Will the USA support the Jakarta generals even if they become embroiled with the Australians?'

The Secretary responded, 'Back in time, 1969 to be precise, the US didn't support Australia's opposition to Indonesia's annexation of West Papua out of concern that would push Jakarta into China's sphere. The current and most past administrations since then have established a strong rapport with the Indonesians in view of their strength in relation to other SE Asian nations. Their relevance, and therefore importance, to the US will continue to be maintained, and even grow, as China expands its influence across that region. The world should not be surprised if our future interests in Indonesia differ from those of Australia.' The Secretary's assuring smile was less than convincing.

'So either way, Summit Gold is screwed?'

'I wouldn't give up hope just yet. The Indonesians may just be full of huff and puff. No one wants to provoke a fight, but if Papua New Guinea draws Australia into any conflict with the Indonesians, the US would be obliged to support the Aussies under the ANZUS Treaty.'

\* \* \* \*

# JAYAPURA

Dressed in *KOPASSUS* uniforms, Bennie's rebel unit bluffed their way into Jules Heynneman's residence where he was being detained, lobbing grenades amidst unsuspecting guards. M84 stun grenades detonated with a thunderous roar, blinding the disoriented soldiers who were then easily despatched. Jules was escorted safely from the building and transported to a vessel standing by offshore.

During Jules' temporary sojourn escape across the Celebes Sea to the Philippines, he contemplated the future in view of his Indonesian assets having been expropriated by the caretaker government. Although he retained substantial monetary assets buried in secret deposits and protected under Singapore's stringent banking laws, the loss of his multi-faceted, Indonesian commercial interests was a bitter blow.

Left to brood with this financial catastrophe, Jules reflected on his relationship with the Free Papua Movement, and how he should be compensated for the years he financially supported Bennie's quest. Jules resented Bennie's ambivalence to the sizeable material contributions he had made since they commenced their journey together, disquieted by a growing cloud of uncertainty as to what an independent West Papua might mean to him.

\* \* \* \*

# SOUTH AUSTRALIA

## WOOMERA
## ROYAL AUSTRALIAN AIR FORCE'S SURVEILLANCE
## AND RESPONSE GROUP

Four hundred kilometres north of the city of Adelaide, Australia's RAAF Base Woomera coupled with the Woomera Test Range covered an area approximately the size of England. As the base lay within the "Red Zone", public access to the aerodrome was not permitted as this was the home of Australia's remotely controlled drone aircraft operation.

Former P3C, RAAF pilot, Flight Lieutenant Des Heyes struggled with constant neck and shoulder ache, swiveling his seat around to face the other two members of his team. They were close to completing a ten-hour shift staring at computer screens that displayed images, beamed back from high-powered sensors on a Northrop Grumman MQ-4C Triton, a remotely-piloted drone aircraft three thousand kilometres to the north. Australian intelligence received a constant feed of information from a fleet of seven unmanned aerial vehicles at the South Australian airfield.

The RAAF utilised the Triton as a high altitude, long endurance aircraft for maritime patrol and other surveillance roles. Flight Lieutenant Heyes was amongst the first Australians to pilot this new generation of drones, which could descend and ascend through challenging maritime weather to gain a closer view of ships, whenever required.

Piloting the Triton through the aftermath of the most recent tropical cyclone, the imagery of a flotilla of ships steaming north-east of Darwin caught his attention, as previous tracking indicated the warships were sailing south-west into the Indian Ocean.

Verification was then sought from the Jindalee Operational Radar Network (JORN). The over-the-horizon radar network monitored air and sea movements across Northern Australia and most of Indonesia, as part of Australia's defence network. The network was so sensitive it could track helicopters taking off and landing in Jakarta more than three-thousand kilometres away.

However, as the effectiveness of JORN was also impacted by extreme weather the Chinese flotilla's turn to the east into the Arafua Sea, had previously been missed.

When confirmed by analysts, the startling aerial intelligence was immediately disseminated by operational staff to Defence HQ in Canberra, and within minutes Australia's Northern Command raised the level of alert to "increased intelligence watch, and strengthened security measures."

\* \* \* \*

# CANBERRA — PARLIAMENT HOUSE

The Prime Minister's bloodless expression reflected his deep concern. 'Did they actually enter our waters?'

'We can't definitively know as the ocean border line still hasn't been ratified since everything was redrawn after East Timor became independent.' The Defence Minister continued to stare down at the enlarged aerial photographs. 'But, if they didn't, they sure as hell came bloody close.'

'This is unacceptable and extremely provocative,' the Prime Minister was almost breathless. 'What purpose would an amphibious craft, capable of carrying such a large number of armed personnel, have, so close to Australian shores?'

'Perhaps they are destined for Kampung Mas,' the Foreign Affairs Minister suggested. 'We have evidence that there could be as many as a thousand ground troops already based in the Autonomous Special Zone of Kampung Mas.'

The RAAF unmanned drone had provided clear evidence that Australia's strategic security environment was being challenged. A Chinese taskforce of five warships had steamed south into the Arafua Sea to conduct combat simulations and other exercises in conjunction with the Indonesian Navy, somewhere between Timor and the eastern-most boundary of West Papua.

The Chinese vessels, a Jiangkai II-class frigate, accompanied by three Luyang III-class destroyers, and an amphibious ship capable of carrying several hundred marines, sailed off the eastern coast of Timor along the Ombai Wetar channel, before heading towards the Torres Strait. The Indonesian navy accompanied the Chinese fleet with two Andau-class patrol vessels, the *KRI Tongkak* and *KRI Ajak*.

This was the first substantial Chinese military exercise in the far-eastern part of the Indian Ocean, and in Australia's maritime approaches.

The Foreign Minister spoke forcibly. 'China is obviously signalling its capability and intention to project force beyond its own shores. They are thumbing their noses at us here by stating that the People's Liberation Army-Navy will go where it wants, whenever it wants, without the need to seek permission to do so from other powers. Australia has a strategic interest in ensuring that China does not establish a military foothold in Indonesia from which it could launch attacks or threaten access to our maritime approaches. Until now, China has not been overtly hostile to Australia. We could be placed under threat by any such military deployment in our nearest neighbour's backyard.'

'There is also the issue of whether the Chinese are violating Australia's Economic Sea Zone with its current offshore rig operation.'

'Have both the Indonesian and Chinese ambassadors front immediately, to explain.' The Prime Minister's face was devoid of colour. This was one crisis he had not expected. 'And get negotiations on the ocean boundary lines with Jakarta back on track!'

Four Royal Australian Navy Anzac-class frigates left their home ports, and sailed north into the area between the Torres Strait, across to Christmas Island. Guided Missile submarines HMAS *Dechaineux* and HMAS *Farncomb* also sailed, leaving their home base in Western Australia, to join the fleet.

HMAS *Canberra* with its four hundred crew, one thousand fully equipped infantry troop, a hundred trucks and armoured vehicles, including Abrams main battle tanks and ten helicopters, sailed for Darwin.

The HMAS *Leeuwin* which had been operating off Timor Leste was ordered to the Arafura Sea, to run a hydrographic check on the Chinese drilling platform *Haiyang Shiyou 1088*. Fitted with hull-mounted high frequency sonar, echo sounders and the ability to tow an array of side-scan sonar, the navy vessel was well equipped to determine whether the Chinese were encroaching on Australia's reserves.

*   *   *   *

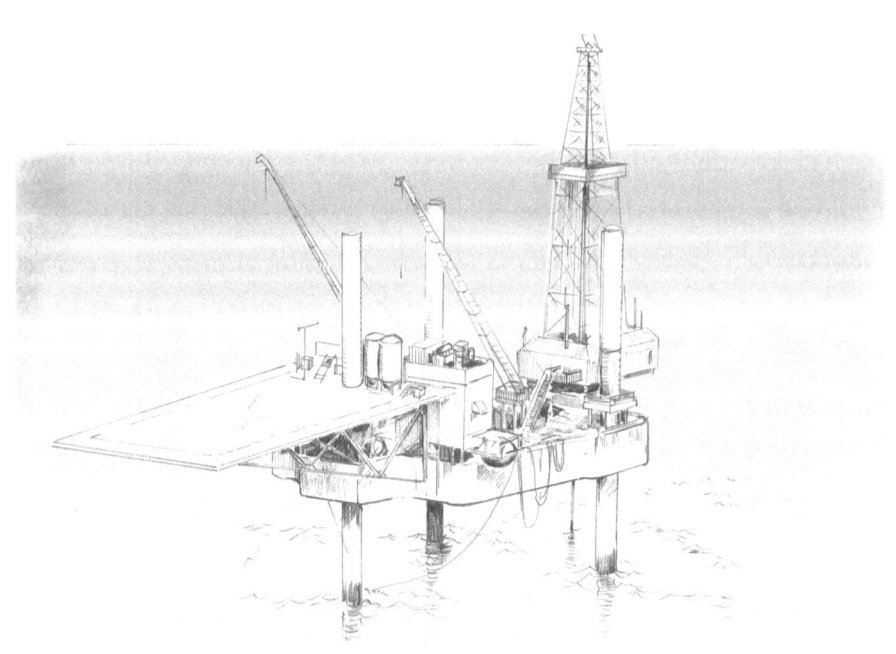

# ARAFURA SEA

## WEST PAPUA — NORTHERN AUSTRALIA

Shen Hao checked the monitor to confirm the rig superintendent's statement, nodded then continued on his rounds. As rig manager, he had absolute responsibility over all personnel, technical and performance aspects on the jack-up rig, *Haiyang Shiyou 1088.*

Shen was proud to have been entrusted with this responsibility as the offshore drilling rig was the most modern of its kind, built in the Qingdao Beihai Shipyard for his immediate masters, the China National Offshore Energy Group.

Shen had been selected for the role not only because of his family connections in Beijing. He had solid experience in the industry and enjoyed knowledge of maritime regulations, essential in his current

231

position, considering the delicacy of the location of the operation. He was acutely aware that the ocean border along the Arafua Sea had not been clearly defined, and that the location of the *Haiyang Shiyou 1088* could be interpreted as being outside the territorial rights claimed by Jakarta.

Shen continued his rounds around the labyrinth of metal railings and machines. Three enormous steel legs had been rooted on the seabed providing stability to the massive structure that resembled a miniature, self-sustaining city. As he passed under a military radar system identical to those evident on Chinese patrol vessels, a Liberation Army Navy commando came to attention. Saluting was not required and not encouraged. The rig was secured by military teams that rotated out of the Kampung Mas Special Autonomous Zone, and Beijing required this not be detectable. Australian RAAF, P-8A Poseidon carried out regular maritime surveillance flights over their position, and Shen took whatever precautions necessary to disguise the military presence.

Teams engaged in the offshore drilling operation were aware that the horizontal, directional drilling they were undertaking might be questionable. Geological surveys indicated a major gas deposit less than ten kilometres to the south of their position, placing the huge gas field's title in possible contention. In consequence, the *Haiyang Shiyou 1088* had secretly commenced covert drilling in the direction of that deposit to penetrate the field.

Shen's team were skilled in this very precise methodology; steering and redirecting the drill head to within centimetres of their target, and deviating the direction whenever required, all executed from the rig's surface control centre.

Having completed his hourly inspection, the rig manager then returned to the communications centre and updated his status report, which was then encoded utilising Chinese quantum communication encryption, a system that simply could not be hacked.

*   *   *   *

# Papuan Highlands

## Mek Mek Village

Alice Heynneman's attention was again drawn by the frequency village women left the compound with small baskets of food. Towards the end of the third day she decided to follow, maintaining a discreet distance.

The steep trail meandered up the slopes, Alice struck by the natural beauty of water plunging down before disappearing into the forest below. When the villager she was tracking paused, and turned as if aware of another's presence, Alice froze, blending into the landscape. Then, where the trail ended with a series of rocky steps, she watched the woman hand the basket to a Mek Mek elder Alice had seen strutting around the compound.

Alice slipped into the thick undergrowth and waited for the woman to return, then slowly crept forward for a closer view of what appeared to be an entrance to a cave. Voices drifted in her direction and, enticed by the oddity of the location, she commenced climbing the steps — only to be prevented from proceeding any further by the *Khakhua–Kumu*.

The witch doctor roared at her. Alice realised she had trespassed and panicked. Turning to flee, an ankle twisted and gave way, sending Alice crashing onto the stony path.

She cast a furtive glance up at the *Khakhua–Kumu* and then back to the sprained ankle. Unable to communicate, she beckoned and waited for the elder to come to her aid; confused when the witch doctor disappeared inside the cave.

A voice called down to her. 'You can't walk?'

Alice craned her neck, stunned when an emaciated, grey-haired figure appeared.

'I asked if you can walk?' This time the voice softened.

Alice shook her head as she gently touched her ankle. 'I think it's sprained.'

'The *Khakhua–Kumu* will call some of the villagers to help you back down the slope.'

'Who...who are you?' Alice peered at the old man.

For a long moment they were captured by silence. Then, 'In this place I am called *Lapun Buna.*'

'You are American?' Alice thought she detected an accent.

The old man ignored the question. He exchanged words with the *Khakhua–Kumu* who then hurried down the trail and disappeared. With small steps he made his way carefully to Alice's side. 'What is your name?'

'Alice,' she replied. 'Alice Heynneman.'

'You came with that other woman.' He cast Alice an enquiring look. 'What are you looking for here?'

'I'm just trying to cross over the border.'

'Why?'

'I worked at the Akumuga Mine. Now it's closed because of all the fighting. I just want to be somewhere safe.'

'And your friend?'

'She's an anthropologist.'

When the old man became silent, Alice thought he may have fallen into a trance. Not another word was uttered until a group of young native men appeared and assisted her back to the village.

Anne sensed something was amiss when the level of village chatter rose unexpectedly. She exited Coleman's hut to find Alice hobbling in her direction.

'How bad is it?' she asked, concerned, bending down to examine the injury.

'Twisted my ankle. It's not all that painful, just feels stiff. I should be okay in a day or so.' Then, 'Anne, you're not going to believe what — '

Anne interrupted. 'More like a week, I'd say. I've suffered ankle sprains from hiking and in my experience you won't be able to put any real weight on that for at least four to five days. As for climbing up hill and dale, it could be much more than that before we can consider leaving for the border.'

'Listen to me! There's an old man living up above the village in a cave.'

Unaware of the elderly Caucasian shuffling towards them until he was directly alongside, Anne suddenly sensed his presence and looked up at the image, silhouetted against a clear sky.

'Don't think it's serious,' he said. 'But it would be sensible to give it rest.'

Anne rose slowly to her feet gobsmacked, staring vacuously, until the import of the moment unlocked her surprise. Suddenly finding her tongue she blurted, 'My God, you're him!' She turned and held Alice by the shoulders almost toppling the injured woman. 'Alice, you've found Michael Rockefeller!'

Struck by those words, a look of pained distress clouded *Lapun Buna's* demeanour. Visibly agitated, he shook his head and turned to walk away. Alice reached out to touch the old man but the *Khakhua–Kumu* interceded, gesticulating wildly, several village men with threatening looks steering the revered man out of harm's way.

Struck by a sadness she could not understand, Alice Heynneman continue to watch closely as *Lapun Buna* shambled towards his hut, both parties oblivious to the knowledge that *Lapun Buna* was Alice's grandfather.

\* \* \* \*

# PAPUA

### Jayapura — *KOPASSUS* Command HQ

Enraged, Brigadier General Didi Sumantri slammed the officer against the wall and held the man there, pressing a forearm across his throat. 'You piece of shit!' The guard commander responsible for holding Jules Heynneman was quickly losing consciousness. 'I should have you shot!'

The officer's eyes bulged then dipped slowly closed as he became limp, Didi Sumantri releasing the first lieutenant who then collapsed to the floor.

Embarrassed by the escape, Didi Sumantri was further infuriated to learn that the navy Makassar-class warship KRI *Tanjung Bungka* would not be arriving at Kampung Mas Port on the other side of the island for another two days. His scheduled inspection of *KOPASSUS* units along the southern Papuan border had been seriously delayed. But, it was the information relayed by the local Akumuga township commander that had earned his wrath.

Discussing an unrelated intelligence matter, the Mobile Brigade police officer commanding the Akumuga settlement revealed that the British woman, Anne Whitehead had left the area without travel clearance and ventured into the highlands. Learning that the foreigner claimed to be conducting research in relation to Papuan tribes, Didi was sceptical that one would undertake such an expedition in such inhospitable country at a time of armed insurrection. Adding to his suspicions, when Didi pressed the police captain further, he was informed that a local mining engineer, Alice Heynneman, appeared to have accompanied the woman.

A conceited smile cracked his lips as he visualised their next encounter.

Brigadier General Didi Sumantri mentally pieced together the puzzle deciding that there had to be a connection to the sightings of the famous American family's heir. With that breaking news, every thread of intelligence buried amongst Indonesian intelligence files had been resurrected and delivered to Didi in Jayapura. Having read the reports mentioning *bule* sightings over time, Didi became convinced that the British woman's activities were possibly subversive in nature, requiring closer scrutiny. He instructed his aide to contact Foreign Affairs and obtain the number of the Indonesian Ambassador's direct line in Washington.

He needed the most current information available relating to sightings of the famous American heir.

Within hours, he had a reasonable idea of the approximate location of the British woman. Summoning his territorial subordinate, Didi ordered a unit of Special Forces *Group 3 Sandi Yudha* commandos to accompany him to Kampung Mas on the first available military aircraft. A team from the 33rd Battalion *Wira Sandhi Yudha Sakti* were deployed to Kampung Mas in preparation for Didi's arrival.

He would determine the validity of the reports citing the long-lost American's presence and in doing so, arrest the British woman and her companion, Alice Heynneman.

\*   \*   \*   \*

## MEK MEK VILLAGE

Stephen Coleman staggered back into the village carrying a field-patched shoulder wound. The Mek Mek chief, *Khakhua–Kumu,* observed as Anne Whitehead cleaned the injury, Coleman relating how an Indonesian forward scout had ambushed him three hours out from the village, when *Lapun Buna* appeared.

Coleman was surprised. 'They know?' he asked Anne.

'Yes. We can talk later.'

*Lapun Buna* looked closely at the damage. 'The soldier will bring others.'

'No he won't,' Coleman assured confidently.

'They're getting closer by the day. Soon, they'll be all over the village.'

'We always knew that day would come.' Coleman looked over at Alice standing quietly near the hut's entrance. 'Tomorrow wouldn't be too soon to head out for the border.'

'I've injured my ankle,' Alice finally spoke.

'She'll need another four or five days,' Anne looked across at *Lapun Buna*. He had not exchanged words with either of the women since their first encounter.

*'Tell the Sanguma.'* The *Khakhua–Kumu* tapped *Lapun Buna* on the arm. *'It is my fault they found you.'*

*'You are my friend, and I do not blame you.'*

Alice caught the one word, *Sanguma,* and cast Coleman a challenging look. 'Isn't it time you told us who you are?' She then indicated to the elderly American, 'At least we know who *he* is.'

The old man lifted a finger to his lips and, with the slightest movement of his head, told Coleman not to say anymore.

'You have a strange way of soliciting help.' Coleman stood and gently touched the wound. 'We'll have a few more days here before moving out. My advice is that you keep to yourselves until then. Alice, you need to be up front about that ankle. If there's any chance whatsoever that you are not fully recovered we won't go until you are. At these altitudes the weather is always unpredictable so the trails will be boggy. At best, I estimate five days to cross and that is assuming we don't run into trouble.' His face hardened. 'The length of the entire border is awash with Indonesian Special Forces. You might be okay if you fall into their hands but I, for one, wouldn't relish that thought.'

Anne and Alice then found themselves alone when Coleman accompanied *Lapun Buna* into his hut.

'What will happen to the old man if the Indonesian soldiers arrive?' she asked Alice.

'Probably nothing much, he hasn't done anything wrong. Besides, he doesn't look well enough to travel any great distance, especially in these conditions.'

'Why do you think he's angry with us?'

'Guess he's been away from Western civilization so long he's upset by the intrusion.'

Anne considered the response. 'Are you going to try to speak to him again?'

'I'd like that. I might give it a try before we leave.' Alice smiled wistfully. 'Up there on the slopes when I fell, he didn't hesitate to see if I was alright. At first I was uncomfortable but when he sat beside me, strangely enough, I felt safe.' Alice became wistful. 'I wish my dad was here right now.'

'Jules? He's a good man,' Anne offered insincerely. 'But I'm not sure he'd be the right person to have here right now.'

Alice conjured up an image of her real father, Bennie Tabuni, wondering where he was at that very moment.

*   *   *   *

# CANBERRA

## OFFICE OF THE PRIME MINISTER

Tracking a course directly along the imaginary ocean lines, separating Indonesia from Australia's far north, the HMAS *Leeuwin* near-missed collision with the frigate, KRI *Yos Sudarso* immediately raised the potential for a naval clash in the disputed seas.

Indonesia moved quickly, boosting its naval presence near Australia's Exclusive Economic Zone, claiming Australian Navy vessels had breached Indonesian territorial waters.

Drawing upon the one hundred and fifty vessels in active service, five frigates, four *Andau-class* patrol boats, Six *Clurit-class* fast missile boats, eight *Pattimura*-class corvettes along with maritime patrol aircraft, were deployed along the southern border with Australia. Radar stations in Papua's Timika and Merauke along with Saumlaki in the Moluccas and Buraen in the East Nusa Tengarra, monitored Australian aircraft and shipping. Sixteen Russian Sukhoi Su-27 and Su-30 "Flankers" were placed on standby. These 11th Squadron fighters could strike deep into Australian territory within one hour from take off.

'Prime Minister, it is imperative that we diffuse the situation immediately.' The Minister for Infrastructure and Transport was in meltdown. 'If the Indonesians move to block shipping through their sea lanes, distribution of food, water, and medicine would cease within days.'

'How is that possible?'

'More than one third of all Australian refined fuel comes from

Singapore and passes through Indonesian shipping lanes. Our total stockholding of oil and fuel on the sea is only two weeks, the supply at refineries only five to ten days with another ten of refined stock in terminals.' Then, with exasperation in his voice, 'Within three days of supply ceasing the pumps at service stations would be dry. This would mean that delivery of frozen and dry foods would also cease within seven to nine days!'

'What would be the impact on our defence forces?' the dismayed Prime Minister asked.

'Obviously we would be deeply affected by any threat to supply. Any major interruption to fuel supplies would abruptly grind our military to a halt. Any turning back of super tankers vital to our supply lines would not only be an instant economic and social disaster, but would also leave us defenceless.' The Defence Minister had long argued for a tripling of the country's fuel holding capacity but had constantly been ignored.

'The super tankers don't fly under the Australian flag. Surely the Indonesians wouldn't block shipping sailing under the "Flag of Convenience" registry?' This, from the Minister for Foreign Affairs and Trade referred to the practice whereby a non-military vessel was registered in a country other than that of the ship's owners such as Panama and Liberia.

'We can't rely on that,' the Defence Minister remarked. 'They could demand a cargo's destination, and if the vessel was to deliver to us then they could very well turn the ship around.'

'This is incredible,' the Prime Minister was appalled. 'What steps are we going to take to ensure safe passage?'

'We don't have the capacity to provide escorts. If the Indonesians move to block supply then we should treat that as an act of war.' The Defence Minister's response was met with defiance.

The Prime Minister stood, stony-faced. 'Let Jakarta be aware that any action on the high seas perceived to be against our national interests will not go unanswered.'

\*    \*    \*    \*

# HAIYANG SHIYOU 1088

## DRILLING RIG — ARAFURA SEA

Radar reported the Australian warship's manoeuvers just five nautical miles to the south of the jack-up rig. Visible also from the platform, the operations manager, Shen Hao, supported the rig superintendent's concerns, that the HMAS *Leeuwin* was most likely conducting hydrophonic sonar surveys directly above the gas reservoir. Because of how the reservoir was shaped additional appraisal drilling was being conducted.

Consequently, the *Leeuwin's* proximity to where the *Haiyang Shiyou 1088* was horizontally drilling required a cessation of activities to avoid discovery.

The area had not been clearly delineated as to whether it lay in the Australian or Indonesian Economic Development Zone and, as such, could be in contention. The situation required an immediate request for direction from his masters, the China National Offshore Energy Group. Upon receiving the report, Beijing ordered the Luy-ang III-class guided missile destroyer, *Xining IV* anchored at the Kampung Mas Special Autonomous Zone port, to intervene. Con-sidering the international ramifications, it was agreed that an Indo-nesian navy ship should also join in the exercise, suggesting that the "Freedom of Navigation" rule would apply. The Indonesian frigate KRI *Yos Sudarso* whose recent encounter with the HMAS *Leeuwin* had initiated the rising conflict, was selected.

Within hours, the *Xining IV* and KRI *Yos Sudarso* sailed into close proximity of the HMAS *Leeuwin*. The Australian defence network JORN over-the-horizon radar network closely monitored these sea movements in the Arafura Sea.

Shen's team was then ordered to resume with their horizontal, directional drilling operations.

*   *   *   *

# PAPUAN HIGHLANDS

A Russian-supplied Mi-35 attack helicopter from the warship KRI *Tanjung Bungka* had flown Brigadier General Didi Sumantri and his eight-man Special Forces commando unit from Kampung Mas, to the Akumuga Mine. His scheduled inspection of *KOPASSUS* posts along the PNG border was put on hold; his primary purpose now to locate the foreigner, Michael Rockefeller, the British woman Anne Whitehead, and Alice Heynneman.

Having been briefed by the local commander, and satisfied he was on the correct course, the group commenced reconnoitre of the mountain area where the Mek Mek tribe might be located.

Didi had previous experience with this version of the Mi-35 attack helicopter. Aware of the issues relating to high-altitude targets, he was counting on the helicopter's capacity to operate flights day or night as low as fifty metres over the forests. Equipped with a target sights system that include a thermal imager, laser range, and location finder, Didi felt comfortable that his quarry would eventually be located.

When the Mi-35's flight path took Didi's unit over the Mek Mek village, upon sighting the helicopter pandemonium erupted throughout the community.

The Mi-35 hovered for several more minutes before the pilots urged the Brigadier General to return to the base camp at the Akumuga mine site for refuelling.

Accompanied by several of the older tribesmen, Coleman, Anne, Alice, and *Lapun Buna* had climbed the slopes and taken refuge in the well-concealed cave. There they remained, until the sound of the helicopter's blades beating through the air, faded with distance.

'They'll be back,' Coleman insisted. 'And next time they'll most likely land and sweep the area.'

'Then we should leave now,' Anne demanded.

Coleman focussed on Alice. 'How's that ankle?'

'I'll manage.'

Coleman turned to his old friend with a questioning look.

'I'm not going anywhere,' the aged American was emphatic. 'They won't harm me.'

'Don't be too sure of that,' Alice asserted.

'You should be safe as long as the Indonesians don't decide to look beyond the village when they return.'

'What are they after? Would it be that aircraft wreckage?' the old man asked, regretting the words the moment they came out of his mouth.

Anne turned with a raised brow. 'What wreckage?'

Responding with a faint smile he said, 'Yes. Isn't that the real reason you're here?'

Alice frowned. 'What's he talking about, Anne?'

Anne shifted uncomfortably on her haunches and looked appealingly to the younger woman. 'Sorry, Alice, I just didn't wish to involve you further than necessary. As it appears that you and I were the only ones in the whole village not to know of its whereabouts, then I guess there's little point in you not knowing also.' Anne glanced around at the others. 'My company designed some of the equipment used in a pilotless American drone aircraft that went missing in this vicinity.' Speaking slowly and without inflection she continued. 'The "eyes" or lenses of the drone use the most sophisticated technology developed, and we can't have this fall into unfriendly hands.'

'Why did they send you?' Alice demanded, peeved at not having Anne's trust.

'Because of my background, my expertise, and the believable story I offered about studying the Papuan hill tribes.'

'And was that really a photo of him?' Alice indicated towards *Lapun Buna* who remained quietly absorbing the exchange.

'Yes.' 'An earlier high-altitude photo reconnaissance run had captured someone who looked European and...' she looked apologetically across to where *Lapun Buna* sat, '...fitted the description of the missing Rockefeller heir.' Anne poked around her backpack to retrieve her GPS cell phone. 'Before the batteries died, I had the coordinates of your location and, as we knew the drone went down somewhere within striking distance then that became part of the cover.' She looked disdainfully in Coleman's direction. 'Had you told me from the outset about the wreckage perhaps Alice and I would be long gone by now and out of danger.'

'Perhaps if you'd been more up front about why you were here,' Coleman countered. 'Do you need to recover those parts from the drone?'

'You've also seen it?'

'Of course.'

'What's the drone's condition?'

'Main body, wings, and tail completed trashed. Nose section totalled. As for the camera section, I have it here.' Coleman disappeared deep inside the cave then after some minutes returned with the broken sensor in pieces.

'This it?' He placed a woven basket on the moist ground.

Anne examined the find and after only a few moments nodded. 'Can we take it with us?'

'I'll take it.' Coleman folded the basket and bound it with twine.

'We'll leave now. Empty your backpacks of everything except the essentials.' Coleman again disappeared inside the cave returning with a Pindad PM2 submachine gun and several spare magazines. 'I'll wait for you back down in the village.' Coleman wrapped an arm around *Lapun Buna*. 'Keep your head down and I'll be back in a couple of months. Try to keep out of sight.'

*   *   *   *

# Haiyang Shiyou 1088

## DRILLING RIG — ARAFURA SEA

Alerted both by their own radar and confirmed by the Australian Defence Network JORN system, when the *Xining IV* and KRI *Yos Sudarso* left the port of Kampung Mas and sailed directly towards the HMAS *Leeuwin*, the Australian warship went to general quarters.

On the *Leeuwin's* bridge, the skipper received a continuous flow of information in relation to the Chinese and Indonesian vessels closing on his position.

When it became apparent that the oncoming vessels were deliberately placing the *Leeuwin* in harm's way, an encrypted "FLASH" signal was sent up the chain of command. "FLASH" messages were reserved for initial enemy contact notification or operational combat messages of extreme urgency, and took precedence over all other messages. Within minutes the ship's situation had passed from the Command Centre to COMAUSFLT, responsible for command of all Navy combat forces to the Chief of Navy, the Minister of Defence and finally, the Prime Minister.

The Captain knew the ship's inadequate armaments would be no match for either of the approaching warships. His expectation was his request for immediate air support to provide the necessary backup against the threat of attack.

Everything the Captain had learned and practised over his fifteen years in the Navy would now determine the outcome of his ship and crew of forty-six officers and sailors. He recognised the

KRI *Yos Sudarso* from a previous encounter, and when the Indonesian vessel cut dangerously across his path, he turned hard to avoid a collision.

The deliberately provocative behavior forced the Australian warship off its intended course and over the precise position above where the *Haiyang Shiyou 1088's* horizontal drilling efforts had just penetrated a significant deposit of methane, natural gas hydrate. This accumulation of methane had migrated along geological faults forming an outcrop just below the ocean floor.

When the drill head chewed into the reservoir, the puncture resulted in a catastrophic gas escape of Olympic pool-sized methane bubbles that grew in size, and quickly floated to within touch of the ocean's surface.

The HMAS *Leeuwin* passed over the enormous bubbles as they burst up to the surface lowering the density of the water. With the sudden release of gas, the warship's buoyancy disappeared as escaping gasses aerated the surrounding sea. Unable to support the ships mass, the ocean suddenly became lighter than air.

Incredibly, the HMAS *Leeuwin* dropped as if it were in an elevator shaft, the hollowness inside the bubble completely engulfing the ship, sending the vessel down to the bottom. Even if there had been sufficient warning for the ill-fated crew, sailors jumping overboard in lifejackets would also have sunk instantaneously.

Then there was silence.

The captains of the *Xining IV* and KRI *Yos Sudarso* stood on their respective bridges utterly astonished when the sea suddenly swallowed the Australian warship. Both immediately thought the HMAS *Leeuwin* had been sunk by a submarine, but when there was no evidence of such a strike, they turned their vessels away in haste, and sailed back to Kampung Mas Port.

In Australia, panicked aides rushed about the capital's halls of power. Parliament was in session when the Defence Minister entered and whispered a message in the Prime Minister's ear, sending him into shock.

'One of our warships, the HMAS *Leeuwin* has been sunk.'

The Prime Minister paled. 'Sunk?'

'There were two warships involved, one Indonesian, and another from the Chinese fleet in the Papuan port.'

'My God! Casualties?'

The Defence Minister shook his head. 'Can't determine yet if there were any survivors.'

Australia's over-the-horizon radar network confirmed that the warship had disappeared from their screens. Over the next hours, navy aerial surveys evidenced loose debris and sailor's bodies which had drifted aimlessly, dragged by seabed currents until finally floating to the surface and away from the escaping gas.

An emergency meeting of the Australian Cabinet was called in response to the loss of the warship.

The Cabinet supported the motion for an immediate retaliatory strike.

It was agreed that the Five Power Defence Arrangements should be invoked, as the original motivation for establishing the Arrangements was to hedge against the resurgence of an unstable, and threatening, Indonesia. However, as there were no concrete guarantees that in the event of an attack the members would support measures in relation to such threats, the Cabinet also invoked, for the second time in its history, the ANZUS Treaty.

As the Australia, New Zealand, and United States Security Treaty provided that an armed attack on any of the three parties would be dangerous to the others, and that each should act to meet the common threat, the Prime Minister made the calls to Washington and Wellington.

The American President was adamant that the USA should not be drawn into hostilities with China. As for Indonesia, the President offered to consider what action he might take to assist in resolving the confrontation.

Disappointed, the Prime Minister informed his New Zealand counterpart of the President's position, angered when the Kiwi leader assumed the same position as the Americans citing rising trade surpluses with the Chinese would be jeopardised if they became embroiled. However, they did offer troop support for deployment to Papua New Guinea within UN guidelines.

It was apparent that Australia would have to act alone. However, in doing so, the Prime Minister recognised the danger of forcing China into play.

Australia would need to send a clear signal to the Indonesian generals.

As Brigadier General Didi Sumantri's Mi-35 hovered directly over the main Mek Mek highland village, three hundred kilometres to the south, the Australian submarine HMAS *Stephenson* moved silently on electric power through the Arafura Sea.

With confirmation of its target and positional data fed into the Shortfin Barracuda submarine's computers, the HMAS *Stephenson* launched two of its twenty Mark 48 ADCAP torpedoes directly into Kampung Mas Port, where the Indonesian warship KRI *Yos Sudarso,* was anchored.

The torpedo was designed to detonate under the keel of the surface target, breaking the ships keel and destroying structural integrity. In the unlikely event of a miss, the submarine's crew knew the torpedo was programmed to circle back for another attempt.

The six-metre, five-million-dollar weapons tore through the ocean at a hundred kilometres an hour, their high-explosive warheads detonating upon impact sending the Indonesian warship KRI *Yos Sudarso* to a shallow grave.

Within the hour the Australian Prime Minister addressed the nation then called the Indonesian Caretaker President, General Sumantri. The Prime Minister advised the General that Australia was prepared to go to war with Indonesia, and that the cities of Jakarta, Surabaya, and Yogyakarta would be priority targets in the event of any further escalation.

General Sumantri threatened the Australian leader and terminated the call. He then summoned his military chiefs of staff.

As news of the conflict radiated, South East Asian stock markets tumbled. The Jakarta Stock Exchange Index collapsed by seventy percent and other Asian markets responded accordingly. Tourist numbers in destinations such as Bali had already declined significantly. However, with the increased possibility of an all-out clash between the neighbouring countries, additional charter flights were required to accommodate the wave of foreigners abandoning the isle.

The United Kingdom called for an emergency meeting of the

United Nations Security Council, to be held within twenty-four hours to discuss the tension between Indonesia, and Australia.

*   *   *   *

# PAPUAN HIGHLANDS

Anne, Alice, Coleman, and their guides trekked in single file through the rough tropical jungle, crossing streams, descending and ascending, continuously slipping and falling whenever the trail was lost in the high grass and thick jungle vegetation.

They had taken a circuitous path wide of Indonesian military border camps. The undefined slippery trail, blanketed with leaves concealing loose stones and sloppy mud, snaked endlessly across challenging ridges.

'We'll rest here for an hour,' Coleman instructed, deeply concerned with their progress on the first day, increasingly hampered by Alice's ankle condition. 'How are you holding up?'

Alice was stoic about her injury. 'So far, so good…'

A guide waved frantically, hushing the group into silence. Coleman moved quickly and pressed the women to the ground. 'Be very still,' he whispered urgently.

Slowly raising his head, Coleman squinted into the semi-darkness and caught sight of two Indonesian troopers making their way through the thick jungle heading in their direction. He signalled the guide to move further into the undergrowth then unfolded the stock of his PM2, holding the weapon at waist level.

The *KOPASSUS* soldiers were almost within reach when Coleman stepped out and opened fire, killing the first trooper instantly, and mortally wounding the other. Coleman pointed his gun at the dying soldier and squeezed the trigger.

'We can't remain here,' he warned, pulling a shocked Alice to her feet. 'We must find another way around. These two would be part of a larger unit and most likely not that far. They would have heard the shots so let's get moving as fast as we can!'

The guide clearly understood, taking the lead and retracing their footsteps. As they descended Coleman could hear the sounds of gunfire spreading across the mountain reaches where they intended on crossing the border. Convinced that the risk of encountering Indonesian forces was too great to continue, and in view of Alice's leg condition, he advised the women that they should turn back with the guide and he would travel on alone.

'Is there no other way around the Indonesian camps?' Anne stooped to recover her backpack. 'Wouldn't it be just as dangerous returning to the village?'

'In the jungle you would be just another target. If you return to the village and the Indonesians take you into custody, being a British citizen would at least keep you safe.'

'But not Alice.' Anne gave him an impoverished look.

'There is no real reason for you to continue.' Coleman tapped the contents of his shoulder bag. 'I can deliver this. It would have made more sense if you had returned to the Akumuga mine then to Kampung Mas and fly out of there instead of attempting this crossing.'

'I'm not letting *that* out of my sight,' Anne jabbed a finger in Coleman's direction. 'If you want to go on alone, give the drone parts to me.'

'You'd never get it past the Indonesians,' Coleman argued.

Exasperated, Anne stood with hands on hips and glared.

Coleman shook his head in annoyance. Minutes passed before

he decided. 'Alright, I'll take you back to the village area. We won't show our faces until we know it's safe. If the helicopter has been back, they would have seen for themselves there's nothing there. If they still haven't returned then we will keep out of sight until I can work out what to do.'

\* \* \* \*

# LONDON

Concerned over the loss of communication with Anne Whitehead, the high-level Anglo American Aerospace Defence Technologies exchange with the Home Secretary resulted in an instruction being sent to the British Ambassador in Jakarta.

The embassy's First Secretary, Political Affairs, (a position always occupied by the MI6 Station Chief), acted immediately calling upon Indonesian resources within the military to initiate urgent enquiries relating to the whereabouts of Anne Whitehead, whose last known contact had been at the Akumuga Mine in West Papua.

Paid informants within the Indonesian Ministry of Defence would also alert their government's central intelligence agency, *BIN*, the *Badan Intelijen Indonesia*. Within hours the search for Anne Whitehead would be passed to all intelligence elements in both eastern West-Papuan provinces. As Brigadier General Didi Sumantri was known to be in the area conducting *KOPASSUS* post inspections, he was contacted directly by the Jayapura Command HQ and informed of the British woman's government's concerns.

\* \* \* \*

# New York

With the sinking of the Indonesian warship, Bennie was convinced a full blown outbreak of hostilities between Indonesia and Australia was inevitable. The timing was opportune to fan Australian resentment, the responsibility for which, Bennie delegated to Marcus Tabuni.

Jules had grave reservations about Marcus' capacity to maximise the potential of the growing antagonism towards Indonesia. Jules had never been supportive of the significant role Bennie had planned for Natan Tabuni's natural son, as Marcus had never displayed the qualities required for leadership.

Jules sensed a slow deterioration in his relationship with Bennie once the United Nations determination for the referendum had been achieved; the source of his resentment, Marcus, whom Bennie had continuously proposed as the first president of the new Republic.

'We still have a few minutes before Marcus' comes online.' Jules checked the laptop to ensure it was ready.

Bennie ran his eyes over the day's schedule. 'Shackleton's meeting is postponed?'

'Yes. He will let us know when he returns from Washington.'

Jules and Bennie had been working together laying the groundwork to attract US investors once the referendum had been held, and a date was determined for Indonesia to withdraw from Papua.

The men were unaware of Alice Heynneman's developing situation, as their last communication had been prior to the women's attempt to trek across the border into Papua New Guinea.

Although Indonesian troops continued their intimidation of the Papuan population in preparation of the proposed referendum, the Free Papua rebels had been ordered not to attempt any major confrontation with the hugely, superior occupying forces. Instead, the freedom fighters continued a campaign of selective guerrilla attacks against the lesser-manned Indonesian posts.

Bennie crossed the room and joined Jules who sat waiting impatiently for Marcus to come online for the prearranged video conference call.

'I just hope this conversation can't be compromised,' Bennie took his seat alongside Jules.

'This *"Poly Cross"* system hasn't been released to the general public as yet. The delay you will sense when we talk is because of the deep encryption implanted in the software. Marcus confirmed he has the copy I couriered to Melbourne.' He nudged his adopted brother with a shoulder. 'Stop worrying. All audio, video and data that passes across this network is fully secure'

Moments passed and Marcus Tabuni's image appeared. 'Hi Bennie, Jules. I have the system up and running. Just hope it prevents others from hacking.'

'Jules assures me that it's completely safe.'

The doubt in Marcus's voice was evident. 'Okay, but let's be as brief as possible just in case.'

'I agree,' Bennie responded. 'I'll start then.'

Over the following hour, they discussed the ongoing mobilisation of the Australian Free Papua Movement's rolling demonstrations across Australian cities, exploiting the mounting anti-Indonesian mood. Social media had been utilised to inundate Federal representatives with calls, demanding the severance of diplomatic ties with Jakarta and immediate recognition of West Papua as an independent state.

'Do you plan on remaining in New York?' Marcus asked.

'We have a few more meetings with Wall Street investment groups over the course of this coming week then Jules and I will fly to Amsterdam for a meeting there with support groups.'

'And then?'

'We'll fly to Singapore for a few days then across to Fiji for another conference with the Melanesia Spearhead Group.'

'Can you come to Melbourne?'

'Yes. I'll let you know once the itinerary is confirmed.'

With their conference call terminated, Marcus wasted no time communicating updates to Free Papua cells across Australia.

The "Poly Cross" encryption was not fail-safe. Once again, Marcus' conversations were recorded and relayed to Indonesian Ministry of Defence's Strategic Intelligence Agency, *BAIS*, via the decoy server German spyware system operating in Sydney. The substance of Marcus' Skype calls were also recorded by Australia's domestic spy agency, ASIO.

Abdullah Siregar, Indonesia's senior spook and head of Indonesia's State Intelligence Agency smiled having read the report. The directive approving the termination of Bennie Tabuni remained active. Mounting such an operation in the USA was never considered due to the absence of appropriate assets.

The intelligence chief communicated details of Bennie Tabuni and Jules Heynneman's proposed travel arrangements, to his agents abroad.

\* \* \* \*

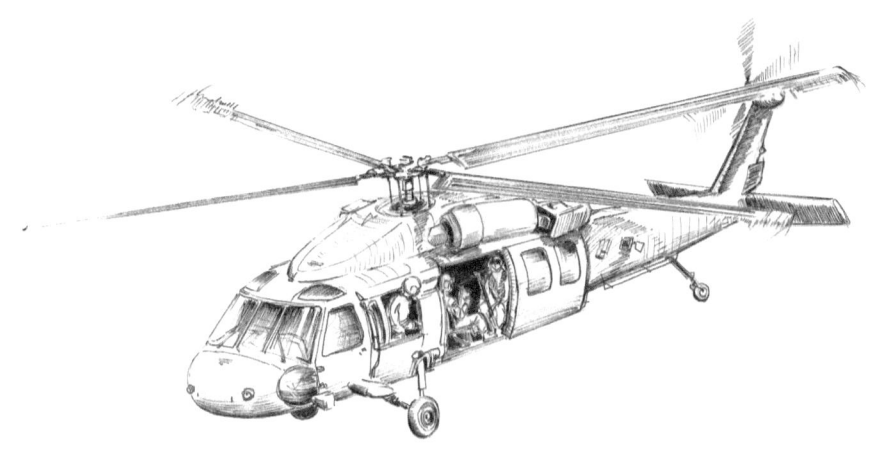

# PAPUA NEW GUINEA

## UN PEACEKEEPER POST

The Sikorsky UH-60 Black Hawk waddled above the ground then with a familiar bump settled on the newly-cleared heli-spot. Lieutenant Colonel Brent Shepherd followed the two, five-man SAS patrol units as they disembarked from the chopper. They were less than five kilometres from the border with Indonesia, their objective to commence patrols from the UN outpost of Erekta along the Fly River, where it formed the boundary between Indonesian Papua and New Guinea. The post was twenty kilometres west of Kiunga, where Papuan rebel troops, masquerading as Indonesian Special Forces, had slain two Norwegian female backpackers and murdered PNG defence elements.

Reports of Indonesian troops violating PNG's territory in pursuit of fleeing Papuan villagers had required an increased Australian defence presence.

The two, five-man SAS patrols would confront any intruders, even penetrate Indonesia's backyard through the rugged terrain and damp, rain-soaked mountains. There had been fire exchanged between UN peacekeepers and *KOPASSUS* raiders, and Brent Shepherd had flown to Kiunga and joined the SAS unit to familiarise himself with the SAS border operations.

\*　\*　\*　\*

# ARAFURA SEA

Australian navy divers from the elite Northern Territory-based Reserve Diving Team "Eleven" were unable to identify any structural damage to the HMAS *Leeuwin.*

By the time the HMAS *Huon III* mine-hunter arrived at the last known location of the warship, the undersea gas release had been capped by the Chinese drillers.

The divers, swimming across the sunken vessel with handheld sonar were bewildered by the absence of any obvious damage to the ship's structure.

When the Prime Minister was informed, he refused to accept the findings. A total blackout on all information relating to the report was immediately instituted.

\*　\*　\*　\*

# JAKARTA

Caretaker President General Sumantri sat in the *Bina Graha* Palace office considering the damning report which projected an outcome should Indonesia and Australia engage in an all-out war. This, together with the reported sighting of the aircraft carriers USS *Ronald Reagan* and the USS *George Washington* in Indonesian waters off Natuna Islands in Riau Islands, had the possibility of US intervention rattling investors.

The impact of the stock market rout had resulted in a Rupiah currency crisis which, in turn, had brought the masses into the streets, demonstrating. Food and other basics had escalated to highs unseen since the Asian Currently Crisis of the Suharto Era.

Entrepreneurs such as Agus Winarko remained in "protective custody", their fortunes devastated. General Sumantri had ordered the seizure of Winarko's assets when their value diminished to a negative level against the billions borrowed from state banks. Ironically, the Government had become the de facto, majority shareholder of the Akumuga Mine in Papua once again.

What concerned General Sumantri most was the rumblings amongst his fellow conspirators that he should consider stepping down. Although senior officers were not expressing their feelings openly he knew, from past experience, that he needed to act immediately to prevent any further decay in his position in power.

The military assessment offered by his general staff was also grim.

Logistically, loading tens of thousands of troops into ships and sailing to Australia would be out of the question. The Australian Navy was a superior force and exposure to RAAF aerial bombing would be disastrous. The analysts projected that should such an attack occur, the estimates were that half of all the country's ships would be destroyed and most of the remaining fleet would be rendered unserviceable. The Caretaker President reluctantly accepted that this would be a critical blow for his Navy. He also begrudgingly acknowledged that although his country could draft more than sixty million into the Army, the Navy did not have the ships to send more than a small number of those into offshore combat.

Additionally he knew that if the Indonesian air force ventured south the distances would require in-flight refuelling leaving the bombers susceptible to attack. Contrary to that, with Australia's northern bases practically on Indonesia's doorstep, the RAAF would be capable of striking all major cities quickly. General Sumantri was appalled with his air force strategist's conclusion: 'Air superiority would be crucial in any conflict and Australia currently enjoyed a greatly, superior position.'

Sumantri rose from a *Jepara*-carved chair and moved to the window pondering his next move, the question foremost in his mind was how to extricate the country from the confrontational predicament he could not win.

\*   \*   \*   \*

# CANBERRA

'If the *Leeuwin* wasn't attacked then what happened?' the Prime Minister demanded. The prospect that neither Indonesia nor China was responsible for the sinking of the Australian warship was deeply unpalatable in view of torpedoing the KRI *Yos Sudarso*.

The United States had agreed to flex some muscle and demonstrate to the Indonesians that any attack on Australia would require intervention by the USA. The Prime Minister had been warned by the Pentagon, that the price of US assistance in any military dispute with Indonesia would be a promise to commit Australian troops to battle, if America was to ever go to war with China.

'Incursions across the PNG border have increased exponentially over the past days. The SAS has engaged *KOPASSUS* troops twice in the past twenty-four hours,' the Defence Minister reported.

'Casualties?'

The Minister disguised a smile. 'None.'

'Do we have anything further regarding Jakarta's overall mobilisation?'

'Our people on the ground report that they haven't summoned reserves as yet but all regular troops have been called to barracks.'

'The question we need to ask ourselves is how much further is Indonesia prepared to go?' the Foreign Minister queried. 'The military is facing the possibility of domestic upheaval and that could work in our favour.'

'And on the downside, there is also the possibility that the country with more than two hundred million Moslems, could now lurch towards extreme religious nationalism, in the event of economic or political meltdown,' the Defence Minister added.

'Then it is agreed that we wait for Jakarta's response once the Americans have shown their hand,' the Prime Mininster decided.

\*   \*   \*   \*

# DARWIN

## NORTHERN TERRITORY

Radio Free Papua: 'The United States Defence Department today announced the arrival of six B-2 Spirit strategic stealth bombers at Australia's RAAF Darwin where the aircraft will be based. The bombers are part of the 509th Bomb Wing at the Whiteman Air Force Base in Missouri, USA.

The Pentagon noted in the announcement that the number of US Marines rotating through Australia's "Top End" has also been increased to three thousand troops.

The move comes as the Republic of Indonesia has announced revised maritime demands on international shipping passing through recognised sea-lanes.

The Pentagon has urged all nations to exercise their freedom to fly and sail in international airspace and waters claimed by Indonesia across the archipelagic state "or risk losing access to these vital lanes".

The US Air Force will continue to fly missions through Indonesian airspace from Guam to Darwin and other destinations despite the presence of surface-to-air missiles and fighter jets in the contested region.

When Radio Free Papua interviewed the Australian Minister for Defence and enquired if the placement of such substantial US assets in Darwin was related to the current tensions between Indonesia and Australia, he refused to be drawn on the deployment. However, we can confirm that sources close to Defence suggested that Canberra asked Washington for a show of force to demonstrate to

Jakarta that any increase in hostilities would be met by both Australia and its allies.'

\*   \*   \*   \*

# Mek Mek Village

Coleman, Anne and Alice had already returned to the Mek Mek village when the attack occurred.

Well suited for high-altitude environments, the Mi-35 helicopter blades chopped into the thin mountain air.

Didi Sumantri surveyed the scene below. 'Destroy everything,' he ordered.

The pilots positioned the destructive machine's chin-mounted turret and fired the twin-barrel GSh-23V 23mm cannon at the thatched huts straddling the forest's canopy-line. The towering, ironwood-stilt-supported shelters disintegrated under the barrage, the timbers shredded into confetti-sized pieces with Mek Mek families sent tumbling to their deaths. Villagers, who just moments before had been staring up in dismay at the hovering Mi-35 were slaughtered in their tracks, others fleeing in terror into the safety of the dense jungle forest.

High on the slopes and hidden from the carnage Coleman and *Lapun Buna* stood inside their cave fearing the worst.

'You can't go down there.' the elderly American insisted.

'Stay here.' Coleman was tempted to take the PM2 submachine gun but decided to leave it behind. 'And don't show your face until I come back.'

Fifteen minutes passed before he was close enough to the Mek Mek compound to comprehend the extent of the carnage visited upon the isolated tribal community. Thatched-roofed huts now lay shattered across the scene; bodies of men, women and children lay crumpled on the ground, the air pierced with the shrill squeals of pigs running aimlessly throughout the decimated village.

The military helicopter's blades had come to rest, Coleman surprised to see such a senior *KOPASSUS* officer standing beside the killing machine. Then, to his alarm, several of the Indonesian troops appeared from the other side of the open communal area shouting and waving to the officer, as they ushered two, half-naked captives into the village.

The bedraggled women were Anne Whitehead and Alice Heynneman, caught bathing at the edge of the village stream when the attack occurred.

Brigadier General Didi Sumantri was genuinely surprised. 'What do we have here?' he mocked, enjoying the women's discomfort as he ran his eyes provocatively over their bodies.

'I'm a Brtish citizen,' Anne snapped, incensed at their predicament.

'Yes, I know who you are,' Didi smiled irritatingly then turned his attention to Alice. *'Kamu lagi ngapain dengan bule ini?'* He demanded, addressing Alice in *Bahasa Indonesia,* demanding what she was doing with a foreigner.

'She is an old friend of my family,' Alice measured her response in English so Anne could understand. 'I'm acting as her interpreter.'

Impatient, Didi cut directly to the chase. 'Where is the old American, Rockefeller?'

The women feigned ignorance, Anne with a shrug.

Didi raised a hand threateningly towards Alice. 'I'll have my men take you both into the bushes if you waste my time. Now, again, where is this old man?'

'There is no American,' Anne lied. 'It must be a misunderstanding.'

Didi's eyes narrowed suspiciously. 'You haven't seen such a person around here?'

Anne gathered her thoughts as she crossed an arm to cover her breasts. 'There are no foreigners here apart from me.' Fearful she might be killed, Anne's mind raced. She glanced over at the unconscious body of *Khakhua–Kumu*. 'Many of the elderly men across the highlands have silver hair from vitamin deficiency.' Confidence returning, Anne became assertive. 'I am an anthropologist. You can check if you want. I have studied these cases in many hill tribes over the years. I haven't seen this old foreigner you mention anywhere around here.'

Didi stepped away from the women and questioned his troops. After some minutes when it became evident that none had seen any evidence of Rockefeller's presence, he ordered his soldiers to bundle the women into the Mi-35 then burn what remained of the village.

*   *   *   *

Coleman emerged from the trees and watched, stony-faced as the helicopter lifted slowly and cleared the treetops then faded into the overcast sky. He hurried back up the slopes to check on his old friend whom he found standing outside the cave, despair carved across his face.

'How bad is it?' He held his hand out for Coleman to take him down to the village.

'It's a bloodbath, though some managed to escape. They've destroyed the entire village.'

'And the two women?'

'Captured by the Indonesians.'

'Take me down to the village.'

'Give me a few minutes.' Coleman unpacked his Iridium 966 satellite phone and ventured outside searching for a signal. Once connected, he relayed what had transpired to Bennie Tabuni, who only hours before, had arrived in Suva, Fiji, having completed his visit with Jules to Amsterdam and Singapore.

Bennie wasted no time in communicating with his commanders on the ground in west Papua. When he learned that the Mi-35 remained at the Akumuga settlement and that additional *KOPASSUS* forces had arrived, he ordered the local commander to investigate and report back to him.

*   *   *   *

# JAKARTA

*'Jancuk!'* Caretaker President General Sumantri cursed in Javanese startling the four-star air force chief. Astonished, he glared in disbelief at the senior officer. 'The Americans flew bombers over our airfields and none of your radar stations knew?'

The US Embassy had officially informed the Indonesian Government after the fact. An unspecified number of B-2 bombers flew from Darwin over to Ujung Pandang where the Indonesian Air Force based Hawk 109s and F-16s, then past Pontianak and their Hawk 209s, and into Malaysia airspace. Without refuelling, the stealth bombers turned and flew over the Roesmin Nuryadi Airfield and a squadron of F-16s in Pekanbaru, and then onto Java and the Iswahyudi Airfield where the latest delivery of Russian Su-35s were based.

'And you believe that these bombers are armed with nuclear weapons?'

'Yes *Bapak*.'

General Sumantri wanted to weep. The message was clear; the United States bombers had been deployed to northern Australia specifically to warn Jakarta to desist from further escalating hostilities with their southern neighbour.

The Caretaker President dismissed the air force general.

Retreating into an abyss filled with gloom and self-recrimination, General Sumantri arrived at the conclusion that, with the United States showing its hand in the manner it had, by sending nuclear-capable strike bombers across the archipelago, the end of Indonesia's domination of West Papua was near.

Infused with an anger born of failure and betrayal by the people of West Papua the Caretaker President summoned his generals. Incensed that West Papua would follow the path of East Timor, the powerful group agreed that if they were to withdraw from the provinces then they would leave nothing behind. Within the hour, troops stationed in West Papua would be charged with the sacking of the provincial capital of Manokwari, and the obliteration of infrastructure across the entire territory.

\*     \*     \*     \*

# WEST PAPUA

In the absence of any United Nations capability to monitor the situation on the ground across West Papua to the Papua New Guinea border, Jakarta's merciless scorched-earth mission was implemented. Troops pillaged then burned. Buildings in Manokwari, Sorong and Jayapura blazed into the night casting an eerie pall of smoke across the landscape. Pro-Jakarta militias joined their Indonesian counterparts attacking Papuans, dragging women and children into the streets, slaughtering entire families as the intensity of their retribution grew. Villages were razed to the ground with scores of Papuans butchered by roaming militias, men castrated and left to bleed to death, women raped, and children murdered in their tracks.

*KOPASSUS* gunships flew into villages killing from the air, while ground troops swept the compounds shooting Papuans and their livestock, even polluting water supplies. The destruction dwarfed that of what occurred in East Timor during the Indonesian withdrawal.

More than ten thousand Papuans fled across the border into Papua New Guinea further exacerbating the refugee explosion already impacting UN resources.

Expatriates were not spared in the frenzy. With no escape from the unprecedented mass assault, tourists were forced from homes and hotels into buses, and transported to the airport for deportation.

Oil and gas project operators were given notice that their safety could no longer be guaranteed, and Indonesian military security was withdrawn from the Tangguh fields and other major resource developments.

When Indonesian troops poured into the Chinese-controlled Kampung Mas City Special Autonomous Zone, they were confronted by China Army Navy marines who stood their ground, and declared the zone under Beijing's control.

As the relentless blood-letting spread from Biak to Merauke, Brigadier General Didi Sumantri stood aloof, monitoring his Special Forces undertaking the total destruction of the Akumuga operation.

The mothballed fleet of hundreds of haul trucks, bull dozers and graders were damaged beyond repair. The conveyor system that fed hundreds of tonnes of ore to the mill was wrecked, and along the three pipelines that carried concentrate almost two kilometres to the Kampung Mas Port, demolition teams prepared the massive task of destroying the entire delivery system.

The Akumuga settlement was not spared. Didi Sumantri's troops burned the near-deserted town to the ground.

The contingent of five Australians was placed under guard at the school building, along with Anne Whitehead and Alice Heynneman.

The Free Papua commander for the Akumuga area reported the situation to Bennie in Suva, Fiji. Bennie considered the situation and then called a journalist who worked with Reuters in Hong Kong. Within the hour, breaking news of Australian teachers and their families being held hostage by renegade Indonesian soldiers in West Papua was released by the agency.

With the international community aware of the situation, Bennie communicated again with the local commander in Akumuga instructing his troops to standby.

\*   \*   \*   \*

# FIJI

'The Akumuga commander has assured me that they won't do anything to jeopardise Alice's safety.' Bennie lowered his voice. 'They will move when it's appropriate.'

'She should never have been involved in the first place.' Jules was angry, agitated, but not only because of Alice's predicament, 'Coleman should have taken better care.'

'We can't blame Stephen. There's nothing more we can do for the moment but pray she'll get out of this unharmed.' Bennie leaned across the coffee-shop table. 'We both love Alice but right now we can't let her situation distract us from why we are here. We should not antagonise the Chinese. Remember, they have veto power at the UN Security Council and Beijing has been dropping funds all over the Melanesian Spearhead Group to buy their influence.'

'The Chinese need to be told that with independence, we will need to reconsider their position in the so-called Special Autonomous Zone at Kampung Mas.' Jules was becoming increasingly aware that their differences regarding how an independent Federal Republic of West Papua would be shaped had become even more apparent. Jules expected a leadership role directing the new republic's economy and investment, whilst Bennie appeared to be leaning away from their previous understanding.

'We will need the British and the Americans, Jules. Having the Chinese also involved might also be in our best interests. Surely you can understand that?'

Jules' demeanour in no way reflected the sense of betrayal that had been festering in his mind.

As they passed through the Peninsula Hotel lobby to attend their final meeting with the Chair of the Melanesian Spearhead Group, Jules spotted a familiar figure he knew he had seen before in London and in Washington. Alerted to the distinct possibility that he was a member of Indonesia's State Intelligence, *BIN*, he pretended not to have noticed the agent.

\*    \*    \*    \*

# AKUMUGA MINE SETTLEMENT

Extreme turbulence jostled the five-man SAS units inside the two Sikorsky UH-60 Black Hawks as the helicopters crossed the PNG border and entered Indonesian Papua. Lieutenant Colonel Brent Shepherd sat silently, mentally preparing for the rescue mission that would take Australian soldiers into direct confrontation with Indonesian soldiers for the first time since the INTERFET force of 1999 in East Timor.

When news of the hostage situation reached Defence HQ in Canberra the closest assets to the Akumuga mine were SAS patrols along the PNG-Papua border. Operations Command ordered Lieutenant Colonel Brent Shepherd to lead the rescue operation. A second UN-designated helicopter was dispatched to the border post to support the airlift of hostages to safety.

Satellite surveillance imagery suggested a number of potential targets where the hostages might be held. Shepherd anticipated resistance, however considering the inclement weather, the cover of darkness and the element of surprise, he was counting on being on the ground no more than fifteen to twenty minutes.

Cruising at close to two hundred kilometres an hour, the Black Hawk crews were within sight of the Akumuga settlement within twenty minutes of their departure.

The Black Hawks landed at the two designated areas indicated in the satellite photos, the assault teams hitting the ground running, reaching their targets before the sound of their arrival could bring the town alive.

When the teams reached the first of the prefabricated buildings they breached the entrances before the sleeping soldiers could offer any resistance. The soldiers' weapons were gathered, magazines removed and thrown outside.

The hostages were nowhere to be seen in either building.

'We're running out of time, Colonel.' An SAS trooper tapped his wrist.

Shepherd leaned down and pulled a corporal's head back viciously. *'Where are the Australian teachers?'* he demanded in *Bahasa Indonesia.*

*'In the school,* the solider gasped. *'With the English woman.'*

Shepherd knew from the satellite imagery which building that would be. Leaving a trooper to stand guard outside the first two targets, he mustered his teams and rushed towards the school where guards, now alerted by the airborne attack, ran outside to determine what was happening.

Having lost the element of surprise, the SAS troopers opened fire immediately removing the threat. Storming into the school building Shepherd found the hostages huddled together in a corner, with a stunned Brigadier General Didi Sumantri holding the barrel of a Glock 19, to a teacher's head.

Recognition followed by shock froze the moment as the two officers recognised each other. Then, when Shepherd realized Alice Heynneman was amongst the hostages he stared incredulously.

'Alice?'

'Brent! Thank God it's you!'

'Get back!' Didi waved the Glock at the SAS troopers who had poured into the room.

'Why are you holding these people hostage?' Brent demanded.

Didi ignored the question and snapped back. 'You are violating Indonesian sovereignty. Get your men out of here.' He glared threateningly. 'Immediately!'

Shepherd knew any of his men could take out Didi without hesitation and with little risk to the hostages. Killing any senior Indonesian officer would greatly exacerbate the growing conflict, let alone executing the son of the Caretaker President.

'Put your weapon down, Colonel,' Shepherd stood his ground. 'My men have orders not to leave without the hostages.'

Didi Sumantri refused, aiming his handgun directly at Shepherd. 'You'll be court-martialled for this!'

'Take a good look around, Colonel. These troopers are acting under UN orders.'

Sumantri hesitated momentarily as he considered what was said. 'The UN has no authority here,' he responded, less confidently than before. 'You are all committing a criminal act. Leave, now!'

When Didi again waved the Glock, one of the Australian teachers seized the opportunity and grabbed for the weapon. In that moment, the handgun discharged. Shepherd pounced, seizing the gun, and disarming Didi Sumantri.

Anne Whitehead's body crumpled to the floor.

For the briefest of moments there was a hushed silence before Alice cried out, 'It's Anne!' She dropped to the British woman's side. 'She's been shot!'

Shepherd stared in disbelief as Anne Whitehead lay dead. He paused, handed the Glock to the closest trooper then bent down and lifted her into his arms. 'Alright, everyone evacuate!'

Sumantri started to move forward, prevented when Shepherd snapped an order to his soldiers. 'If he follows, shoot to kill!'

Didi paled in his tracks.

Alice hurriedly followed Shepherd outside. 'Take me with you,' she pleaded.

Shepherd adjusted the dead weight in his arms then nodded. 'Come on then, get moving!'

The hostages were ushered outside and hurried to the waiting Sikorsky Black Hawks, where the pilots idled the slow beating helicopter blades in readiness.

The last of the assault team climbed aboard as Brigadier General Didi Sumantri, now armed with one of the discarded *KOPASSUS* rifles, appeared, and commenced firing at the departing troops. An SAS trooper responded, firing his MP5K from the waist, spitting three-round bursts of fire at the Indonesian officer's feet, and sending Didi scurrying back inside.

The two assault teams, along with the hostages and the body of Anne Whitehead were transported across the border to Kiunga where an RAAF Beechcraft Super King Air had been positioned to repatriate the hostages. The SAS teams remained behind to later redeploy to the border area, while Brent Shepherd accompanied the Australian hostages together with an emotionally-devastated Alice Heynneman, to the military base in Townsville.

Anne Whitehead's body was flown directly to Port Moresby where the British High Commission made arrangements to have her remains flown home to England.

The Australian Defence Jindalee Operational Radar Network had monitored the two helicopters' operation from commencement to completion, from more than three-thousand kilometres away. Patrolling the air corridor above the Torres Strait between Northern Queensland and the Papua New Guinea-West Papua border were two, RAAF 3 Squadron F-35 Lightning stealth fighters supported by an in-flight tanker. The fighters, armed with "Sidewinder" air-to-air missiles swept the skies in the event the Indonesian air force, Russian Sukhoi Su-30 fighters, that had been relocated from Makassar to Merauke only days before, attempted to endanger the hostage rescue mission.

\* \* \* \*

# QUEENSLAND

Alice Heynneman sat apprehensively alongside Brent Shepherd who wished he could hold her hand. Immediately upon arrival at the RAAF Base, the hostages were provided with a full medical examination then transported to the Army military base. The Australian teachers and wives were interviewed separately and released to their families. The interviews were conducted by an officer introduced as a public servant from the Department of Foreign Affairs and Trade but, in reality, he was a member of the Australian Secret Intelligence Service (ASIS), responsible to the Minister for Foreign Affairs.

'Good morning, Colonel, Miss Heynneman. My name is Scott Davies.' The officer shook hands with Brent and led them into a windowless room. Then, with a well-rehearsed smile, he moved to place Alice at ease. 'Firstly, there is nothing for you to be concerned about, Miss …' He paused. 'May I call you Alice?' Again, with the disarming smile he continued. 'The purpose of this interview is to corroborate what we already know, and to offer confirmation that Canberra has approved issuing you with a temporary stay visa.'

'Valid for how long?' Brent cut in.

'Initially, six months.' The senior agent looked directly at Alice. 'But don't concern yourself about that right now as the question about your ongoing status is not something to worry about.'

'Thank you,' was all Alice could find.

'Right.' The officer placed a tape recorder on the table in front of

Alice. 'Hope you don't mind?' Again, with that smile. 'It's just a for-mality. Okay, let's commence with who was responsible for the Brit-ish woman, Anne Whitehead's death?'

Alice was ready. She had apprised Brent Shepherd of the events commencing from when Anne had arrived, their trek into the moun-tains, in search of Michael Rockefeller and the role the other for-eigner the Mek Mek called *Sanguma* had played in their failed cross-ing into Papua New Guinea. When Alice related what Anne had revealed regarding the underlying purpose for her journey into the highlands, that in her wildest dreams she had not imagined actually finding Rockefeller, Brent Shepherd knew he had to alert his superi-ors upon arrival in Townsville. Within hours, a senior ASIS officer had been delegated the task of interviewing Alice to determine what happened to the American drone.

'As the others present will confirm Anne was shot when one of the Australian teachers attempted to disarm Sumantri.'

'Why were you and Anne being held by the Indonesians?'

'The village where Anne and I were staying had been attacked by Sumantri's Special Forces. We were taken back to Akumuga and locked up with the teachers.'

'Tell me more about why you were in the village.'

Alice glanced at Brent. He nodded, and over the following hour, Alice repeated the story she had given Brent.

'So, when you were taken captive, where was Michael Rockefeller and this chap, what's his name again?'

'The Mek Mek called him *Sanguma*.'

'Did you learn where he was from originally, or his real name?'

'Rockefeller was hiding further up the mountain outside the village in a cave. The other man stayed with him. I'm not sure where *Sanguma* came from as we never had any real discussion about that. My guess is that from the way he spoke, he could have been English, perhaps South African. Even Australian.'

'And this *Sanguma* chap still has the drone parts you described?'

'Yes. He carried the parts when we tried to cross the border and back to the village when that failed.'

Another half-hour passed before the interview came to a close. 'We will need to know your movements while you are in Australia at all times Alice. Is that clear?'

'She is staying with my uncle in Sydney. I'll provide the details before you leave,' Brent offered.

'Fine,' the officer seemed satisfied. 'But I need to stress the importance of your not discussing with anyone, and I mean anyone, about the drone. Is that clear, Alice?' The smile had now vanished, a threatening touch now evident in his voice.

'I understand.'

'The media will want to interview you and I believe that this is unavoidable, so let's go through what questions might be asked and how you should address these. Okay?'

When the briefing was completed, the ASIS officer departed. Brent explained that he could not be part of any media coverage, and would wait until she had spoken to the Press before catching up again. Alice was then led into another area where, upon entering, she was caught off guard by the clamouring media and television cameras that filled the room.

'How long were you hostage, Alice?'

'Tell us about who shot the British anthropologist, Alice!'

'Alice, Alice! Did you meet Michael Rockefeller?'

When it became apparent that she was not responding, one of the female reporters called for the gathering to settle down. 'Come on guys, give the lady a chance.' The volume dropped as the reporter took advantage of the moment. 'Hi, Alice. I'm Carol Holmes from the ABC. Would you tell us in your own words what your relationship with Anne Whitehead is...' She paused, 'Was?'

Gathering her composure, Alice drew a deep breath and looked slowly around the room, conscious that whatever she said would be reported widely. 'Before I go there, I want to make a statement about what is happening across West Papua and then challenge you, and the rest of the international media, why you have not been more supportive of my people.' Alice felt the cavity in her stomach but still she proceeded. 'I won't speak about how West Papua fell into Indonesia's hands as that is old history and generally ignored by Australians and the rest of the Western nations. What I do need for you to understand is that even as we stand here in this safe environment, thousands of West Papuans are being slaughtered by Indonesian militias and government forces. The entire Papuan landscape is in a state of lawlessness with Indonesian troops engaged in rampant criminality and revenge killings because we dare to claim and pursue our right to be an independent state.' Alice paused again, for affect. 'I have witnessed the brutality of Indonesia's military machine, the butchering of pregnant women with their unborn babies cut from their bodies and discarded in the dust, native Papuan men beaten then castrated and left to die, young girls of eight years old and sometimes less, raped and then murdered, their bodies thrown into wells to pollute village water.'

Alice stopped, ran the back of her hand across her eyes and steadied herself before continuing. 'And yet, we see little evidence of this genocidal behaviour being mentioned in your newspapers or on your news broadcasts.' She felt the anger rising along with her new-found confidence. 'What do we Papuans have to do, so you will open your eyes and ears to what is happening right on your doorstep?'

'Jakarta blocked the international media from reporting there,' someone at the back of the room called out.

'That's a weak excuse,' Alice challenged. 'There has been no shortage of foreigners pouring in and out of the area pumping our oil and gas overseas, our gold and copper, our timber and other resources. Church organisations have been releasing reports of the carnage but, for whatever reason, your media hasn't raised any significant level of interest with the general public. Mark my words, by the time Canberra sends more Australian troops into West Papua it will be too late for many.'

'What makes you believe Australia would put boots on the ground in West Papua?'

'Because they are already there ...' Alice left this hanging intentionally.

The room erupted, the reporters calling loudly over each other to have their challenges heard.

'Did you see the Aussie troops yourself?'

'Where were these soldiers operating?'

'Can you confirm that Australian forces are actually on the ground in West Papua?'

Alice raised her hands in the air until the room became quiet. 'I'll tell you what I know to be fact.' She folded her arms defiantly. 'It was

Australian Special Forces that flew into Akumuga on the Papuan side of the border to rescue the Australian teachers.'

'Not UN Peacekeepers?' the ABC reporter queried.

'One of the helicopters had United Nations emblems but the other was Australian. The soldiers who got us all out of there were Australian SAS.' With this, there was a sudden flurry of activity as some of the reporters hurried from the room to call their stations.

'Are you certain, Alice?'

'Yes. I am positive.'

'Where there any Australian troops killed or wounded?'

'None that I'm aware of, but there were a number of Indonesian *KOPASSUS* soldiers killed when they opened fire on the Australians.'

'*KOPASSUS*?' A woman in the front raised her hand.

'Indonesian Special Forces. They were the ones who captured Anne Whitehead and me and took us to Akumuga where the teachers were being held. They *were KOPASSUS* because the officer in charge is General Sumantri's son.'

A collective gasp of disbelief filled the room.

'Can you confirm his name?' A reporter extended his phone, recording the interview.

Alice did not hesitate. 'Didi Sumantri. He led the attack on the Mek Mek village killing men, women and children. I can bear witness to those events. I can only hope for a time when Sumantri can be summoned as a war criminal and tried for genocide and crimes against humanity at the International Criminal Court in The Hague.'

Cameras continued to roll as Alice accepted a tumbler filled with water.

'Alice, is it true you actually met with Michael Rockefeller?'

'Yes, I believe so.'

'You're not sure?'

'Anne Whitehead embarked on her trek into the Papuan highlands to determine if the aerial photographs of a figure she had could be Michael Rockefeller.' Alice knew she had to be careful now with what she could, and should not reveal. 'Anne believed the elderly American we found was indeed Michael Rockefeller.'

'Is he still where you found him?'

'I would expect so,' was all Alice would say.

'Did you spend much time with him?'

'Yes, some. At first he avoided us but after a few days we did exchange a few words.'

'Did he pass on anything you can give us?'

'Not really. He is quite old and fragile and it was obvious he didn't enjoy having us around.'

'Come on, Alice, you've had contact with one of the great mysteries of our time and that's all you have?'

'We didn't communicate much. Most of the time we were in the Mek Mek village he remained distant.'

'Didn't you take any photographs at all?' A tabloid reporter asked suspiciously.

'Yes, we did until our batteries died.' Alice dropped her eyes to the floor as the incident came flooding back. 'All our gear was destroyed by Sumantri and his soldiers when we were captured.'

She inhaled deeply. 'I'm sorry but we'll have to leave it there for now. I'm still not a hundred percent so if you wish to catch up again I will be in Sydney from tomorrow. Give me your contact details and when I'm up to it I'll give you a call. Okay? Thanks.'

*   *   *   *

Alice would not receive her wish to see Didi Sumantri tried by the international community. Surprised when the two Black Hawk helicopters arrived at the Akumuga site and by the rapid events that ensued, the local rebel commander immediately signalled Bennie in Fiji. Shortly thereafter, upon learning that Alice was amongst the hostages evacuated by the assault teams, Bennie agreed when the rebel leader decided to take advantage of the moment and seize Didi Sumantri.

Two hundred Bougainville-trained rebel soldiers moved under the continuing cover of night and attacked the *KOPASSUS* post. None of the Indonesian soldiers were spared. Refusing to surrender, Brigadier General Didi Sumantri died under a hail of bullets.

His body was taken outside and tied to the flagpole. The Indonesian flag, *Bendera Merah Putih* was taken down and replaced with *The Morning Star.*

Jakarta would not learn of Didi's death until army support units arrived the following day.

*   *   *   *

# FIJI

## Peninsula Hotel Suva

'So you met Alice?' Bennie had initiated the call to Stephen Coleman.

'Yes. Wish I could've done more for her.' Coleman's voice was cutting in and out; Bennie struggling also with a persistent, overlapping echo.

'She's safe in Australia. You need to abandon that location and get out of there as soon as you can.'

'I plan on doing just that as soon as you've arranged for your local commander to come and remove the ordnance we've stockpiled here.'

'They're on the way. They should be there no later than tomorrow morning. There's little time to spare now. I should also tell you about CNN reporting they've identified Michael Rockefeller in the area. It's front page news everywhere.'

'Shit!' was all Coleman could find to say.

'That's not all. General Sumantri's son has been killed at the Akumuga site. We're expecting reprisals, and as the Indonesians will be aware of the Rockefeller sightings, then you should consider that as well when you're finalising your exit.'

Coleman digested the information. 'That complicates things even more. If your teams don't arrive by tomorrow morning then I will head out and leave everything for them to clean up here. Agreed?'

'I'll let the commander know.'

Stephen Coleman sat outside the cave entrance quietly considering his options. There was no doubt in his mind that with world-wide attention focussing on the whereabouts of Michael Rockefeller, what remained of the scattered Mek Mek community would soon be overrun.

Following the destruction and deadly violence visited upon the Mek Mek, Coleman had done whatever he could with the limited means at his disposal, attending to the wounded. Survivors had slowly dribbled back to the charred remains and gradually commenced rebuilding their village, and he did not know how to tell them, that it was all likely to happen again.

Coleman's thoughts turned to his old friend, *Lapun Buna* who remained ensconced in the cave. He knew that the obstinate fellow would never leave, not that he was in any condition to travel. Alone, Coleman was confident that he could find his way across the border undetected without the encumbrance of others. This was a skill he had acquired over the many years of living in such environments. The question now foremost in his mind; how to prepare *Lapun Buna* for what would surely come?

\*     \*     \*     \*

# WASHINGTON

## US STATE DEPARTMENT

'The Australians alerted our Defense Liaison Officer in Canberra.' The US Secretary for Defense was on the phone to his counterpart in the State Department. 'We don't have confirmation as to who this character they're calling *"Sanguma"* might be, but Langley has suggested that it might be a former Australian government man turned mercenary by the name of Stephen Coleman.'

'Who's he working for?'

'We don't know for sure but it's most likely he's been running weapons into the area for some time, supplying the Free Papua Movement.'

'What's your next step?'

'Langley says they can have a Black Ops team in and out within twenty-four hours.'

'You want me to take this to the President?'

'Yes. We feel that the window is closing rapidly with all this attention about Rockefeller in the news. The USS *Fitzgerald* is currently positioned south of the New Guinea border with a Seal team on standby. We'll use one of the Sikorsky choppers to ferry the Seals into the target, retrieve the drone equipment and offer Rockefeller passage out if he wants to leave.'

'Rockefeller's repatriation being the cover if the mission comes unstuck?'

'That would be the official line.'

*   *   *   *

# Mek Mek Village

Stephen Coleman's curiosity was aroused when *Lapun Buna*, obviously in deep discussion with the injured *Khakhua–Kumu* abruptly ceased talking when he entered the cave. A knowing look was then exchanged between the men, the *Khakhua–Kumu* rose and leaving without so much as a word, acknowledging *Sanguma's* presence.

'What's his problem?' Coleman squatted alongside his elderly companion.

'The entire village is on edge.'

'You know we could still get you stretchered out of here if you're willing to leave.'

'I'm not leaving.'

Coleman expected this response. 'I'm going to head out tomorrow as soon as the weapons have all been removed.' He looked sadly at his friend. 'Are you sure you won't reconsider?'

The old man casually flicked an ant off his foot. 'Everything I need is here.'

'You should not have let that British woman leave without telling her your story.'

'Too late now. Besides, what difference would it have made?' He looked annoyingly at his feet as another ant encroached. 'It wasn't the Rockefeller story that brought the Indonesians on their killing spree, was it?' He leaned forward and pinched an ant between thumb and finger, squeezed, then cast the dead insect away. 'It's that damned aircraft wreckage that's brought death and destruction to the Mek Mek.'

Coleman rose. 'When I leave, you know I won't be returning?'

'I expected as much.'

'Just wanted to make sure you understood.'

The cave became quiet. Coleman, sensing there was little left to be said made his way down the mountain trail to spend his last night amongst the villagers.

\*   \*   \*   \*

# JAKARTA

Caretaker President General Sumantri had become increasingly distraught as news of his son, Didi filtered through from Akumuga. At first, fearing the general's wrath, aides attempted to soften the news by suggesting information regarding Didi's end remained unsubstantiated by any reliable military source.

A *KOPASSUS* field officer was despatched from Jayapura, arriving eighteen hours after the attack. He found Didi's body still perched against the post's flagpole. Shocked to discover the entire unit had been annihilated to a man, witnesses were interrogated to determine what had really transpired.

The officer then called Jakarta and informed the Palace Commander who, in turn, relayed the news to General Sumantri, that Australian troops had arrived under the cover of darkness and attacked the post, killing his son.

Enraged, General Sumantri summoned his Chiefs of Staff to the *Bina Graha* Palace office and demanded they prepare for an immediate attack against Australia. The generals understood that declaring war against Australia would be tantamount to inviting the Americans into any such confrontation. Indonesia was precariously close to the brink of social and economic collapse, a situation these senior officers were aware could eventuate, if they were to pursue military action against their southern neighbour.

A heated exchange erupted resulting in Sumantri arbitrarily sacking all three Chiefs of Staff. The generals refused to accept their Commander-in-Chief's dismissal, instead, directing Sumantri step aside and restore the presidency to Abdul Moewardi. The country's second-most-powerful general who headed the nation's Strategic Army Reserves, *KOSTRAD*, informed Sumantri that he no longer had the support of his military.

Staggered by the challenge to his authority, coupled with the loss of his son Didi, General Sumantri reluctantly acquiesced, accepting that he could not survive in power without the support of his generals.

Within hours, when news broke that their democratically-elected President, Abdul Moewardi had been reinstated to office, the Australian Prime Minister was the first to call.

\*　　\*　　\*　　\*

# MEK MEK VILLAGE

Coleman rose early to prepare for the arrival of the rebels. He climbed back up to the cave where he found *Lapun Buna* lying prostrate on the ground as if praying before an idol.

Bending down to wake the elderly American, Coleman turned his friend onto his side, shocked when there was no response. Startled with movement from behind he glanced over his shoulder to find the *Khakhua–Kumu* standing, silhouetted in the entrance. The witch doctor stepped forward and placed an open palm against the dead man's bare chest, then wiped the dried, pooled saliva that had dribbled down his chin.

An upturned piece of coconut lay close to the body and when Coleman reached for the shell, the *Khakhua–Kumu* beat him to it. Instantly Coleman knew the *Lapun Buna* had been poisoned.

*'Lapun Buna give this for Sanguma,'* Coleman understood even with his limited knowledge of the Mek Mek dialect. The paper had been torn from the diary in Coleman's backpack. The brief note simply said, *"Stephen, Forgive me for leaving in this manner. I cannot live with what is to come. Please remember your promise to me. Khakhua–Kumu will have my body cremated. With God we rest."*

Coleman locked eyes with the witch doctor knowing that the *Khakhua–Kumu* would have been complicit in his friend's suicide. Tribesmen, with faces and bodies painted in bright pigments and adorned with larges shells and plumage, were already assembled outside the cave. They carried *Lapun Buna* down to the village where, to Coleman's surprise, a wooden funeral pyre had already been prepared.

*Lapun Buna*'s body was taken into his hut and prepared. After the testicles were removed his remains were washed then wrapped with mango leaves.

Village women, their bodies painted with mud, gathered as *Lapun Buna*'s body was placed on the structure. The *Khakhua–Kumu* stepped forward and ceremoniously leaped around the pyre setting fire to the timbers. As the flames licked higher and higher the villagers rhythmic wailing filled the surrounds, while lines of warriors stomped their feet in unison. Dogs barked at children who danced around kicking dust into the air, emulating their elders. Coleman backed away from the pyre as the heat grew consuming his friend's earthly remains.

Suddenly, women screamed and pointed to the sky. Coleman shielded his eyes from the sun, the familiar chopping sound of a helicopter approaching sending villagers fleeing in all directions and abandoning the ceremony.

The Sikorsky landed, the aircraft's blades further fanning the funeral fire. Coleman remained motionless as a team of six Seals leaped from the helicopter and ran directly to where he stood.

'Name and nationality?' the lead commando demanded.

'You have no authority here,' Coleman countered.

'Are you Michael Rockefeller?' Again he was challenged.

Coleman crossed his arms in defiance. 'No. But if you're looking for someone who might shed some light on that, you're too late.'

The remaining Seals had already spread out and secured the village already abandoned by its terrified inhabitants. The team leader pointed his MP5 submachine gun at Coleman's head.

'Don't fuck around. We know someone here has taken parts off a downed drone and my guess is that it would be you. Now we don't have time for any crap. On approach we sighted a large group of soldiers moving up the mountain in this direction.'

Coleman's mind raced. He knew that would be Bennie's rebels heading for the village to remove the ordnance stored in the cave. If they arrived before the US Seals departed there could be a bloodbath. 'I have what you want. My guess it's the drone's sensors. The parts are stored in a backpack further up the mountain.'

'And the condition of the drone?'

'Totally destroyed. There's nothing left that would of any relevance.'

'Let's go!' The commando gripped Coleman by the arm and

pushed. He led the Navy Seal up the trail to the cave where he surrendered the drone's parts.

Upon returning to the village, the funeral pyre had burned itself out and the body transformed to ashes and charred bones. Coleman knew that when the villagers returned, the remains would be scattered widely, and the skull secreted away by the *Khakhua–Kumu*.

The Seals regrouped and prepared to depart. 'We have orders to offer you a ride.'

Coleman hesitated. 'No thanks. I'll take my chances here.'

'No, you're coming with us. Just for the record …' the commander jerked his head at the smoking remains. 'Was that Michael Rockefeller?'

Coleman shrugged. 'Guess the world will never know.'

\*   \*   \*   \*

# SYDNEY

Jules' resentment percolated as he sat listening to Bennie outline his strategy for Marcus to return to West Papua in preparation for the referendum. He continued to look out the Hyatt Regency window towards the city, his back to the others in the interconnecting hotel suite

Jules and Bennie had arrived from Fiji the evening before. Acting on Bennie's instructions Marcus had located Alice through the media and asked her to attend the meeting. Marcus' communications remained compromised providing Indonesian *BIN* and ASIO with details of his contacts' movements.

'I expect the UN will announce the deployment of forces to oversee the referendum within the next days.' Bennie grinned at Marcus. 'Once the outcome has been accepted by Jakarta their troops must withdraw. Then you'll both be able to return home.'

'What will the timetable be, moving forward?' Marcus asked.

'If we consider what transpired with East Timor then I would hope that immediately following the referendum, the UN will create another multinational, military-peacekeeping force and assume control over the West Papuan administration, until the first elections can be held. I am going to propose a joint-interim arrangement between the UN presence and ourselves to consolidate our position. Considering the damage done by the Indonesians to the infrastructure, I estimate it will take around a year to organise the political parties and then a further six to twelve months, to actually hold the election.'

'How confident can we be that our party will rule?' Marcus asked.

'We already have that undertaking from the majority of representatives. They know that independence could never have been realized without the commitment we have made over the years.' Bennie looked Marcus directly in the eye. 'And with that support, you should be the first President of the Republic of West Papua.'

The statement reinforced Jules' concerns of being sidelined. But, to avoid open conflict he remained silent, willing his attention to a flock of seagulls crossing Darling Harbour, as the birds twisted and turned over unsuspecting, perambulating tourists.

Marcus checked his watch. 'Do you want to go somewhere to eat?'

Bennie shook his head. 'We still have more to discuss. Order room service.'

Marcus threw a cashew nut at Jules back to get his attention. 'What do you want for lunch?'

Without displaying his annoyance, he turned. 'Don't order for me. I'm having coffee in the lobby with a business colleague once we've finished here.'

'Alice?' Marcus passed the room service menu.

'Not for me either thanks. I need to head back to the North Shore shortly as Brent's uncle is expecting me.'

Bennie and Marcus continued discussing strategies for keeping the media's attention on issues relating to the imminent referendum. Feeling there was nothing further he could contribute to the conversation Jules decided to leave. 'I expect to be back in a couple of hours.'

'I'm off also,' Alice announced.

They left together, exiting the room as the lunch trolley entered the hallway. As their paths crossed, the waiter deliberately dropped his eyes to avoid contact, the fleeting glimpse of the man prompting recognition, reminding Jules of a face he had seen before. A thought crossed his mind and he paused, mid-stride, turned, frowned then continued on his way to the lifts, parting company with Alice in the hotel lobby.

'Someone, get the door!' Bennie was heading into the toilet when the buzzer sounded.

'Your lunch order, sir,' the Indonesian State Intelligence agent wheeled the trolley into the suite, his eyes searching for Bennie, the primary target. Someone coughed in the bathroom. Marcus lifted the silver-plated food cover to check his order, and with this opportunity the assassin struck, driving his blade deep into Marcus Tabuni's chest.

The sound of a toilet flushing alerted the former Group 3 *Sandi Yudha* Special Forces soldier to Bennie's imminent return. He crouched, placing a free hand over Marcus' body covering the blade's point of entry.

Bennie strolled into the room, shocked to see Marcus doubled over on the carpet. 'Marcus?' Bennie rushed over to the body and fell to his knees. 'Marcus ...? Marcus, what happened?'

The assassin leaned back revealing the bloody wound and Bennie's jaw dropped in surprise as a Fairbairn-Sykes knife flashed, slicing Bennie's throat from ear to ear.

\* \* \* \*

Less than thirty minutes had elapsed when Jules returned to his suite. He entered, removed his jacket and called, 'I'm back!' He walked through the open, interconnecting door where the crumpled bodies of Bennie and Marcus lay.

Blood spatter trailed over the furniture, leaving a distinctive path across the wallpaper, down the beige curtains to the carpet.

Awash with trepidation, Jules stepped carefully forward for a closer view of the bodies, his heart skipping a beat at the sight of Bennie's distorted grimace in death. Jules stepped over to where Marcus lay on his back, instantly reeling back in shock when a faint gurgling moan bubbled from his mouth. 'He — help — me ...' he coughed, blood trickling from the corner of his mouth.

Jules stepped back from Marcus' partially raised, outstretched hand, his mind in turmoil. The room phone glared back at him challengingly. He knew he should call for help. Lost in thought as to whether he should withdraw from the scene and leave, Jules snapped back when Marcus mumbled his name. With mixed emotions he stared down at the man he called brother. Shifting his gaze to Bennie's corpse then back again to Marcus, Jules arrived at his decision. He called reception and raised the alarm.

*　　*　　*　　*

The assassination of an international entity and the attempted murder of a leading political activist were covered widely in the media.

Having been interviewed, Jules was permitted to leave the scene. He called Alice and informed her of Bennie's death. Although deeply shocked when she received the news Alice did not hesitate in proceeding to St. Vincent's Hospital where Marcus was being treated. There they had to battle their way through the throng of cameras and other media, the Federal Police escorting the couple to the intensive care unit.

'Did they bring Bennie here also?' Alice asked.

'No, Alice,' Jules held an arm around her shoulders. 'There needs to be a full medical examination due to the circumstances of his death.'

'When do you think we can see him?'

'I'll ask.' He kissed her on the side of her face. 'I'm sorry. I wasn't there when it happened.'

Alice responded gravely. 'In a way it's lucky you weren't.'

An armed police officer checked their credentials then permitted Jules and Alice to the patient's bedside where the surgeon was speaking to an attending nurse.

'Are you family?'

'Yes,' Jules nodded. 'How bad is it?'

The surgeon slowly shook his head. 'Considering the extent of the damage it's surprising he arrived at the hospital alive. A lung was punctured resulting in tension pneumothorax. The hole created by the knife acted as a one-way valve, letting air into the chest, but not letting any air escape. When this occurs, with each breath, more air collects in the chest and air completely collapsed the lung'.

'Will he make it?' Alice needed to know.

'The paramedics most likely saved his life. They used a syringe to remove air to reduce the trauma. We inserted a chest tube to make sure the lung stays inflated and doesn't collapse again. The nurse will continue to check his breathing, heart rate and blood pressure. As you can see, he is being given oxygen'.

'When will he be able to talk?'

'Come back tomorrow afternoon.'

Jules nodded and took Alice by the hand. 'We'll come back then.'

\*   \*   \*   \*

# JAKARTA

Prepared for his address to the convened national assembly Indonesian President Abul Moewardi raised his head from prayer and
waited for the delegates to come to order.

'*Bismillahirrahmanirrahim,     Assalamu'alaikum     warahmatullahi*
*wabarakatuh,*
*Honourable Members of the People's Consultative Assembly, Members*
*of the House of Representatives of the Republic of Indonesia.*

*We have called this extraordinary session today at the start of a new era,*
*following an unsettling time of trial and tribulation.*

*We have overcome an attack on our democracy which has cost the lives of*
*many of our fellow countrymen. Now we must face the reality of change and*
*find a consensus which will satisfy the Constitution and meet the demands of*
*our motherland, Ibu Pertiwi, to breathe new life into a vibrant, coherent, and*
*stable nation.*

*My fellow countrymen, as Indonesia again embraces this new opportunity*
*we must recognise from what we have experienced, that democracy cannot*
*solve the problems of political instability, economic crisis, national unity, ethnic*
*conflicts, separatist rebellions, or social dislocations.*

*We have entered a new era with a rapidly evolving political landscape*
*that challenges our national principle of Unity in Diversity — and in order*
*to uphold a harmonious relationship with our neighbours we are obliged to*
*consider what has brought Indonesian to brink of disaster.'*

The President continued at length, presenting to the assembly how he had previously hoped that by providing a Commonwealth system of government to the people of West Papua, the province would have remained within the Republic. He apologized for failing to achieve this objective and appealed to the representatives of other restive provinces, not to follow the same path that the Papuans had decided upon.

Finally, in closing, he sought the approval of the People's Consultative Assembly, and Members of the House of Representatives to prepare for the separation of West Papua.

*'It is now clear that the people of West Papua will participate in a vote to decide their own future and that will undoubtedly result in a separation of that territory from our great archipelagic state. It is also apparent that rogue elements within our military have brought great shame upon our people.*

*Therefore, in view of the United Nations support for the proposed referendum mentioned here today, I propose an immediate withdrawal of all Indonesian military forces from the provinces of West Papua and seek your approval to commence discussions with the relevant United Nations authorities to enable an international presence to oversee any transfer of power.*

*I encourage you in your deliberations to support the outcome of the imminent referendum to be held in the two provinces that represent all of West Papua.*

*Terima kasih,*

*Wassalamu'alaikum warahmatullahi wabarakatuh.'*

That evening, the decision to separate with West Papua was passed by the narrowest of margins. The President was informed, and Abul Moewardi issued the order for all Indonesian forces to commence withdrawing from the distant provinces.

\*   \*   \*   \*

# SYDNEY

'When will he be well enough, to be released, Doctor?' Alice enquired. This was the third day she had accompanied Jules to St. Vincent's Hospital where Marcus remained in care.

'His injury was severe. Most of his pain and discomfort will diminish over the next few days but a full recovery will take at least several weeks, even after severe symptoms pass. He needs to have complete rest for two to three months.'

'That long?' Jules was surprised.

'I've already had a long talk with Marcus. I warned that he not travel too soon and certainly not contemplate flying for a minimum of three months. He knows that he should only engage in low-impact activities such as walking, and I strong recommend he only do so if accompanied. Marcus is aware that if he resumes regular activities too quickly then he would be in danger of another collapse.'

'What are the long-term effects?' Alice pressed.

'Generally speaking, once the collapsed lung has completely healed there are few, if any, long-term effects. But, having experienced a collapsed lung once only increases the likelihood of it occurring again.'

'Then he would be house-bound for at least three months?'

'He could take short walks out. He understands that up to half of all people who've experienced what he's been through most often have a further incident with their lung collapsing within a few months of the first event. He needs to remain under home care and be aware of any symptoms during the rehabilitation period.' The surgeon led them into the room where Marcus was propped up with pillows. 'I'll leave you with our patient. No more than twenty minutes today please.'

Jules forced a smile and shook Marcus' exposed foot playfully, while Alice bent over the bed and kissed him on the forehead. 'How do you today, Marcus?'

Marcus spoke, his head half-buried in a pillow. 'Most of the pain is gone.'

'The doctor says you might be here for another week or so,' Alice was saddened by his appearance; the sunken eyes and inwardly curved cheeks affirmed the seriousness of his condition.

'The doctor explained what to expect.' Marcus paced his breathing as he spoke slowly. 'And in view of what's happened, we need to discuss the decision I've made about the future.'

'There's time for that when you've recovered.'

'No, I don't think we can wait.' He smiled weakly at Alice. 'Considering my condition and the timing of the referendum I won't be of much use to anyone.'

'Nonsense,' Alice exclaimed. 'You're the head of the Free Papua Council. Once the referendum is held and we move to the next phase, your position to lead the country will be widely supported.'

Marcus looked down at the tubes hanging alongside his body. 'What happened to me almost cost me my life. I've given it a great deal of thought, especially since we've lost Bennie. Everyone's already given so much. The referendum is going to take place whether I'm still involved or not.' Marcus swallowed a lump in his throat and blinked tears from his eyes. 'I'm sorry. I don't think I have the strength to do what is needed. I'm going to resign my position as President of the Council.'

Alice snapped a glance at Jules then back to Marcus. 'Don't make any decisions about that now. Wait until you've had a few weeks to recover. You're still in shock.' Alice recalled the doctor's earlier comments that patients often experience depression and other psychological distress following surgery.

Jules leaped in, anger filling his voice having processed what was said. 'You can't abandon everything we've all worked for with the snap of a finger, Marcus.'

Alice placed her hand on Jules' arm with a look of reproach.

Marcus lay quietly for a few moments gathering strength then responded. 'You've not heard everything I want to say, Jules.' He paused when a nurse entered then waited for her to leave the room. He lifted a hand towards Alice to hold. 'Now Bennie is gone we three are the only ones left who know that you are his daughter.' Marcus squeezed Alice's hand softly. 'I intend on informing the Council that I propose you take my place. I want you and Jules to assume the leadership together and do what Bennie would have wanted.'

'Me?' Alice was staggered at the suggestion. 'That's nonsense!'

Taken aback by Marcus's announcement Jules stared blankly at the patient. The implication of having Alice assume the leadership position would offer the perfect opportunity for Jules to play a significant role in the management of the future republic. He cast a determined look in Alice's direction.

'It's not such an absurd idea.' Quickly, he ran the possibilities through his mind. Support for Alice would be substantial once their support base was made aware that Bennie was her father. She was of solid Papuan stock, had a sound education and background and was already known to the media. 'If Marcus feels he's not up to it and throws his support behind you, then you should do what is best for the people.'

'You're both crazy!'

'Not so.' Jules argued. 'Think it through…'

'It's ridiculous!' Alice insisted, although the proposition did have appeal.

'It's what Bennie would have wanted,' Marcus implied.

'He never suggested I should become involved.'

'The situation's changed,' Jules remarked.

Marcus' breathing became shallow and the attending nurse terminated the visit.

'We'll come again tomorrow,' Jules said. 'And if you're up to it we can discuss everything then.'

Leaving the hospital, Jules insisted they continue the conversation. Alice agreed and at Jules' suggestion they caught a taxi to the Sheraton. There they crossed to Hyde Park and settled on a bench close to the fountain.

'Marcus was never going to be a great choice, you know.' Jules was now committed to the idea of Alice assuming the leadership of the Council.

'He was Bennie's choice.'

'I feel that decision was wrong from the outset.'

'How so?' Alice appeared genuinely confused.

'When we were children, the three of us were about as close as blood brothers might be. As adults, that changed. We all grew apart philosophically. I was keen to build a business career, Marcus was actively engaged in politics, and Bennie seemed to prefer more of a mentor role towards us both. As an activist, Marcus succeeded but something happened to him when he was incarcerated. He changed. Then, once he was permitted to stay in Australia, over time I could see that he lost most of the drive that had been evident before.'

'Why then did Bennie still support Marcus, paving the way for him to become the Head of the Papuan Independence Council?'

'I guess Bennie knew I could not realistically be considered for that role. Natan Tabuni may have raised me as one of his own but he made me aware of my Dutch heritage. Bennie however, was denied knowing anything of his parentage. Natan either didn't know or refused to divulge how Bennie came to be part of the Tabuni family.' He wrapped an arm around Alice's shoulder. 'What is obvious, you have a lot of Papua in your veins. It's time you changed your name back from Heynneman to Tabuni.'

Alice leaned into Jules' shoulder. 'You've also been my father.'

Jules gave her a comforting hug. 'Time to step up, Alice Tabuni!'

'Do you really think it would work?'

'You have the education, knowledge, love for the Papuan people, and once everyone knows that Bennie was your real father, there will be a clear path for you to secure either the leadership, or at least a major position in any future West Papua government.'

Alice started to ponder the possibility. 'I don't have any political experience.'

'I'd be there at your side.' Jules was enthused at the prospect of having Alice in a position of power to recover, and protect, his vested interests. 'Together we could deliver Bennie's dream.'

Alice leaned away and turned to face the man whose name she had borne throughout her life. 'If I were to agree, it would be on the condition you would be there for me, to guide me, to protect me.'

Jules took her hand. 'I wouldn't have it any other way.'

*   *   *   *

# Hong Kong

Stephen Coleman completed the banking formalities closing his accounts at the HSBC. He then returned to the rented room across from the Dorsett in Wanchai, packed the few clothes he had acquired upon arrival, and headed to the airport on Chek Lap Kok.

His new passport listed Coleman as Stephen Jenkins, retired, citizen of New Zealand.

Having parted company with the American Seals team in New Guinea Coleman flew to Fiji. It was there he learned of Bennie's assassination. After a lengthy discussion with Jules it was decided that their future would be best served by terminating the relationship, Coleman then closing down his operation and departing for Hong Kong.

As the airport express train barrelled through the concrete jungle Coleman smiled inwardly at the prospect of relocating to Koror Island in the Republic of Palau where he intended to spend his remaining years. He would no longer participate in the clandestine operations that had consumed a life spanning decades across Asia's restive zones.

*   *   *   *

# Sydney

Jules and Alice worked together preparing the announcement. A week to the day from when Bennie Tabuni was murdered, Jules arranged for a press conference to be held on the steps of the University of Sydney's Law School building in Camperdown.

The local Free Papua Movement chapter had succeeded in widely promoting the event, attended also by the international media. When the crowd fell silent she commenced.

'Good morning and thank you all for being here.

'My name is Alice Tabuni. Some of you may know me under another name, Alice Heynneman.

'Following the assassination of Bennie Tabuni and the attempted murder of the Head of our Free Papua Movement, Marcus Tabuni it became immediately clear to the international community that extremists continue to work against the realisation of an independent state of West Papua.

'Please bear with me as I refresh our memories as to how we all arrived here.

'In 1962, America was the first to betray West Papuans by creating the "New York Agreement". The Australian government was next to follow. This nation previously supported Papuan independence but abandoned my people by reversing its policy and then supported an Indonesia annexation instead.

'Then the United Nations participated in this injustice by agreeing to the transfer of all authority over West Papua to Indonesia in 1963, based on the premise that Indonesia would allow Papuans to determine whether we wanted independence or to be a part of Indonesia.

'The New York Agreement clearly required that all men and women in Papua that were not foreign nationals had the right to vote. Instead, declared West Papua a "quarantine territory".

'In 1969 when the United Nations oversaw the so-called Act of Free Choice they permitted Indonesia to handpick a thousand Papuan men out of a population of three quarters of a million inhabitants and corrupt the outcome, proclaiming the one thousand had voted unanimously for integration with Indonesia. From that time the majority of Papuans has continued to resist the Indonesian occupation, always with deadly response.

'Human rights were ignored, activists were murdered, political assassination, imprisonment, torture and even total annihilation of village communities became the norm. We were not permitted to raise our flag, *The Morning Star* and singing of our national anthem always attracted retribution.

'Our lands were ripped away and given to non Papuans, under the Indonesian transmigration scheme designed also to dilute the Papuan demographic.

'The number of dead resulting from the cruel Indonesian military will never be accurately known, but estimates suggest that this figure could be as many as five hundred thousand. We should be very clear, these acts were nothing short of genocide and those responsible should be brought to justice.

'The international community pushed the plight of the Papuans into a corner where they didn't have to look, permitting the destruction of West Papua and the genocidal acts perpetrated by Indonesia, to go unpunished. No one can deny that this is a stark indictment of the global indifference in the face of unprecedented human suffering.

'This will hopefully change with the imminent referendum to be held to determine not "if" but "when" we Papuans will finally have our freedom and independence.

'Now to the purpose of my announcement today.

'I am Papuan by birth. My father was Bennie Tabuni. Because of my father's high profile in supporting the West Papuan Government in exile, and the many threats attempted against his life, in order to protect me from danger I was given my uncle Jules' surname, Heynneman.

'As an infant, a young child, a teenager, and continuing to today I have been blessed to have been cared for by Jules Heynneman, and although my relationship with Bennie Tabuni was an unusual one, I know I also enjoyed his love as well.

'I spent my career as a senior engineer working with the Akumuga Mine in Papua and, although I have not been actively engaged in the political arena, I have maintained a close relationship with those at a leadership level. Marcus Tabuni, as you are aware has led the Free Papuan Council for many years.

'The people of West Papua owe Marcus a great deal for his leadership, integrity and dedication in the pursuit of a free West Papua. Sadly, due to the cowardly attack on Marcus he has informed the Council that he can no longer manage the role of leader, and has asked me to assume that position to provide stability through the execution of the referendum and, if the people find me worthy, to participate as a member of the transitional administration until elections can be held to determine the Republic of West Papua's government.

'I have been informed that the members of the Council have supported my appointment and that of Jules Heynneman, as senior counsel. In short, with effect immediately, Jules and I will continue building the foundations for what will be required subsequent to the referendum.

'Together, we will install leadership and credibility with the international community and pursue the expectations of the West Papuan people.

'I accept that the path ahead will not be an easy road to travel. My hope is that the international community will support the outcome of the referendum and offer the hand of friendship in our endeavour to realise a free and independent Republic of West Papua.

Thank you.'

Within hours, government agencies in Canberra, Washington, Jakarta, London and Beijing went into overdrive to determine what opportunities, an Alice Tabuni-led future Republic of West Papua might offer.

China's ambassador in Australia was the first to publically congratulate Alice on her ascension to the leadership role, deliberately avoiding mention of Beijing's vested interests in maintaining its position in the Kampung Mas Autonomous Zone. Drilling by the *Haiyang Shiyou 1088* had been suspended under instruction by the United Nations until such times sea borders between Northern Australia and the future Republic of West Papua were clearly defined by both nations.

Asian stock markets remained rattled. Agus Winarko avoided insolvency by bribing the Indonesian courts and General Sumantri commenced his rapid slide into obscurity.

David Shackleton, president of the Summit Gold Mining conglomerate communicated with Jules Heynneman, seeking clarification on where the US interests would stand once power had been transferred to the new government of West Papua. Shackleton was informed that Summit Gold would be offered a managerial role only with respect to the Akumuga Mine as the operation would be nationalised by the future government.

*   *   *   *

With the United Nations Security Council Resolution allowing for an international peacekeeping force for West Papua being passed, a multinational military force, INTERWEP (International Force for West Papua) was created. Troops from eighteen nations totalling twenty-five thousand were deployed across the territory. Amongst these, an Australian contingent led by recently-promoted, Colonel Brent Shepherd.

With the withdrawal of Indonesian troops foreign journalists were finally given access to the former provinces.

For the first time, evidence of the incalculable devastation and atrocities caused by the brutal forces was revealed, staggering the international community. Estimates placed the number of Papuans killed in the previous six months at fifty thousand with a quarter of a million more, displaced. Almost all schools, homes and buildings had been destroyed and the electric grid no longer existed.

Fortunately, the oil and gas fields remained operational. However, the damage to the Akumuga Mine was substantial.

United Nations observers estimated the cost of rebuilding the emerging nation would exceed $2 billion.

When the referendum for West Papua self-determination was concluded an overwhelming majority voted for independence.

Under UN supervision, the first Assembly of West Papuan leaders was created and a draft constitution prepared. Parliamentary elections followed. The election of the Republic's President was then also held. Under the Constitution, the President appointed the Prime Minister as the functional head of government.

*   *   *   *

# MEK MEK VILLAGE

Now fully recovered from his injuries, the *Khakhua–Kumu* climbed down from his newly-constructed hut. Slowly he approached the two white men and their guides who had arrived at the village earlier in the day, seeking background information relating to Michael Rockefeller's time amongst the Mek Mek.

The Western journalists were taken to the cave where the *Lapun Buna* had spent his last hours, the interpreters explaining to the inquisitive foreigners that upon his death, the elderly American who had spent more than fifty years living amongst the Mek Mek community had been cremated, his ashes spread across sacred ground.

When the *Khakhua–Kumu* was questioned about the other white man whom the villagers called *Sanguma,* the journalists met another dead end.

\*   \*   \*   \*

# KOROR ISLAND

## REPUBLIC OF PALAU

Stephen Coleman, aka Stephen Jenkins sat in the Island Bar at the Cove Resort nursing his fifth Heineken for the day. He pushed an unfinished meal of mangrove crab aside and yawned. 'How about cranking up the volume?' he asked the Melanesian barmaid. She curled an eyebrow then pressed the remote for the sixty-inch screen attached to blue walled-backdrop, behind the bar.

Coleman's attention was fixed on the screen watching the Republic of West Papua, Presidential inauguration ceremony broadcast live from Manokwari, the new nation's capital.

When President Alice Tabuni appeared and was greeted with a thunderous reception Coleman's face split into a wide grin. The screen's view widened and Jules Heynneman could be seen standing to Alice's right, the thought crossing Coleman's mind that the Papuans might want to keep a close eye on their newly appointed Minister for Finance and Investment.

As the ceremony dragged on, Stephen Coleman's mind drifted, his eyes misting as the alcohol assumed charge. The memory of the elderly American known to the Mek Mek as *Lapun Buna,* and the secret he had taken to the grave, took the former mercenary back in time.

⁕   ⁕   ⁕   ⁕

# THE MISSIONARY TOBIAS

Stephen Coleman recalled Tobias relating his story, cataloguing the scars which had led him into his self-imposed exile. At the close of his revelation, the elderly American had insisted that Coleman only refer to him as *Lapun Buna,* that he respect his right to anonymity.

329

Having secured Coleman's pledge not to reveal his secret to others, Brother Tobias had disclosed all.

'I was born in Boston to poor and deeply religious parents. I guess it was my mother who influenced my decision mostly, to enter the brother-hood and become a Xaverian missionary. I had completed my High School Diploma and was eager to travel overseas. At eighteen, I commenced the Novitiate stage and towards the end of two years I had become restless and unsure of the vocation that had been chosen for me. Around that time I strayed, commenced drinking secretly and this led to my involvement with a married woman. Before long, I was the antithesis of everything a man of the cloth should be. One night when I had been drinking, apparently I wandered into someone's home and was beaten up by the beastly woman who lived there.

When my misadventures became apparent within the brotherhood hierarchy in 1961 I was given the choice of leaving the Xaverians or under-taking a two-year mission to Western New Guinea as it was then known. This landed me amongst the cloistered Asmat cannibal tribes along the south coast.

The tribal men were primitive and practiced every taboo known to the Western world. Men had sex with each other, shared wives, drank each other's urine, killed their neighbours and hunted human heads.

Confronted with the constant threat that at any time I could do some-thing that would antagonise the primitive tribes-people, I constantly struggled to cope. That's when started drinking the local tuak and totally lost direction.

When Michael Rockefeller crawled out of the mangroves and was brought to the village, his arrival almost cost me my life. At that very moment I was in flagrante with Vavine, the thirteen-year-old daughter of an Asmat elder. If we'd been discovered it would have been the end for me. Fortunately, the girl slipped away out of my hut unseen. I don't know if you are familiar with the Asmat and their other barbarous ways. Vavine happened to be already married to one of the chief's sons and if she'd been found naked with me, my head would have ended up on a stick.

I remember that Rockefeller was in a real bad way. He had been mauled near to death when they found him. The village women cleaned his wounds and treated him with traditional cures. Vavine was amongst those who were constantly at his side. I didn't believe he would survive but he did. Within a week he was reasonably coherent and on the path to recovery. He never did reveal that he was a Rockefeller.

There was already deep resentment towards foreigners when he came to the Asmat community. This had come about when Max Lapre, a Dutchman, had ventured into the area with a force of armed police and ordered the execution of five of the elders, just to stamp his authority over the primitive people.

I could never be sure of what happened next. Rockefeller appeared to be recovering when suddenly approaching Christmas Eve, he simply vanished. It was as if he had never existed, or at least not in that village. In retrospect, I believe his disappearance was a "Swanggi" revenge killing; he was taken away to an adjoining village and cannibalised in secret, so I wouldn't know.

Those responsible never mentioned the incident.

The villagers were not aware of his importance until foreign teams arrived scouring the mangrove-ringed coastline, searching for the missing heir. I never did understand why Rockefeller had not revealed his identity. A couple of years later when I was living in the Akumuga mining camp I read his story and thought that he withheld who he was, perhaps because he felt his family name would have no significance in this distant, and unfamiliar corner of the planet.

After he went missing, there had been an exhaustive search by land, sea and air. Of course, they had no chance of finding any trace of his body.

I recall that when rumors circulated that Rockefeller had made it to shore and had then been eaten by the Asmat, the Dutch government were vehement in their denial of any such possibility. I read somewhere that he was declared dead by drowning and would have thought that would have been the end of the story.

Several months passed before it was obvious that Vavine was pregnant. When she died giving birth to a fair-skinned child with obvious European features, the village elders took her death as a sign and threatened to sacrifice her baby. I couldn't raise my hand and reveal that the infant was mine. I knew I had no choice but to remove the child from the village.

I was familiar with a highland community that had converted to Christianity and decided to take the baby there for safety. I arrived on Natan Tabuni's doorstep and because the child was so close to death, we had him immediately christened. I didn't feel the need to explain all the circumstances surrounding the boy's background and the Tabuni family agreed to raise him as one of their own. They named him Bennie. I returned to the Asmat community and remained in the area for a further five years. Then I was assigned to overseeing the spiritual needs of the newly-created Akumuga mining settlement.

It was there that I became consumed by my dependency on alcohol. I proceeded to break every conceivable vow made by man, sleeping with *the whores shipped in from Java and ignoring my commitment to over-seeing the spiritual needs of the community.*

*What happened there burned a deep hole into my conscience. I stuck it out for awhile until I had a moment of crisis and decided to give it all away. I wrote home and explained that I was leaving the Brotherhood then packed the few meagre belongings I had, and erased myself from the life I had known.*

*I was aware of the isolated hill tribes and decided to remove myself as far away from Western civilisation as possible. Lost in the highlands I stumbled into the Mek Mek community and have been here ever since.*

*Bennie Tabuni is the fruit of my loins.'*

\*    \*    \*    \*

Coleman's reverie was interrupted when the bar attendant flicked the remote to another channel. Wrapping his mouth around the bottle of Heineken, he drained the remaining contents effortlessly then tapped the counter for another.

With the beer grasped in one hand, he slid off his stool and meandered outside to catch the last vestiges of day, evanesce into night across the landscape he now called home.

The sky darkened. Lightning flashed and a thunderous roar rocked his surrounds. He turned his face to the heavens, raised the bottle in salute, and smiled at the thought of Tobias sitting together with Michael Rockefeller in their heavenly surrounds.

\*    \*    \*    \*

# Author's Note

*Indonesia occupied what we now know as West Papua, the last Dutch East Indies' possession following years of bloody confrontation and, finally, through a tacit agreement signed to appease the United States of America and the Commonwealth of Australia, in New York, in 1961.*

*In 1962 the Soviets had struck a billion dollar arms deal with the world's largest Moslem nation that galvanised the Americans into action. John F. Kennedy intervened, pressuring both the Dutch and Australians to desist from supporting West Papuan independence, offering the resource-rich prize to the Indonesians.*

*On 1st May 1963, Indonesia became the new colonial power in West New Guinea. The elected West Papuan Council was disbanded, the official flags banned, as was singing of the West Papuan national anthem and the founding of any new political parties. This, in contradiction to the agreement signed in 1961 which provided for the indigenous people to be given the right of self-determination, and the option of independence.*

*In their role as so called 'caretakers', Indonesia's Special Forces killed more than thirty thousand Papuans as part of the government's successful efforts to influence the 1969 plebiscite.*

*Although the United Nations claimed the referendum would be an 'Act of Free Choice', for the indigenous inhabitants who had been disenfranchised by the flawed United Nations'-sponsored plebiscite, the outcome could not have been more disastrous. One thousand and twenty-six tribal representatives were chosen to represent the voice of the entire West Papuan population. Intimidated by Jakarta's killing machine the result was inevitable.*

335

*In 1969, supported by Australia and the United States, the former Dutch territory became Indonesia's Twenty-sixth province.*

*The historic and political parallels between East Timor and West Papua cannot be ignored.*

*Jakarta's bitter and brutal exit from Dili in the latter part of 1999, clearly wounded national pride, a contributing factor in the selection of targets by the Jemaah Islamiyah extremists, in the devastating Bali bombings in 2002.*

*In Europe, there is growing support for the international community to revisit the flawed 1969 West New Guinea plebiscite. Some member nations of the European Community, including The Netherlands, have suggested that the United Nations might consider reviewing the implementation of the referendum with the purpose of determining whether the process was, in fact, democratic.*

*And, more recently, driven by anti-Australian sentiment the groundswell has become evident amongst Western Pacific island states which, in concert with their African counterparts such as Zimbabwe, have become increasingly vociferous in their calls for such a UN resolution.*

*And, surprisingly, the lead has now been taken up by Ireland.*

*However, the situation is more than problematic for Australians.*

*Should the United Nations support a call for a new plebiscite to be held in West Papua, such action would undoubtedly become the genesis of any future confrontation between Australia and Indonesia — fertile ground, indeed, for the growing number of militant religious groups (both Christian and Moslem) that fester throughout the great archipelago that is Indonesia, referred to lovingly as "Ibu Pertiwi".*

**Kerry Boyd Collison**
**Melbourne**